"Make love to me, Jesse—I want you to."

"Lauren, think about what you're saying...." He was here as her bodyguard, to keep her safe from some nut who wanted to hurt her. As much as he wanted to, he couldn't make love to her. "I think it's time I found the spare room."

"He was going to rape me," she stated, revealing what she couldn't tell the sheriff. "He doesn't just want to kill me, he wants to rape me first."

Jesse stilled instantly. "I won't let that happen."

"I've never—" She couldn't just come right out and say *I'm a virgin.* "Please. I don't want the first time to be—rape." She touched him; then her warm mouth found his lips.

Jesse made no attempt to disguise the effect she was having on him as he hauled her against him. "Still feel the same? Or has this dampened your thirst for knowledge?"

In answer she pulled his shirt from his belt.

Dear Reader,

When two people fall in love, the world is suddenly new and exciting, and it's that same excitement we bring to you in Silhouette Intimate Moments. These are stories with scope and grandeur. The characters lead lives we all dream of, and everything they do reflects the wonder of being in love.

Longer and more sensuous than most romances, Silhouette Intimate Moments novels take you away from everyday life and let you share the magic of love. Adventure, glamour, drama, even suspense—these are the passwords that let you into a world where love has a power beyond the ordinary, where the best authors in the field today create stories of love and commitment that will stay with you always.

In coming months look for novels by your favorite authors: Linda Howard, Heather Graham Pozzessere, Emilie Richards and Kathleen Korbel, to name just a few. And whenever you buy books, look for all the Silhouette Intimate Moments, love stories *for* today's woman *by* today's woman.

Leslie J. Wainger
Senior Editor and Editorial Coordinator

Loving
Lies

ANN WILLIAMS

Silhouette Intimate Moments

Published by Silhouette Books New York

America's Publisher of Contemporary Romance

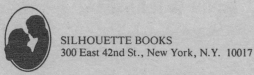

SILHOUETTE BOOKS
300 East 42nd St., New York, N.Y. 10017

ISBN: 0-373-07335-6

First Silhouette Books printing May 1990

Books by Ann Williams

Silhouette Intimate Moments

Devil in Disguise #302
Loving Lies #335

ANN WILLIAMS

gave up her career as a nurse, then as the owner and proprietor of a bookstore, in order to pursue her writing on a full-time basis. She was born and married in Indiana, and after a number of years in Texas, she now lives in North Carolina with her husband of twenty-three years and their four children.

Reading, writing, crocheting, classical music and a good romantic movie are among her diverse loves. Her dream is to one day move to a cabin in the Carolina mountains with her husband and "write to my heart's content."

To Paula Oates,
a friend in Haltom City, Texas.
Thanks, and good luck.

Prologue

Leave it off!"

Lauren's right hand froze in mid-reach, inches below the pull chain dangling from the middle of the ceiling.

"Who's there?" she asked, narrowed eyes darting around the room in an attempt to penetrate the darkness. For long moments there was only silence, the kind of silence that makes your skin crawl and the hair stand up on the back of your neck. The kind of silence that screams you're not alone.

"Who is it? Is that you, Jimmy?"

Jimmy Henderson, one of the older children who visited the library, loved playing pranks on people. One of his favorites was to hide in the dark and jump out at some unsuspecting person when they thought they were alone.

"This isn't funny, Jimmy. And you know better than to sneak off into the back of the library at closing time. What would you have done if I hadn't come back here before leaving? It's Saturday, and no one will be here again until

Monday. Your parents would have been worried sick when you didn't turn up, and you'd be one hungry little boy by the time Monday morning rolled around.''

A soft, sibilant laugh caused her heart to beat out of sync. That laugh didn't belong to a mischievous ten-year-old boy. Goose bumps rippled along the exposed skin of her arms and legs, causing her to shiver and rub both bare arms. A squeaky, scratching sound had her eyes flying toward the window, a rectangular patch of lighter dark in an inky stretch of blackness. But it was only a branch from a bush hitting the glass.

"W-who is it? Who's there?"

Her heart began to pound fiercely; her body shook with each thud, and her head filled with the sound of the blood rampaging through her veins.

"T-this isn't funny, you know—and whoever you are, you're trespassing. The library is closed now. Please leave, or I'll be forced to call the sheriff.''

Laughter filled the room, a hard, ugly sound that ended abruptly. Again there was silence, and then a faintly audible sound reached her ears; it sounded like fabric brushing against a smooth, solid surface.

Twisting around, she again tried to pierce the darkness with her eyes, but all she could make out were shadows and indistinct outlines.

The room was used to store extra books, papers, tables and chairs, shelves, decorations for the holidays, and anything she thought she might be able to use again. Because of the small budget allotted for the library, nothing was ever thrown out.

When a tingling sensation slid down her arm, she shivered convulsively and, looking up, realized she was still reaching toward the light cord. Maybe if she stretched a little higher—whoever it was hiding in the murky shadows couldn't see any better in the dark then she could—maybe—

"Don't move!" The rasping whisper sounded closer, and infinitely more threatening.

She should have kept the door to the hallway open, allowing some light to spill into the room, instead of entering the darkened room out of habit. Rotating her head from side to side, Lauren glanced around in growing fear, seeking the source of the voice.

The only thing the search accomplished was to show her how he had seen what she was doing. The door behind her had drifted open an inch, allowing a narrow band of light from the hallway to flow into the room. Unfortunately it fell on the window, reflecting back a clear image of her straining arm and twitching fingers.

She might just as well be standing in a spotlight. Angry, frightened, but nevertheless growing tired of this little game, Lauren decided to let him do his worst. Whirling suddenly, she made a headlong dash for the door.

When she was barely inches from freedom the door slammed shut, echoing loudly throughout the building. Fear gripped her with uncontrollable intensity, threatening to destroy reason with blind panic.

This man obviously wasn't here because he'd wandered off and forgotten the time and, on being found, decided to have a bit of innocent fun with the librarian. She knew without the shadow of a doubt that, whoever he was, he'd waited, patiently waited, for *her*. She knew it the same way she knew she would have to fight her way out of this situation, whatever the cost. Fear made fierce fighters of the meekest, and Lauren was normally a mild sort of person.

"What do you want?"

"That's a funny question for a librarian to ask. Since I'm here, in a place filled with books, I must want information."

Lauren waited, knowing there was more to come. It was evident by his tone.

"Or maybe—" he continued, "I just want the librarian...." That horrible laugh again.

Adrenaline flooded her system, and strangely, though she was shaking with terror, inside she became deathly calm. All her senses came suddenly, sharply alive. She could distinguish every tiny, separate hair on the backs of both arms. She could feel the silence beating against her skin like soft waves beating against a shore.

Kicking off her high heels soundlessly, bending her knees slightly, she braced herself for the attack she felt certain would be coming at any moment.

A hard arm wrapped suddenly around her neck from behind; a second arm slid beneath both of hers, drawing them behind her, trapping them between her body and his.

"Whore," he condemned her. "You're not so high-and-mighty now, are you?"

His breath flowed deceptively gently across her ear. Lauren's insides clenched at the words. Oh, God, was this going to be rape?

"I'm n-not a—what you called me," she protested.

A laugh wheezed along the sensitive skin of her face. Swallowing quickly against the bile its whiskey scent elicited, she twisted her face aside.

"No?" he answered her angry denial. "Well, the whole town thinks you are. A slut who sleeps with Mexicans."

He was a coward whose courage obviously came from drink or he wouldn't have attacked her in the anonymity of a dark room. But knowing that didn't keep the hurt and humiliation caused by the words from slicing through to her soul.

Surely the town wasn't calling her that? They couldn't be so low-minded. The man she'd dated exclusively until six months ago had been Spanish, but he'd also been good, hardworking, well educated by anyone's standards. Raul Estevez had been a respected teacher in the local high school.

He was also dead. Raul Estevez had been killed the past April, along with two other men. The whole thing was still something of a mystery, one Lauren had felt partly guilty at causing.

It had been six months since the murders, and she had finally begun to accept the whole thing for what it was, an event beyond her control. She was not responsible for the death—only the man who had pulled the trigger was guilty of that.

The death of the quiet but strong man whom she had been coming to care deeply for was not of her making. In thinking that it was, she had been viewing herself in an unrealistic light, giving herself a power over life and death that was only God's right.

"That's a lie!" she denied vehemently, straining against the arm at her throat. "Everyone in town knew and respected Raul. The whole town was at his funeral to pay their last respects to a man they liked and admired."

While she was speaking her attacker began to exert pressure on both arms locked behind her back, thus drawing her up onto her toes. At the same time he tightened the arm pressed against her windpipe, causing her words to sound thin and breathless.

"The whole town knows you're a traitorous bitch. And I can't take the chance on your spilling your guts about what you know."

With each word he drew her a little higher. Her arms strained, and her shoulders felt as though they were being torn from their sockets; she couldn't keep back an agonized gasp.

"I'm n-not a traitor. I don't know w-what you're talking about. P-please—" It galled her to say the word. "You're hurting me."

She could feel his chest expand and contract with his laughter. "Hurting you? Good, that makes me feel re-e-eal good. And before this night is over, I'm going to feel a whole lot better."

"Why are you doing this? I don't even know you. Who are you? Can't we talk about this? If I've done something to make you angry, tell me. At least give me a chance to—"

Her words were cut off abruptly as he tightened the hard muscled arm biting into her windpipe, shutting off her air.

While she'd been talking, she'd also been thinking furiously. There must be some way to break the hold he now had on her. It was a good one from his standpoint; he'd chosen well, despite his inebriated state. He could choke the breath from her in an instant, or break her neck if he liked—anytime he liked.

Also, with her arms pulled back as they were, he could dislocate both her shoulders with one quick move. Lauren was familiar with both holds because she had taken a self-defense course while she was in college. A campus at night could be hazardous for any woman, especially one as small in stature as she was.

The man had obviously counted on her being frightened, which she was. He also kept her off balance by keeping her on her toes. What he hadn't taken into account were her small size and the deft agility her self-defense instructor had soon detected in his pupil.

He was mouthing vile, graphic descriptions of what he was going to do to her before he put an end to her life, and that cost him his edge. He was so caught up in the lurid details that his attention wavered, and he allowed his hold on her to relax ever so slightly—not much, but enough.

In one swift move, by drawing her knee up and kicking forward and back, Lauren caught the man with her heel dead center in the groin. His arm tightened reflexively against her throat, and for an instant she thought she'd been done in by her own cleverness.

With her lungs burning for air, gagging, unable to either draw a breath or to swallow, Lauren struggled to stay conscious. Her toes danced madly inches above the floor. White lights burst behind her eyeballs, and blackness began to engulf her mind, while hoarse, pain-filled curses beat against her eardrums.

I'm dying! I'm dying! No! I won't let this happen, I won't let myself be throttled like a plump chicken for Sunday dinner. I have to fight it—fight him!

A sudden surge of strength shot through her like a charge of electricity, surprising her as much as her attacker. Lauren squirmed and fought against his hold.

And then, unbelievably, miraculously, she was free—free to draw in long, deep, wheezing breaths of sweet, fresh air. Dropping to her knees, she rubbed at her bruised and aching throat with one hand. Shaking her head to clear it, she scrabbled around on the floor with her other hand, searching for her shoes.

After finding them at last, she fastened shaky fingers on first one and then the other. With a shoe held in each hand, the sharp spikes pointing outward like weapons, she lurched to her feet and fell out the door. After slamming it swiftly behind, she wrenched the lock in place.

Behind her, she could hear the sound of his muttered oaths. Her skin prickled at the foulness in his voice. For several long seconds she stood completely motionless, sagging against the door, her ear pressed to its panel.

"I'll get you, bitch! If you breathe one word of this to anyone," he gasped, still in pain, "I'll get you. You better keep your mouth shut like you been doin' about the other time, too.

"Remember, I know who you are—and I know who your friends are. Accidents are easy to arrange—especially to a pregnant woman," he threatened meaningfully.

Oh, God, Lauren thought. He was talking about Carrie. He knew that Carrie, her best friend, was pregnant. Who was he? What did he want from her? It had been too dark to make out his features, and he had been careful to stay positioned behind her.

She had to get to the sheriff! Sheriff Slade was Carrie's husband; he'd know what to do.

A little voice inside reminded her of the last time she had gone to the sheriff with information. As a result three men had been killed—the former sheriff and a custodian at the local grade school, along with Raul.

Perhaps if she hadn't hesitated, a small voice whispered, as she was doing now, those three men would still be alive.

Leaning back against the wall, she drooped in indecision. The man hadn't only threatened her, but Carrie, as well. Would he carry out his threat? Would he do injury to her best friend and her unborn child if she went to the sheriff? Could she take the chance that he still might hurt them even if she kept quiet?

It was a no-win situation. If she didn't tell and he tried to do something to Carrie, it would be her fault. At least by telling Rand, he'd have the option of trying to protect his wife and child.

The man who'd attacked her had to be crazy; there was no telling what he might do after this. Rand had to know. She would never be able to forgive herself if she caused injury to her best friend and her baby. She'd already felt too much guilt to live with in recent months, whether real or only imagined on her part.

Rubbing the back of one hand down wet cheeks and across her nose, Lauren moved away from the wall. A sudden, sharp noise from inside the locked room halted her in her tracks. She knew that sound. He was at the window.

Darting down the hall to the front of the building, running as fast as her unsteady legs would carry her, Lauren sobbed and gasped her way toward the lighted windows at the end of the street.

The sheriff's office was only half-a-block away. Please, she prayed silently, let either Rand or Kalan be there, not one of the other deputies who she knew only by sight.

Reaching the office door at last, she threw it open and stumbled inside, stunning the two men sitting with feet propped up on their desks, carrying on a desultory conversation.

Deputy Kalan Holtzer jumped to his feet first and hurried toward Lauren's disheveled figure.

"Lauren! My God, what's happened?"

Rand stood more slowly, but moved around the other man to take her by the shoulders. Lauren gasped softly as his fingers bit into her already sore flesh, and then she hurled herself against his big chest.

The sheriff glanced over her bent head toward his deputy, meeting the other man's look of puzzled compassion with one of his own.

"Lauren, honey, are you hurt? Do you need a doctor? Can you tell us what's happened to upset you so?"

Gathering the tattered remnants of her thoughts together, Lauren pulled back. Still in the shelter of his arms, she looked up at him from beneath tear-drenched lashes and whispered, "I was attacked—at the library."

"Kalan—"

The other man grabbed his hat and headed toward the door. "I'm on the way."

"Do I need to call the doctor?" Rand gently asked the woman still trembling in the shelter of his powerful arms.

"No." She shook her head and allowed him to lead her to a chair. "He didn't hurt me—except for a few bruises."

"Can you tell me what happened—everything, from the beginning?"

Rand knelt by her chair and offered her a handful of tissues from the box on his desk.

Lauren told him as she remembered it, mentioning that at first she had thought the intruder was no more than a small boy playing a practical joke. When she got to the part about the man's ugly accusations and threats, she hesitated.

"Is that it?"

"N-no. He called me names, and he mentioned Raul."

"Raul—was he a friend of his, do you think?"

"Spanish, you mean? Oh, no." Lauren shook her head vehemently, causing her short dark curls to fly about her face. "He was very clear about what he thought of Raul and—" She looked down at the tissues she was shredding in her lap. "He called me a—name. He threatened to kill me.

"Rand..." She touched his arm. "He threatened Carrie."

His glance locked on hers as his broad frame stiffened and a hard, angry glitter darkened his normally mild hazel eyes.

"He mentioned Carrie by name?"

"No, but I know what he meant. He said a lot of things, mostly filth, but he told me to keep my mouth shut about something—only I don't know what he was talking about."

Pushing the hair back from her hot forehead and damp cheeks, she looked at the man across from her with confusion plainly written in her dark eyes.

Rand stood and moved across the room to the radio. He called one of the other deputies and told him to make a fast trip out to his ranch, where Carrie was alone. He instructed the man not to disturb her if everything appeared to be all right, but to stay there until he came to relieve him.

Turning once more to face Lauren, he asked, "You said he mentioned Raul, did he say anything else—about how he died, for instance, or anything about the other two men who died with him?"

Lauren knew it must have been a hard question for him to ask. One of the other men to die that night six months ago had been his father, the former sheriff.

She shook her head. "He only mentioned Raul, and my... relationship with him. But he sounded like a bigot, a man who doesn't like Mexicans."

Sitting on the corner of his desk, Rand stared contemplatively at the toe of one boot for a long moment before meeting Lauren's eyes.

"Do you think this attack on you could have anything to do with what happened six months ago?"

"I don't know, but I don't see how. I thought you'd decided that Aguilar, the custodian, killed your father and Raul, then died from wounds inflicted by your father during the struggle."

Rand walked to the large square window that looked out on to the street and stared in the direction of the library. It looked dark and quiet. Kalan would have called by now if he'd found anything noteworthy. So the man must have gotten away before he arrived on the scene.

He was angry at the thought of Lauren being attacked, especially in town, so close to the sheriff's office. Was there no place a person could expect to be safe anymore?

But despite his anger, he couldn't deny a flicker of excitement, as well, though he was doing his best to smother it. Was this the clue he had been searching for, for over six months? The clue that would prove his personal theory that a fourth man was involved in the shootings? The real man responsible for the deaths of Grant Slade, Raul Estevez and Hernandez Aguilar.

Rand had proven that Aguilar was involved in smuggling illegal aliens, along with anything else he could get his greedy hands on, across the Mexican border. What he hadn't been able to prove was whether Aguilar had worked alone or in conjunction with someone else—the infamous *El Personaje no Presente*, "the man without a face," the man sought by both Mexican and American authorities.

Gazing at the bent head of the woman in the chair, Rand speculated about her part in all of this. Could she know something she hadn't told him? Something she wasn't aware of knowing herself? It wasn't a pleasant thought. Not if *El Personaje no Presente* was involved. The man was ruthless.

He'd heard rumors that the man was purported to live somewhere around the border town of Del Rio. Others swore he lived closer to Brownsville. Rand had someone down there right now trying to learn what he could about the man and report back to him. He had a hunch that *El Personaje no Presente* was responsible for his father's death, and he wouldn't rest easy until he proved it and saw the man brought to justice.

Lauren was frightened now, but nothing compared to how she would feel if she were aware of the thoughts going through his head at the moment. Her life could be in grave danger. *El Personaje no Presente* protected his true identity mercilessly. Rand suspected that might be the reason Aguilar had been terminated. If the man had even conjectured who *El Personaje no Presente* might be... What if that were the piece of information hiding somewhere in Lauren's mind?

The real problem was how to convince her of the seriousness of the situation. He knew how independent a person she was. She wouldn't sit still for having her movements curtailed, or someone watching her every moment of the day. He couldn't afford the manpower involved in that kind of a move anyway.

Maybe he could persuade her to let him use her as bait to trap the killer. After all, she was already in danger. No, she'd never agree. And if Carrie ever found out he was even thinking of using her as a decoy...

Maybe there *was* a way to protect her. One she needn't even be made aware of. And it wouldn't require him to lose a single man-hour from his deputies. Tonight had proved one thing to him. As long as whoever was responsible went free, no one would be safe in this town, least of all Lauren.

He'd do it! He was the authority in this part of the country. He was sworn to uphold the law and bring the guilty to justice. Sometimes that meant taking chances for others as well as himself. He'd protect Lauren to the best of his ability, and he'd see the man responsible for his father's death brought to justice at last.

The office door flew open, and Kalan entered, removing his hat as he crossed the floor. His eyes went immediately to those of his superior.

"Nothing. The window was open in the storeroom, but there wasn't even a sign of a struggle. I've got Herbie dusting for prints."

"I guess that's it, then, for now." Rand laid a comforting hand on Lauren's thin shoulder. "You want to stay out at the house with Carrie tonight?"

"No, I'm fine. And I wouldn't want to have to tell Carrie what the man had said about—you know—her and the baby. I just want to go home and take a hot shower and wash the feel of his hands off me." She shivered and twisted her hands together in her lap.

"I'm going to send Kalan home with you. Your car will be all right parked where it is for tonight. I don't want to frighten you any more than you already are, but you need to take some precautions until we catch this man.

"Don't drive alone at night on secluded roads. Don't walk alone, especially at night. Try to stay where there are plenty of people. And be sure to keep all your doors and windows locked. And stay out of situations that are potentially dangerous. Got that?"

Lauren nodded solemnly.

Kalan handed her the shoes he had found in the hallway outside the storeroom, and while she put them on, Rand told him to stay with her tonight.

Lauren didn't protest Rand's plans for her car or for herself. And when, at the door, he gave her a brief, hard hug and told her that he would see nothing happened to her, she felt safe for the first time since the attack.

This was one time when Kalan's normally solicitous air and protective attitude were more than welcomed. There was not one single person she could name at the present moment who she would rather have sleeping on her couch than the man with the large black gun in his holster who was riding quietly at her side.

Chapter 1

The air was hot and heavy; it had a waiting quality that played havoc with the nerves. Dark stormclouds rolled silently across the horizon, blocking the sun, as Lauren pulled out of her gravel drive and onto the unpaved road that led from her house into the town of Chance.

Her head felt like a balloon, and a dull ache beneath both eyes signaled the imminent change in weather. Neither the weather nor her headache gave much promise for the day ahead. There were other reasons for her headache, too, but she didn't want to think about them right now.

The ache across her cheekbones grew to monumental proportions. A strong breeze sprang up outside, blowing dust and debris across the yellow compact car's path. Grains of sand pelted the windshield like drops of rain. The steering wheel pulled beneath her hands as the car's small frame shook under the onslaught.

An unexpected sound drew her attention to the rearview mirror. She looked up in time to see a streak of black appear as though from out of nowhere and come roaring up behind her, then, in the next instant, swerve out around her.

This stretch of the road was narrow and full of potholes from the torrential rains native to Texas. She reacted instinctively by jerking the steering wheel to the right, a sign of her frayed nerves, and felt the car almost leap off the road and onto the uneven shoulder.

It bumped along for a few hundred feet, hitting rocks and deep ruts, the wheel bucking and jerking in Lauren's tense grasp. She felt her bones rattle and her teeth jar together before she at last managed to gain control of the machine.

Once she had the steering firmly in hand, she stopped to sit for a moment, gripping the wheel tightly. Breathing a sigh of relief, an angry glitter sparking in her large dark eyes, she stared at the thick cloud of reddish dust left by the motorcycle's passing.

Jesse Tyler. There was no mistaking to whom that particular shade of flowing, blond hair belonged. Besides, no one else that she knew of rode a big black monster of a bike like the one Jesse rode—except on occasion, Jesse's pal, Hank.

She was furious that his reckless driving had nearly caused her to wreck her car. She muttered dire imprecations beneath her breath about what she would do to him if she ever got the chance, and made threats of calling the sheriff to report his excessive speed.

After a moment, when the dust of his passing and the intense anger it had sparked had settled, Lauren started her car's engine and pulled slowly back onto the road.

About five miles farther along she came upon the big black-and-silver motorcycle sitting at the edge of the road. A man in a black T-shirt delineating strong shoulder and back muscles was bent over it.

As Lauren drove by, he paused in what he was doing, turned his head over his shoulder and looked up. The expression of fierce concentration on his classically handsome face changed immediately to one of relief. His lower jaw dropped open as though to call out.

Lauren purposefully depressed her gas pedal and went sailing past. She was gleefully satisfied to see his features reform themselves into an expression of surprised disbelief as she left him behind in a choking cloud of dust similar to the one left earlier by his passing.

About a mile farther along she began to slow the car's speed. That had not been a very neighborly thing to do. Obviously he was having trouble with his machine. And though they weren't really friends, she felt guilty for leaving him stranded so far from town.

Then Rand's words of caution the night of the attack came back to her, and she continued on without turning back. Rand had told her not to get herself into any situation that was potentially dangerous.

Given Jesse Tyler's reputation with women, she considered *him* potentially dangerous on a lonely back road. Though not personally acquainted with his abilities in that area, like anyone in town who had ears with which to hear, she'd heard of his status as a reputed lady-killer.

She soothed her conscience now by reminding herself that *she* hadn't run *him* off the road. And besides, she thought as she glanced at the round digital clock on the dash, she was already late for work.

Jesse fanned the dust from in front of his face with a grimy hand and stared at the disappearing bumper of the little yellow car. He guessed he deserved that. He hadn't intended to run her off the road a ways back. He was in a tearing hurry to get to town and just hadn't anticipated coming upon her the way he had. He knew he drove too fast. The sheriff had cautioned him about it often enough. But he was normally a safe driver.

He figured he owed Miss Lauren Downing, the town librarian, an apology. The prospect of apologizing didn't bother him much. It would give him an excuse to become reacquainted with her. He remembered her from school, and he'd seen her around town several times in the last year since he'd returned home.

He was a few years younger than she was, he knew, but years older in experience, he reckoned. He'd thought her attractive when they were in high school, but she was beautiful now.

The age difference was hardly worth mentioning—as far as he was concerned. If the gossips were to be believed, and he had firsthand experience on just how "accurate" they were, Lauren wasn't much of a social person. Not that she didn't participate in town affairs, she just didn't date much. At least, not before Raul Estevez, and no one regularly since him.

Raul Estevez had been a friend of Jesse's. It was a real shame he was gone. And if he had his way, someone would be paying for his death—soon.

A bolt of lightning split the sky, and thunder growled overhead, capturing his immediate attention. While he had stood lost in thoughts about Lauren, the impending storm had moved closer. If he didn't want to get a drenching, he knew he had better get his bike fixed, and fast.

Fiddling with the coil beneath the seat of the motorcycle, he speculated about the cause of the problem. He wondered if there could be a crack in the case, causing the bike to start, splutter and stop. For the last fifty miles or so his journey had been broken intermittently while he stopped to re-evaluate the problem.

After a close inspection of the machine's internal workings, he did indeed discover a crack in the coil's casing. That meant he'd have to get a part to replace it, and quickly, if he didn't want to be immobilized permanently. And for that he'd have to travel to the larger town of Del Rio, across the mountains.

After fastening the seat back into place, he straddled the powerful machine. Turning the key with a few mumbled words of encouragement, he was pleased to hear the engine cough and then come to life. In moments he was following the trail left by Lauren's earlier passing, feeling the wind whipping his hair out behind.

As he drove slowly past the library, located on the town's main drag, he saw Carrie Slade, the sheriff's pregnant wife, climb from their truck. She gave a cool nod in answer to Jesse's cocky wave and turned quickly away.

Jesse was well aware of what Carrie Slade thought of him. Her opinion was echoed by nearly everyone in the whole town.

If he had allowed it, the picture the town had of him could have played havoc with his self-esteem. But he rarely did that to himself. For now it was enough to know he was doing what *he* felt was right.

A large drop of rain splattered on the faceplate of his helmet, and he decided this was not the time for introspection. He had an urgent meeting to attend, and he was almost half-an-hour late.

The meeting had been arranged over the telephone nearly a week ago, and it was important that he be there. A matter of life and death, he'd been told.

As the run-down facade of Pete's Cantina loomed up on his right, Jesse concentrated on getting his cycle off the street unobserved and parked out of sight in the alley behind the bar.

When that had been accomplished to his satisfaction he ran through the heavy downpour to the green painted door at the back of the building. This room belonged to Rosalita Mendez, one of the sexy barmaids Pete employed. Knocking three times, two long and one short, he waited for admittance.

"Good morning."

Lauren glanced up quickly, then smiled into Carrie Slade's beaming face.

"Carrie! What are you doing out so early, and in this storm?" Her friend was eight months pregnant with her first child. She'd had two previous miscarriages, and Lauren worried about her.

Lauren put aside the cards she was updating and watched as the other woman shook her umbrella outside the door, then folded it and placed it in the stand near the entrance.

"I had some shopping to do in town, so I figured I'd stop in and say hello."

The truth was that she was worried about Lauren; shopping was only an excuse to drop by and see how she was. She'd been concerned about her ever since Rand had told her about the attack a week back.

And if the startled expression on her friend's face when she'd first spoken was any indication, Lauren wasn't as calm about the whole affair as she had been pretending.

"There are lines beneath your eyes deep enough to lose a truck in," Carrie accused without preamble. "I know you aren't sleeping at night. I told you to get a watchdog instead of that damned bird."

"Daniel is a watch-bird. And he's all the protection I need."

"Hah!" Carrie snorted loudly as she moved to lower her cumbersome weight into a chair beside one of the reading tables.

"What good is a bird going to do you if that maniac comes back looking for trouble? A dog could protect you."

"Daniel might out-cuss him—if he tried," Lauren answered her friend solemnly. "Besides, I like Daniel."

Carrie stared at her friend for a long, silent moment, and then, recalling some of Daniel's more colorful epithets, laughed. "You'll never guess who just came roaring into town." Knowing Lauren's penchant for being stubborn, she decided to drop the subject of the dog, but that didn't mean she was through with it—just yet.

"Jesse Tyler," Lauren answered without hesitation and to her friend's amazement. "No, I haven't become suddenly psychic," she continued when she saw the startled look on Carrie's face. "Who can miss the way he thunders in and out of town on that monster machine of his? And, besides, we, er, crossed paths this morning on my way to work."

Watching Lauren pick carelessly at the edge of the desk, Carrie asked, "What's he done now? That boy is forever getting into trouble."

"Well, I'd hardly call him a boy. He can't be more than two or three years younger than we are. That makes him about twenty-three, by my figuring."

"Yeah, well, then when is he going to grow up and start acting like an adult?"

Recalling the way he'd come tearing up behind her without any warning that morning, Lauren had to admit that his behavior hadn't seemed very adult. Carrie was undoubtedly correct; Jesse needed to act in a more responsible manner.

"How is it going with you and Kalan? Have the two of you been able to spend much time together lately?"

Carrie's second abrupt change of subject came as no surprise to Lauren. Her friend was forever extolling the man's virtues and inviting the two of them to dinner on the same night.

Lauren glanced up, then quickly looked away. The question of her relationship with Kalan Holtzer, or lack of one, could have been a point of conflict between the two women if she'd let it.

Carrie, happy and secure in her marriage, and in the knowledge of her pregnancy, was positive that all life's problems would be solved for Lauren if only she would open her eyes to Kalan Holtzer's excellent attributes and accept him as husband material.

She simply couldn't understand Lauren's hesitation in snatching the man up. And Lauren couldn't seem to make her realize that, while Kalan was indeed a fine figure of a man and would make some woman an admirable husband someday, that woman wasn't Lauren.

The spark that ignited between a man and woman, letting them know they belonged together, was missing with Kalan. Lauren had had a taste of what that spark could mean in her relationship with Raul. And she knew that she couldn't settle for anything less with someone else.

When Lauren didn't immediately respond to Carrie's question, her friend took up the threads of the conversation straight away. She had guessed where Lauren's thoughts lay.

"Raul was a good man, Laurie, but he would be the first to tell you to get on with your life. Besides, you yourself said that your relationship hadn't gotten much beyond the good friends stage."

"I know all that—I'm just not ready yet."

It was easier to fall back on that than to try to explain once again that there was something missing in her response to Kalan.

"I'll know when the time is right."

"I hope so, Laurie. You know, you can be awfully hard on yourself sometimes. We all have shortcomings, they aren't exclusive to you. Ease up on yourself. We all love you."

Lauren smiled and nodded. "Right." She crossed her heart solemnly, as they had as children. "I promise to accept the very next offer for a date, whether it's from Kalan or any other presentable male. Okay?"

"Okay." Carrie laughed and began to lift herself from the chair. "It's time I was getting on about my own business. Besides, I see a couple of people coming up the front steps."

Lauren watched her friend leave, knowing that they had talked all around the real purpose of her visit, the question she had wanted to voice and yet hadn't. Did Lauren remember anything more about the attack? Could she add anything to the description she'd given earlier? Had she remembered anything more about the time back in April when she'd found the note—the note involving the murders?

The answer was still no.

The morning dragged by slowly. Usually when the weather was cold or damp, or both, people wanted a good book to wile away the dreary hours.

Today, however, only a trickle of people had made their way to the library, and Lauren found herself feeling surprisingly lonely.

About an hour before lunch she looked up to see the sheriff enter the building after shaking the water from his Stetson. He wiped the mud carefully from his boots onto the doormat, and Lauren hid a smile at the thought that Carrie had trained him well.

"How you doin', Lauren?" he asked as he closed the door on the staccato sound of the rain.

"Haven't had much business today. How about you? You come to find a good book to keep you busy this afternoon? I'll bet any self-respecting criminal has the good sense to stay inside on a day like this," she teased him with a grin.

Rand grinned back and shook his head. "I didn't come for a book. Thought I'd stop by and make sure you haven't had any more scares like that one last week."

Coming to lean against the checkout desk, he propped a hip against its side and rested an elbow on its smooth surface.

"Haven't heard a peep out of him, thank God. You know, I still can't imagine what he meant about me keeping my mouth shut." Meeting the man's piercing gaze, she shrugged her shoulders. "I've thought and thought about that day, the day I found the note—it was right there, under that table—" She pointed across the room. "And there's nothing, not a thing, I haven't already told you."

Rand veiled his disappointment at her words. He'd come by hoping that perhaps now that the fright had worn off something might have surfaced in her memory, jogged loose by the attack.

"Well, don't worry, or try to think too much. If you try too hard, whatever is there—if there's anything at all—might just stay hidden."

"I'll remember that, and I'll try to relax."

From the darkness of the circles below her eyes and the lines of tiredness at the corners of her mouth, he didn't put too much stock in her answer. She was worrying, all right, and she wasn't getting much sleep. For a moment he even wondered if she was telling the truth about not knowing anything more about the man who'd attacked her.

There must be some way to help her. Some way to find the man who'd terrorized her. And, in so doing, perhaps find the answers to the questions surrounding the death of his father. But right now he didn't know what that way might be.

"Well, guess I better go earn my pay." Straightening, he picked up his hat and turned away.

"Oh, by the way..." Lauren halted him with her words. "I forgot to ask Carrie when she was here earlier, but I wondered if I might borrow your truck Saturday. Kathy Richards is filling in for me that day because I have a donation of books I need to pick up in Freemont, and I thought I'd stop and do some shopping in Del Rio."

"You goin' alone?"

"Yes, why?"

Rand slapped his hat against his thigh in a nervous gesture. He was torn between the need to warn her against the trip alone and the thought that maybe this was the chance he'd been waiting for to trap the man responsible for his father's death.

He knew that those lonely, winding canyon roads offered all kinds of opportunities for an accident, should someone want to stage one. He should at the very least tell her to be cautious, yet he didn't want to scare her too much and keep her from going.

"I can't stop you from goin'—" his conscience wouldn't let him get by without the warning "—but it would be best not to."

Lauren lifted her chin and looked him straight in the eye. "I won't be kept on a string—or chained to town like I'm the one who did something wrong."

"Well, don't stay too late, and don't stop anywhere along the way unless there are plenty of people around. I'll make sure the truck is serviced and full of gas before you pick it up."

What little color there was in Lauren's pale face drained away, and a spark of fear dulled the shine in the dark eyes meeting his. "Do you think there's a chance someone—*he*—might follow me?" she asked uneasily. "It's been over a week—and there was just that one time...."

Rand calmed her fears with a shake of his head. "I didn't say he would follow you. I just want you to be careful. Just be prepared for anything unexpected, out of the ordinary.

"There's no reason to panic. I seriously doubt you'll ever hear from the man again. He's probably lying low, figuring he put the fear of God into you and there's no need to worry about you now. He might not even be in the area any longer."

But Rand hoped he was. As much as he hated himself for wanting something that could put Lauren in danger, he hoped he was.

"You think he's gone?" Lauren took a deep, measured breath and felt the turbulent beat of her heart begin to slow. "I'm not a coward, Rand, but there's something so—" she gripped her elbows and shivered "—so frightening about some faceless person threatening you, threatening to kill you—" She shivered again.

"I know, honey." He stepped close enough to touch her shoulder reassuringly and felt like a two-faced pig. "You know I'll do everything in my power to see you aren't hurt again." Tipping her chin so that she met his eyes, he asked, "Trust me?"

Lauren nodded and smiled slowly. "I have to, don't I? You're the sheriff. And besides, Carrie wouldn't be my friend anymore if I didn't."

Rand heard the sneering voice inside telling him he should forbid her to go or, at the very least, tell her the real dangers involved. But he silenced the voice by assuring it, and himself, that her going was not of his doing, and that he'd see she was protected every step of the way.

Though he hadn't mentioned anything to Carrie about the threats on her life, Rand had taken them seriously. And it was straining his abilities to keep a watch on both women. It would be impossible to protect the two women indefinitely.

Carrie's safety he could manage himself, but Lauren's future well-being was another matter.

As he left the library, Rand glanced up at the gray, weeping sky overhead and prayed that a solution would come to him—soon. The more time that was allowed to pass after a crime, the less likelihood there was of finding viable clues with which to solve it.

There had been nothing in the storeroom after the attack to identify the man—not even a partial fingerprint. And if he was correct in his theory that the three deaths were all due to the same man—well, any clues were welcome, any at all.

Lauren spent the rest of the day in a fog. The trip to Freemont loomed like a dark cloud on the horizon. The pleasure had gone out of it with the sheriff's words of warning. Several times she almost picked up the phone and told Rand she'd changed her mind.

She'd spent more than a few nights in the last week sitting up talking to Daniel, her cockatoo, because she couldn't sleep for worrying. Daniel was a new addition to her household, but one she was glad she'd made.

After hearing of the attack, Carrie had advised her to get a watchdog—a big one. But the care of a dog was more than she felt able to handle. And besides, she thought it would be a lonely life for the dog with her gone all day long. Birds didn't seem to need that much attention.

But Daniel was a lot of company for her, and when she talked to him, occasionally he talked back. He swore a blue streak, too, whenever he sensed someone's approach. She had no idea how he sensed their presence; maybe birds had the same sixth sense dogs had.

Lauren continued to rack her brain for an answer to the question, why? Why had the man come after her? But there was simply no logical reason for the assault. She could think of nothing she knew, or suspected, that would in any way incriminate anyone in the murders that had taken place in April. Besides, the police considered the case closed.

Questions plagued her, waking or sleeping. She asked herself things like, could there have been a fourth man involved in the deaths? Could he be the man who had attacked her? But then she had to ask herself, why? What possible motive could he have for thinking her a threat to him?

The presence of a fourth man had never even been established to her knowledge. Was she only clutching at straws? Or was there something—something she didn't *want* to remember—buried deep within her psyche? But why wouldn't she want to remember? Could it be something that incriminated someone she knew?

Chapter 2

Lauren drifted aimlessly through the throngs of people. If anyone had been observing her very closely they would have noticed how her glance strayed to the window of each shop as she passed.

She'd been doing some early Christmas shopping, for Carrie and the coming baby, since just after noon. And the feeling of being watched, stalked, had grown steadily, until she found herself watching the face of every passing stranger and wondering if he was the one. The one who was following her, causing her skin to crawl, looking for an opportunity to strike.

At first she told herself the idea of being followed was ridiculous. She knew no one had pursued her from Chance. On the roads she had traveled that morning it would have been easy to spot a tail.

Of course, if it was someone who *knew* she was going to be in Del Rio that day, he could have come over ahead of time and waited for her. The thought of someone wanting to hurt her, possibly someone she knew, brought back the feeling of sick dread that she had experienced the night she was accosted in the library. It returned each time she had to go into the storeroom for supplies.

Though she tried as she made her way through the crowds of shoppers, she was unable to overcome the feeling of being on tenterhooks, or the anxious desire to make a headlong rush from the mall to the comparative safety of the truck.

Lauren quickened her stride as the bank of double doors at the entrance came into view, then shouldered her way through. A group of people in a hurry to get inside pushed their way in as she exited, causing her to lose her hold on her packages.

"Oh, sorry—" she said.

Glancing up, she met the strangely veiled, vividly blue eyes of the man she'd all but knocked down in her precipitate bid for freedom.

Lauren swallowed quickly, feeling momentarily light-headed as she tried to fix her fear-befuddled mind on the face of the man holding the bundle she had rammed into his chest.

"That's okay, my fault," he said quickly.

A flicker of a smile lifted the edges of his beautifully-shaped mouth and then quickly died out at her lack of response. The hands gripping the package moved into view as he held it out to her.

"I believe this belongs to you."

Lauren nodded and, still without speaking, tried to add it to the mountainous heap in her arms. But it was an impossible feat to accomplish. However she had juggled them all earlier, she couldn't seem to get a grip on them all at once now.

"It's okay, I'll carry it to your car," he offered. "That *is* where you're headed, I hope," he added with a slightly raised brow.

Lauren noticed, inanely, that the brow was a couple of shades lighter than the blond hair feathering his forehead and cheeks. Redirecting her eyes to a spot beyond his left shoulder, she gave a short, sharp nod in answer to his question and took a step back away from him. His sudden appearance had come as a shock. Could *he* be the one? But no. She remembered that he'd been out of town at the time of the attack in the library. They were blocking the exit, and people were attempting, impatiently, to move around them.

Laying a hand on her shoulder, he assisted her out of the line of traffic with a surprisingly gallant gesture. Lauren was at a loss for words, but feeling something more was required, broke into breathless, indignant speech.

"Your chivalry now doesn't excuse your behavior of yesterday. If you remember, you nearly ran me off—"

"I remember," he broke across her words. "And I want to apologize to you for that. I admit I drive too fast out of habit, but I don't usually make a habit of running pretty librarians off the road and into the ditch."

There was no denying the sudden thrill that rushed through her at his words. Or the instant captivation the blue eyes created as they met and held her gaze with an intensity that left her breathless.

Any further indignation—or speech, for that matter—was beyond her, though she did manage to break the hold of his eyes. They made their way across the parking lot to the blue-and-silver truck in silence.

Jesse lifted the bundles from her unresisting arms and, along with the one he carried, stacked them carefully in the back of the truck, as confused as Lauren by the silver thread of attraction that seemed to be drawing them together.

He had always thought she was attractive; he'd even had a crush on her his first day of high school. But she'd been out of his reach then as a popular senior, and she was every bit as much out of his reach now.

He could admire her from afar—and did—but from afar he hadn't felt this awful yearning to reach out and touch the brown curls framing her heart-shaped face, to rub them between his fingertips to see if they were really as silky as they appeared. From afar he hadn't felt this burning need to lean over and taste the hesitant smile on her pink lips, to see if it was as sweet as it always looked.

What the hell was wrong with him? Women were a dime a dozen in the places where he'd been the last few years. He didn't need the complication of courting a woman like this, a woman who had love and marriage bred into her soul.

Lauren felt an immediate and painful tightening in her chest as she watched the play of muscles beneath the blue cotton shirt. Jesse had gained a few pounds, filled out in an alarmingly sensual manner, since they had been in school together. When had it happened? She didn't recall his being this virilely appealing a few years ago before he went into the military. Maybe the military weren't lying when they claimed the ability to build men. And what a man!

Jesse turned, catching her glance, and for a moment neither of them could look away. Lauren felt as though she were swimming in a sea of thick honey, and for a brief moment she lost all sense of time and place.

A car revving its engine somewhere close behind backfired, startling her into an awareness of her surroundings. What was she doing, standing here staring at Jesse Tyler as though mesmerized. What was wrong with her sense of propriety? Her only excuse was that she'd never had a conversation with the *notorious* Jesse Tyler before, and she was decidedly out of her element.

"I—well—if you'll excuse me—I have to be going—" she began disjointedly, backing away and coming solidly up against the side of the truck.

How the mighty are fallen, she thought with a faint self-deprecating sneer. She should be telling him what she thought of him and that monster of a bike he rode so recklessly about the countryside. Just because he had apologized, that didn't make what he had done any less dangerous. And instead, here she was letting him make her feel and act the fool.

But Jesse wasn't ready to let her go. He kept pace with her as she backed away from the truck and made her way to the driver's side. There he stopped her from climbing inside with a quick question.

"Are you headed back to Chance?" he asked suddenly, turning the full force of his smiling blue eyes on her face. Eyes the exact shade of the Texas state flower, the bluebonnet.

Swallowing tightly, Lauren nodded silently. This man was dangerous—with a smile like that, no wonder he had the reputation he did. What woman, old or young, could resist his lure—even one bound to hold him in contempt?

"I'm headed home, w-why?"

"I wondered if I might beg a lift? I hitched a ride over here to pick up a part I ordered for my bike, but I can't find anybody going back that way."

The grin had diminished somewhat, and Lauren could think clearly once more, but she felt crowded and uncomfortable by the way he stood so close, his eyes trained unwaveringly on hers.

Would she be foolish to give him a ride? It was getting late, and by the time they drove the distance through the twisting canyon roads it would be dark. She didn't really know him—not all that well—even if they *had* lived in the same town more or less all their lives.

"Yes, all right, I'll give you a ride."

Fool! You were told not to get yourself in any dangerous situations. If driving alone with Jesse Tyler isn't dangerous, nothing is.

Ridiculous, she argued with herself. Jesse hardly had to resort to force to take a woman. From what she'd been led to believe, they practically fought to be next in line for his favors.

"Thanks." He smiled again, directly into her eyes.

Lauren felt an odd breathless sensation and stepped quickly around him.

"I want to get started right away. I don't like driving home from here after dark. So where do we pick up your motorcycle part?"

"It's around the south side of the mall. We can stop and get it on the way—if that's all right with you."

Lauren almost flinched with nerves when he took her arm and assisted her into the truck, then carefully closed the door. Her flesh burned from his touch. Keeping her eyes on the cars in the distance, she waited for him to join her inside.

Jesse directed her to the outside door of the automotive store, and she watched, under cover of her lashes, as he climbed from the truck and sauntered, with loose-limbed grace, inside. In a moment he returned, the muscles in his upper arms bulging as he lifted the heavy box into the bed of the truck.

Seated inside once more, he gave her a grin and said, "All set, let her roll."

Now that they were ready to leave, Lauren felt even more apprehensive about the sense of what she was doing. It was about a two-hour drive to Chance, but somehow she knew it would seem a whole lot longer today, with Jesse at her side.

She didn't realize how close the confines of the small sporty truck were until her hand accidentally brushed his hard thigh as she pulled the seat belt around her and clipped it into place. Jerking her hand back instantaneously, she stared apprehensively from the tight muscled leg to Jesse's face.

At the sudden contact Jesse's head swiveled slowly in her direction. Their eyes met, and Lauren felt as though he had looked behind her eyes and read her thoughts.

"I don't usually wear one of those," he said after a long, oddly taut silence, nodding toward the seat belt. "But since you're driving—" he shrugged "—I wouldn't want to get you into trouble." He fastened his own in place.

Lauren's heart skipped a beat, and she felt a sudden surge of some emotion she didn't care to identify. The air between them seemed to vibrate. Glancing hurriedly away, she started the truck, all her concentration on the task at hand.

Sneaking a sidelong glance at him, she wished he was still the fresh-faced youth of the past. It would have made this trip more to her liking. Feeling attracted to Jesse Tyler was more than she could handle right now. It was a ridiculous idea at the best of times.

She was years older than he was, she admonished herself, attempting to bolster her flagging confidence. And there was absolutely no reason for her to stand in awe of him. Jesse was definitely not a figure of authority. On the contrary, he was someone who flouted the need for such elemental things as order and respect. His history as a teenager proved that.

The town of Chance was relatively small, and Jesse's parents' spread was several miles from town. Even with Lauren being the town's only librarian, their paths didn't cross much. Most of what she knew of him was hearsay, learned from other people's conversations. She wasn't one to listen and form her opinions from gossip, but she'd seen his wildness with her own two eyes on a couple of occasions.

Even knowing that, she couldn't keep her glance from straying to him warily as they moved out of town and headed west from Del Rio. He was hardly a reassuring sight for a woman of Lauren's untried femininity. In tight faded jeans and a dark blue cotton shirt that matched the color of his eyes, he challenged every woman whose path he chanced to cross.

Lauren's eyes traveled down from the shoulder-length, wheat-blond hair, over the front of his shirt and paused momentarily at the spot where a button was missing, just about the middle of his brawny chest. Curly gold hair peeped through the opening, and her eyes hurriedly moved on.

The long sleeves of his shirt were rolled up past his muscular forearms to his elbows. Lauren couldn't remember ever feeling quite so enchanted by a man's wrists and elbows before. Her eyes slid down his long muscled thighs and over bent knees to his scarred western boots. The trip had just begun, and already she felt as though she'd been riding for hours at his side.

The silence inside the cab stretched and seemed to heighten the tension building between the two occupants.

Finally Lauren broke into speech. "Are you back in town to stay, or are you thinking about leaving again?"

"Haven't decided. There's a big world out there, and I haven't seen nearly enough of it." Was he reassuring himself, or just making conversation?

"You seem to travel around quite a lot." There was a question in her voice that he chose to ignore by turning to stare out the window. "You've been in the military, I understand," she tried again in a conversational tone. For some reason it was impossible to sit this close to him and remain silent.

"And just what else do you understand about me?" he couldn't help asking in a soft voice.

"I . . . don't know what you mean."

"Don't give me that. I'm sure you've heard plenty about that wild man Jesse Tyler."

There was a teasing quality to his words, but a darker, deeper note to the tone of his voice. Lauren didn't know quite how to take what he'd said. Should she laugh and admit to hearing the gossip about him, or pretend ignorance and change the subject?

"It doesn't matter," he went on. "I know what's said about me, and I'm immune to it. 'Sticks and stones' and all that."

He laughed. But a small prick somewhere inside let him know just how false his words were, and had been for a long time now.

Lauren felt a sudden need to apologize to him, but wasn't quite certain why. Somehow she'd hurt him—yet that seemed ridiculous. Hurt Jesse Tyler with words?

"Look, I don't usually listen to gossip. And I don't judge a person on what's been said about them."

"Then you're a mighty rare individual," he said skeptically. "Most people are ready to believe anything they hear, then embellish it before passing it along."

"But—I really don't—I mean I hear it of course, but I don't—"

"Forget it," he muttered after a short pause.

With his hands clenched on his thighs, he looked out the window at the passing scenery. Since when did the opinion of one person—and a woman he barely knew, at that—make a difference to how he felt?

After a moment of tense silence he shifted in the seat and crossed an ankle over his knee. He spent the next few miles staring sightlessly at his fingers, plucking at a loose thread on one boot.

The truck swept along the highway past the flat desert countryside into the steadily rising inclines of the Tinaja Mountains. At times the road ran parallel to the Rio Grande, which in places was hardly wide enough to be called a stream.

In the distance, massive white limestone cliffs gave way to strange structures of dark basalt, interspersed with haunting shapes composed of hardened volcanic ash. It was a country of extremes, extreme contrasts, extreme loneliness and deprivation, and extreme beauty.

Glancing at the big-knuckled hands lying loosely in Jesse's lap, Lauren saw him give a slight shiver. The sun was slipping past the tall rugged spires in the distance, and the early October night had taken on a chilly air. Leaning forward, she switched on the truck's heater.

"Are you thinking of taking a job while you're back?" The road was lonely, and she needed an escape for her building uneasiness.

She had never known Jesse Tyler to do anything but work his father's spread and raise Cain—mostly raise Cain.

"Yeah, I got a job lined up at Sam Tindle's feed store at the end of Main Street."

Aware of every move he made, Lauren squirmed restlessly in her seat. When she rested a hand on the gear shift, his knee bumped against her wrist. They both started, and she quickly pulled her hand away, the delicate inner skin of her wrist feeling as though it had been branded.

The air inside the cab became stifling. Sweat trickled down between Lauren's breasts, and her hands stuck to the steering wheel. The windows fogged up.

"Is there anywhere in particular you'd like me to drop you off?" she asked, secretly relieved, as they descended from the mountains and passed into the small valley where the town was situated.

"Anywhere is fine," he answered abruptly.

Pulling up directly in front of the lighted porch, so she wouldn't have to cross the dimly lit parking lot, Lauren shut off the engine and turned slightly in her seat.

Hoping to end this trip on a positive, joking note, she whispered in a serious tone, "I know all about you, you know—even your big secret."

Jesse's hand became motionless on the seat belt, and his guarded eyes rose to meet hers, a breathless, waiting quality in their stare.

Feeling confused and somehow out of her depth at his reaction, she forced a smile. "I was only teasing—I meant you're a nice person. Not at all the kind of person you're said to be—"

Reminding someone of unfavorable gossip about them was hardly the way to lead into a compliment, she realized. Or to let them know you've been pleasantly surprised by their behavior. With a wide-eyed stare, a hand at her wayward mouth, Lauren whispered, "I mean—I didn't mean—"

Jesse's hand reached toward hers, hovering briefly without making contact. "It's all right. I think I understand what you mean." He grinned.

"You know, you're not at *all* like I expected you to be," she blurted all at once. And then, embarrassed, "I-I mean your reputation— that is—"

"Jess!"

Hard knuckles rapped on the passenger window. A round face topped by tight dark curls grinned in at them.

"Jess, my man, get the hell out here, boy."

Clicking the seat belt from around him, Jesse paused long enough to glance back at Lauren, something disturbing in his eyes. "I am, you know," he told her. "I'm every bit as bad as my reputation. All I've thought about this whole trip is how to get you into bed."

Lauren gasped, flushed a brilliant shade of red and stared open-mouthed at him.

Jesse exited the truck, grabbed his friend by the neck and grinned. "Hank."

"Hey man, where the hell you been? Come on, let's go get a brew. There's this new waitress down at Pete's." Hank fanned his face with one hand.

"Hold on a minute," Jesse told him. Leaning down to the window, he asked, "Will it be okay if I leave my box in the back of the truck for now? I'll be around to pick it up in a couple hours."

"This is Sheriff Slade's truck. If it isn't here when you come back, try the lot behind the sheriff's office," she said, unable to meet his glance. After a moment, another face replaced Jesse's at the window.

"Hi, Miss Downing." Hank grinned shyly.

"Hello, Hank. I haven't seen you in the library for a while."

"No, ma'am, the ranch has been keeping me pretty busy. I been out of town a lot lately on business for my dad."

"Well, don't be a stranger. I've gotten in several good mysteries since I last saw you."

"Yes, ma'am, I'll see you soon."

"Tell your brother, Paul, I found that book he thought he'd lost. It was stuck in with some books in the adult reading section."

"I'll tell him," he promised as he straightened up and backed away from the door.

Climbing slowly from the truck, Lauren watched the two strut off down the street, clapping each other on the back, laughing and talking.

A snatch of their conversation came back to her, and she heard Jesse ask Hank laughingly when he had learned to read. He hadn't cracked a book the whole twelve years they'd been in school together. And if it hadn't been for him, Hank never would have made it out of kindergarten.

She didn't hear Hank's answer, but she saw Jesse threaten Hank's jaw with his fist, laugh and look back over his shoulder in her direction.

Why had he said what he had just before leaving the truck? They had been getting along pretty well until then. And she'd been convinced that at least some of the things said about him were lies—until he'd ruined her impression with that last damning statement.

"Hi."

Lauren glanced up into Deputy Kalan Holtzer's friendly face. "Hi, yourself. What are you doing skulking around the library parking lot?"

"I'm skulking with an ulterior motive. How about a cup of hot coffee?"

Kalan moved to join her beside the vehicle and draped a companionable arm around her shoulders, gave her a brief hug and let the arm drop. It was as far as he dared to push their friendship at this stage.

Jesse chose that moment to look back over his shoulder as he and Hank rounded the corner heading for Pete's Cantina. His stride didn't so much as falter to hint at the chaos of emotions he felt at the sight of the deputy's familiarity. In the next moment he lost sight of the couple.

"Sure, come on." Lauren took Kalan's arm. "We'll see if Kathy has any made, but it's closing time, and we may have to make our own."

"That's okay with me," the man walking at her side answered slowly. "Lauren..."

"Yes?"

Pausing on the steps, she looked inquiringly up at the man whose shoulder came to the top of her head.

"Was that Jesse Tyler I saw get out of the truck just now?"

"Yes, why?"

"His reputation precedes him."

"I know."

Screwing her face into a frown, she murmured, "I gave him a ride back from the city. We literally bumped into one another there." After an infinitesimal pause, she added, "You may think I'm crazy, but I wonder if his reputation isn't a bit exaggerated."

"No, it isn't." He shook his head. "He's just about done it all."

"Oh." Looking off in the direction Jesse and his friend had taken, she murmured softly, so Kalan had to strain to hear her words, "That's basically what he said."

"Is there something you want to tell me?"

"No." Putting on a smile for his benefit, she shook her dark curls decisively, forcing Jesse Tyler—and his disturbing effect on her equilibrium—out of her mind. "Come on, let's find that coffee."

Later that evening, Lauren sat before the fireplace with an open book across her knees, thinking about the deputy. In many ways Kalan reminded her of Raul.

That made her wonder if she had gone along with dating Kalan for that very reason. Had she been trying to find

Raul, or what she thought they might have had if he'd lived, with Kalan?

Until Raul's death she'd felt almost as though she was leading a charmed life. She was doing work she loved in the town where she'd grown up, among the people she knew and loved. And she thought she might have found the man she could grow to love and plan a future with.

But fate, as it has a way of doing, had stepped in and made her realize that only the gods lead charmed lives. And she was only mortal.

If only she had ignored the note she'd found beneath one of the reading tables that afternoon back in April, perhaps she wouldn't be sitting here now, trying to make sense out of the upside down turn her life had taken.

First there had been the murder, then the attack, and now she found herself attracted by the likes of Jesse Tyler. Though she had told him she didn't put stock in gossip, it was hard to turn a stone-deaf ear to so much of it, in such a small town, about one person.

The phone on the table beside her rang, startling her from her gloomy thoughts. Lifting the receiver to her ear, she spoke into it.

"Hello?"

"It's me. I just wanted to let you know I like that little outfit you got today. It'll look real cute on a baby. Pink, wasn't it?

"You expecting your friend to have a girl? Or are you just in the habit of knowing things you shouldn't?

"You didn't pay any attention to me when I told you not to tell anyone about our little meeting in the library. I'm going to have to punish you for that. You hear me? You've been a bad little girl, and I'm going to have to make you pay— make you learn that when I tell you not to do something, you better listen." The tone of the harshly whispered words rose as he spoke, and his breathing became fast and irregular.

Lauren clutched the phone tighter against her cheek. He knew about her trip to the city. He knew about the purchases she'd made. How could he know—unless he had followed her?

The feeling of being watched, stalked, hadn't been her imagination after all. The hand holding the phone began to shake, and her stomach fluttered as if a million butterflies were trapped inside it, trying to find their way out.

Where was her way out—out of this nightmare?

"Who are you? Why are you doing this? Why don't you leave me alone?" she cried, before slamming down the receiver and burying her face in her hands.

What was she going to do? He knew her phone number, he knew her friends, he'd followed her today all the way to the city. Who was he? What did he want from her? Was he crazy?

Shoving herself to her feet, she forced herself to reach for the receiver again. She had to call the police. A sharp noise from outside caused her to stop all at once and stand fearfully in the middle of the room, hardly daring to breathe.

"Oh—oh—trouble!" Daniel squawked. "I'm hungry—time to eat."

Lauren was torn between a hysterical need to laugh at the bird and the very real fear she felt tightening the nerves in her stomach. Lurching toward the door, she checked the safety locks, some newly installed, and stood leaning against the wall, staring at the phone.

This was ridiculous; the man couldn't be in two places at once. He couldn't be on the phone to her one second and at her door the next. She was losing her sense of proportion. Why didn't she just call the sheriff and tell him what was happening? He'd protect her *and* Carrie. Rand Slade would see that nothing bad happened to either one of them.

She was again reaching for the phone when her hand froze inches from it as it suddenly rang. Fingers knotting into a fist, she hesitated before lifting the receiver once again to her ear.

"Why did you hang up?"

The whispered tones were becoming familiar, but they still caused the hair to stand rigidly up on the back of her neck.

"Leave me alone! You're sick. You need to get help before you really hurt someone!"

After slamming the receiver down once more, she unplugged the phone to keep from receiving another call.

"Help! Erk! Help me! You need help!"

Daniel stood on his perch, squawking away, turning his head from side to side and lifting first one foot and then the other, his curved beak snapping shut on each word.

Lauren walked over to his cage and stopped for a moment to whisper a few soothing words to the large white bird with the beautiful fan-like crest on his head. He responded by putting his beak against the bars, and when she leaned down he made a kissing motion against her cheek.

The few minutes she spent with Daniel soothed her jangled nerves, and she had her fear under control when she reconnected the phone and dialed the sheriff's number.

It was after eleven, but the phone at the office was answered immediately by a deep voice she didn't recognize. A few seconds later Rand's reassuring tones came down the wire to her.

"H-he—called—"

Her voice broke, and she swallowed hard before continuing, attempting to bridle the fear that swamped her immediately upon mentioning . . . him.

"Lauren? Is that you?"

She took a deep breath and nodded against the receiver, all the terror she'd felt during the conversation with the madman charging back.

"Yes, it's me. He called just now—he's been following me—he knew all about where I went today and what I did."

The panic in her voice escalated until she hardly recognized the high squeak as her own.

"Did he threaten you again?" Rand asked.

"Yes, he said he was g-going to have to p-punish me—because I'd been bad. He's sick, Rand. He has to be—he talked crazy. I'm really frightened this time. He was following me! What am I going to do?"

"I'm coming out there. I'll be there as fast as I can. Will you be okay until I arrive?"

"Yes." Her teeth were chattering, and her hands felt icy cold, but she nodded and repeated, "Yes. I'll be fine, just hurry—please hurry."

It was a little longer than a few minutes, but when Rand knocked on the door he had Carrie along with him, and Lauren was unbelievably comforted by the other woman's presence.

Lauren told Rand what the man had said while Carrie made coffee for them all. No one really wanted the coffee, but it added a more normal note to the proceedings.

"I think it's time we put a trace on your phone here, and at the library. Then, the next time he calls, we got him."

"I forgot to tell you..." Lauren looked at Rand with fear-dilated pupils. "He knew I went to you the other night. That's why he said I had to be—punished."

Rand patted the cold fingers bunching the edge of her jacket into a wad and said, "Of course he knew you came to me. He knew you would when he told you not to. You did the right thing. It isn't your coming to the sheriff that's making him do this, Lauren. It's like you said earlier, he's sick.''

Carrie poured them each a cup of coffee and sat down on the couch beside Lauren. "I'm going to stay the night with you. It'll be just like old times, when we were in school."

For the first time since the phone call, Lauren smiled, a bit tremulously, but a smile nevertheless.

"Not quite like old times." She nodded at Carrie's increased waistline.

The three laughed, and after a few added words of reassurance to Lauren, Rand made a final check of all the locks and kissed his wife. "Don't worry, either of you. Someone will be right outside all night. I'll stay myself as long as I can, but if I have to leave, Deputy Holtzer will take my place."

Lauren lay wide-eyed for a long time, listening to Carrie snore softly in the big bed beside her, questions chasing themselves around inside her head.

Who in the town was hiding a streak of insanity? The kind that caused him to want to play this sick game with her? Who considered her a threat to him? Why?

Round and round they went, questions with no answers.

Finally, her eyes drifting closed, the last thought she was conscious of was of Jesse Tyler. He'd told her he was bad, as bad as his reputation made him out to be.

Just how bad was that?

Chapter 3

The sheriff was out bright and early the next morning. After taking his wife home, he decided to pay a call on Jesse. When he couldn't find him in the room behind Pete's where he sometimes stayed, Rand knew where to look next.

There was an old garage about a mile outside of town that was owned by an old high school buddy of Jesse's, and he figured he'd be there, working on his motorcycle.

Sure enough, when Rand pulled around behind the building and moved to the front on foot, he could hear a familiar off-key whistling coming from inside. As he stood in the open bay window he saw motorcycle parts strung out in a line leading from the bike. Jesse had the machine propped up on its center stand, with the front wheel tilted downward and the back one raised off the ground.

"Looks to me like you could use a good mechanic."

The whistle stopped in mid-note as Jesse looked back over his shoulder. "Yeah? You know any that work for free?"

Rand shook his head and moved into the cool interior of the building. The weather had gone crazy lately; one day it was cold, and the next it was so hot you could fry an egg on the street outside his office window. Today, though not yet noon, it was already ninety degrees.

With his hands in his pockets Rand watched the younger man work. It would no doubt surprise the townspeople to learn that their sheriff liked and respected Jesse Tyler.

But then, he knew things about Jesse no one else in town was privy to, except for Jesse's parents.

Jesse Tyler worked for him as a snitch. In the big city he would have been called an undercover cop. Or at least, that was what he would be called if he gave in to Rand's blandishments and officially joined the force.

The young man seemed to have a natural talent for acting out whatever role he was playing at the time. He blended into a group with amazing agility. But at the present time he was undecided about whether police work, or work as a deputy sheriff, was what he wanted to do with the rest of his life.

His involvement with the law had begun five years ago when he went to Rand's father and divulged information that he had gathered about a drug dealer working the high school campus.

Jesse had a pretty wild reputation at the time, but Grant Slade was willing to listen when Jesse admitted that he was only giving him the information because drugs bought from the dealer had been responsible for the death of a friend of his a few months before.

The relationship that grew between him and the elder Slade was a turning point in Jesse's life. He could have gone either way, but with the sheriff's encouragement Jesse entered the military after high school graduation and signed up to train as an MP.

When he finished his hitch and came home he agreed to work undercover for the sheriff's department as long as no one knew what he was doing, while he made up his mind if it was going to be his life's work. A year later, he was still undecided.

To this day, no one, not even his best friend, Hank Benton, knew about his helping the authorities to find and arrest the drug dealer in high school. Or that he still worked for Rand on various cases where his abilities came in handy.

At the present time Jesse was following up leads on the smuggler known as *El Personaje no Presente*, the man Rand believed was at least indirectly responsible for his father's death. Jesse wanted the man who had killed Grant Slade every bit as badly as Rand did.

Jesse straightened away from the bike, wiped his hands on a greasy rag he pulled from his back pocket and walked across the stained concrete floor to an old beat-up refrigerator resting in one corner and giving out a steady hum.

"Want one?" he asked, as he lifted a can of beer above his shoulder without turning around.

"You know better than that," Rand replied without hesitation.

Jesse shut the door and pulled the tab on the can as he turned to face the other man.

"Just checking. What are you doing here? I thought our 'association' was supposed to be kept quiet. Why else have I been skulking around Pete's back room, meeting with you where no one can see?"

"Yeah, yeah." Rand dispensed with his objections impatiently. "You got a minute? I need to talk to you about something important."

Propping himself up against the wall a few feet from Rand, Jesse took a long swig of beer and nodded. "Sure, go ahead." Then he chugalugged the remainder of the cold, bitter-tasting liquid and wiped his mouth with the back of one large hand. "But if it's about that report I made the other day, I told you everything I learned—it's all written down in triplicate.

"*El Personaje no Presente* is reported to be based somewhere around Chance. Of course, he's been said to live somewhere around Brownsville, too. The word is out that he's looking for a new partner. And if you keep calling me back here, I'm never going to learn anything else." Jesse eyed the other man meaningfully.

"I know all that. I read your report. At the moment I'm more concerned with what's going on right here in town. And I think you know what that is."

Jesse stared at the silver can in his grease-stained fingers. "The librarian? Oh, look, damn it, I told you the other day, I'm not a baby-sitter."

"She was followed to Del Rio yesterday."

"Yeah, I know." He'd had to borrow a car from one of his friends to follow her.

"No, not you. The man you were supposed to be protecting her from was there, too."

"What? I didn't see anyone. Are you sure?"

"I'm sure—he called her last night, late. The poor kid was nearly hysterical when she called me to report it."

"What's he want from her? You said she claimed he threatened her unless she keeps her mouth shut. What does she know that he's worried about?"

"That's the question. She can't remember anything to account for our man's nervousness."

"Well, can't you hypnotize her or something?"

After crushing the empty can in his hand, Jesse sent it sailing across the room, where it landed dead center in the trash barrel.

"That works well in TV and movies—but this is real life," Rand muttered disparagingly.

"So, what do you want from me? I can't make her remember anything. And if you want a bodyguard for her, ask your deputy—what's his name—to take the job. I like what I'm doing. I don't want to have to stay in town here and stand guard over a neurotic female."

His conscience pinched him a bit over the word neurotic. Lauren was not, he knew, neurotic. But the idea of spending a lot of time in her company bothered him too much to consider doing it.

"You don't understand," Rand explained. "This man—this maniac—hounding Lauren could be the very man we're after."

"What are you saying?" Jesse frowned.

"I'm saying we know that six months ago Hernandez Aguilar was a smuggler. What we don't know for certain is who he was working with. When he died, that cut the tie to whoever it was. Now, just suppose the reason he died was because he knew something he shouldn't." He had Jesse's full attention now.

"Suppose that what he knew was something so closely guarded that he *had* to die." Rand eyed the other man closely. "You following me so far?"

"Yeah, I get the picture. You're saying Aguilar could identify *El Personaje no Presente*." Jesse shook his head, ran a dirty hand through the tangled blond strands, and shook it again.

"It sounds pretty farfetched to me. *El Personaje no Presente* means *the faceless one*. And that's just what he is, faceless, nameless. His trademark is getting rid of anybody who can identify him. No one knows what he looks like— and if anyone has guessed who he is, they're keeping quiet about it 'cause they want to stay alive."

"But what if I'm right, and the man after Lauren is *El Personaje no Presente*? You've just said he's a killer, a ruthless one. You want her death on your conscience?"

"I don't want to baby-sit the town librarian," Jesse protested strongly. "Let Holtzer do it. I understand they're friends. That would be a better match."

"I'm not asking you to marry the woman, damn it, just keep her from getting killed."

Jesse reached for the package of cigarettes shoved up under the sleeve of his white T-shirt and offered Rand one.

The other man shook his head. "Carrie wants me to quit before the baby comes."

Jesse clicked his tongue. "Women!"

Rand drew a deep breath, inhaling the other man's smoke and agreed silently with him.

"Besides..." Rand returned to the immediate problem at hand. "I don't have enough men to assign one to Lauren permanently, for who knows how long a time, and that's why I want you to do it. You're good at disguises. Disguise yourself as a gentleman and it will all work out."

Jesse eyed him disparagingly. "That supposed to be funny?"

The sheriff could see no sign of the man's weakening, so he played a stronger hand. "Late last night, when the creep called Lauren, he told her she had been a bad girl—and he had to punish her."

"Jeez!"

"Exactly," Rand agreed. "This guy sounds like a real loony tune. And what I don't need right now is someone running around town threatening women and creating havoc."

"You know this isn't my usual line. I'm okay going around the dives across the border and ferreting out information, but this—" Jesse shook his head.

"The guy could be the man who killed my father and Estevez," Rand reminded him. "And if, as I suspect, it's *El Personaje no Presente* we're after here, it fits right in with what you've been working on."

"Naw," Jesse protested. "He's smart, and mean as a snake when it comes to his work, but his work is smuggling, not terrorizing women. What the hell would he want with a librarian? Now, if you told me he was trying to kidnap her to sell her into white slavery, I might buy that."

"What if there's something she can tell us about him?"

"Like what? You think she knows who he is?"

Rand pulled his hands from his pockets without immediately answering and strode over to the refrigerator. Taking a can of cola from inside, he took a long pull before answering. "I think there's something locked inside her head that she isn't aware of, and that may be the link we're looking for that will give us his name.

"And that's another reason why I want you to stick to her like fleas on a dog. I want you to get her to talk. Be her friend, jog her memory about what this maniac has hinted at. And try to get her to remember exactly what happened from six months ago, when she found that note, the one she gave to my father that led to the murders. Somehow, it's all tied together."

"Whew! You don't want much. And just how do you propose I get all this information? I don't expect Lauren Downing is panting at the idea of making Jesse Tyler her bosom buddy."

Rand ran a finger down the side of the sweating can and shook his head. "You'll think of something. I don't need to tell you how to do your job." He looked up directly into Jesse's narrowed blue eyes.

"Just a damn minute, here. I'm not a gigolo. And since when did you take up pimping?"

Rand's face flushed with anger. "I'm not suggesting you carry things that far. But this man we're after is a killer—I know he's the same man who is responsible for Dad's death.

"Damn it! I want him!" He crushed the can in his hand, spilling the cola onto the floor without either man noticing.

"I thought Lauren Downing was a friend of yours?"

"She is—that's why I'm trying to protect her. But I'm a cop, too, and this is our one big break—a chance to bring in *El Personaje no Presente*."

Jesse watched the other man, felt his pain. He too had loved the elder Slade. And if there was a possibility that he could learn something from a closer association with the librarian, why was he hesitating?

Because you're smart enough to know when you should turn tail and run, a little voice from somewhere inside whispered knowledgeably. The librarian is a face from your past that you've never quite been able to label and put aside. She attracts you like a bee to honey. And you're scared of her. Scared to look too deeply into that fear and see just what's causing it.

"I don't think Lauren is deliberately keeping anything back." Rand's words brought Jesse back from his not so enviable past. "Whatever it is she knows, I don't think she's aware of knowing it. But the man who's after her is afraid she'll remember—or figure it out—and that's why he has to silence her. I'm trying to save her life."

Dropping the cigarette butt onto the concrete, Jesse ground the fire out with his heel. He knew he'd give in and do what Rand wanted. The thought of Lauren's life being in danger would make him, if nothing else.

"There's just one thing that I find wrong with your theory. Why did he wait so long to come after her? It's been six months since the murders. Why now? Why not right away?"

"Yeah." The sheriff rubbed a hand around the back of his neck tiredly. "I thought of that, too. It doesn't make sense, does it? The longer he waits the better the chance Lauren will remember. So why wait at all?"

Jesse shrugged and moved toward his bike. "Maybe the guy was out of town."

"Right, visiting a sick relative."

Jesse picked up a wrench and hesitated for a moment, then looked up at Rand. The same thought had entered the other man's head.

"What if it *is El Personaje no Presente*, and he *has* been out of town on business—the business of smuggling? Where does that leave us?" Rand asked. "Do we check up on everyone who's been out of town for the last six months?"

Jesse shrugged and bent over the motorcycle. "It's an idea. There are several people I can eliminate right now, but I'll wager that one of those I don't eliminate is our man."

He worked in silence for a few minutes, then looked up when the other man continued to stand watching him. He'd already half made up his mind to do as Rand wanted, but he felt bound to offer one last protest.

"Okay, what do you want from me?"

"I told you, I want you to keep an eye on Lauren."

"Come on, Rand. Get real. Take a good look around you. Can you find one thing, one tiny thing, that leads you to think the librarian and I have anything in common? It would never work. She'll suspect something right away, unless you plan to tell her up-front what I'm doing hanging around."

The sheriff shook his head. "That wouldn't work, either. The lady is determined to go her own way. Carrie suggested she get a watchdog after the first attack—she got a bird."

"A bird." Jesse laughed.

"Yeah, a talking bird."

"What does she plan for the bird to do, talk the man to death?" Making an adjustment on the new part he'd put in place, Jesse grinned and laughed aloud. "You see what I mean? We just don't go together. I still think you should get Holtzer to keep an eye on her. That would suit them both much better than trying to force me into her life."

"You're probably right about that, but like I told you, I can't afford the lost man-hours. It has to be you. Besides, no one is likely to suspect your real motive in hanging around an attractive woman like Lauren—"

"Wait a minute—" Jesse straightened quickly, the screwdriver he held pointed in Rand's direction. "I thought we worked that out already."

"Come on, Jesse, it's the only way it would work. In the beginning I can get you into the library, but after that you need to have a reason to stick close. Can you think of a better reason than being smitten by the lovely lady?"

"With friends like you, no one needs an enemy." Jesse slammed the screwdriver down angrily.

Clenching a fist and smacking it against his other palm, Rand barked, "I want this bastard!"

"I understand—"

"No, I don't think you do. It isn't only for Dad, though that's a large part of it. It's the whole thing, the smuggling, the killings, and now Lauren. He has to be stopped."

"Okay," Jesse conceded, "I'll do what I can. But I refuse to romance the woman under false pretenses. There has to be something between two people for that to work, and there is *nothing* between Lauren Downing and me," he denied heatedly, refusing to admit to a disturbed sense of balance on his trip back to town the day before.

"All right," Rand said approvingly and grinned.

"So what do I do now? I'm supposed to start work at Tindle's Feed Store in the morning," Jesse reminded him.

"No problem, Sam owes me a favor or two. I'll take care of it. Just go into work as planned, but don't be surprised if you aren't employed there long."

"That's supposed to relieve my mind?"

Jesse shook his head. He had a feeling that by the end of the week another black mark would have been added to the long and growing list of Jesse Tyler's misdeeds.

"You know, if you'd go to work for me properly, everyone in town would know the real you—*and* the job you've done to help keep them all safe while they're snug in their beds at night."

Jesse laughed without humor. "If you let my past work get out around town, I'd probably wake up one night, in my own bed, with a knife stuck between my shoulderblades."

Rand didn't agree or disagree with that. The work Jesse was doing was important, and he wasn't about to do or say anything that would jeopardize his friend's continuing to do it. He just wished Jesse would give in and join the sheriff's department openly. Honest young men, like Jesse, with a flair for police work, were hard to find, and he was doing his level best to keep him—he just hoped his best was good enough.

After Rand had left, Jesse quickly finished his work on the bike and began to give some considerable thought to what he had agreed to do. The town bad boy and the town librarian? It sounded like a black comedy to him. No matter what Rand said, he refused to play the lovestruck younger man, mooning over an older woman who wouldn't give him the time of day.

That really bothers you, doesn't it? a sly voice inside his head queried. Age has never been a factor in your relationship with a woman before. Why now? Afraid you won't measure up? What about all that experience you were congratulating yourself about having the other day? She really got to you, didn't she?

"Hell, no!" he muttered aloud, arguing with himself. "No woman has ever gotten to me. I don't need a steady woman hanging around to bolster my self-image. I'm sufficient unto myself."

After putting away the tools he'd been using and cleaning up his mess, he forced the chiding voice from his head. Lauren Downing was just a woman he used to know in school, an old friend—no, an old acquaintance—who he'd barely thought of in years, someone he'd lost touch with despite their living in the same small town.

But as he worked, pictures flashed into his mind. The wind blowing through her short cinnamon-colored curls. He'd always thought of them as brown, but in the sunlight the other day he'd realized there was a red cast to them that the sunlight had brought out.

There was a small brown mole just above her lip, a scant inch or two from the dimple he'd seen flash in her left cheek once or twice during that ride. He didn't remember it from when they were in school.

But then, why should he? He'd been too young to run in her crowd, and too shy to expect someone of her beauty and intelligence to notice him. That year, the year he was a freshman, must have been the last time anyone could ever refer to him as shy, he thought, grinning.

"Jesse, you in there?" Hank Benton sauntered into the garage. "I heard about a pair of saddlebags this guy I know has that might fit your bike. You interested?"

"Where did you come from?" Jesse asked a bit sharply. Had he seen the sheriff leave? No one except his parents, not even Hank, knew of his work for the man, and he wanted to keep it that way.

"I came in Dad's truck. I'm supposed to be hauling feed from town. I thought you were working at the feed store, but old man Tindle told me you had bike trouble and couldn't start till tomorrow. He said he thought you had mentioned something about using a friend's place to fix it today."

Hank shrugged. "What's the matter? You got a woman hid out here—somebody's wife?" Screwing up his eyes, Hank peered into the shadowy recesses of the building.

"Don't be dumb, man. You know I don't fool around with married women."

"Yeah, I know, I was only kidding. Besides, with someone like Rosalita Mendez in your bed, what would you need with another woman?" Hank asked enviously.

Jesse didn't bother denying the allegation. He knew there was nothing between the two of them and hadn't been for a long time now, but it didn't hurt anyone for people to think there was.

And besides, it gave him a good excuse to hang out at Pete's place long after hours, when he needed to meet Rand or gather information about whatever he happened to be working on at the moment.

Pete's place was a veritable hotbed of gossip about who was smuggling what, and when and where—if you knew the right people.

"Come on, let's go look at those saddlebags." Jesse slipped his arm around his friend's shoulders and led him to where his bike, now in perfect running order, sat parked in the shade of a mesquite tree at the side of the building.

He watched his friend pull the black-and-maroon helmet over his dark curls and spotted a fading bruise on Hank's chin. He didn't need to ask where he'd come by it.

"What's your dad going to say about you leaving the truck here? You want to take it and follow me?" Jesse asked. He didn't want to be responsible for any more trouble between Hank and his father.

"The hell with him," Hank replied as he fastened the chin strap over the bruise. "I'll park it inside the garage and lock it up. He'll be mad 'cause I took longer to get the feed than I should, but he won't know I left the truck here."

Hank strode toward the truck, climbed inside and drove it into the garage, then closed the door with its broken glass and snicked the lock into place.

"Somebody comes along, they're bound to see the truck," Jesse warned him.

Hank straddled the bike and patted the seat, ignoring his words. "Come on, let's go."

As his friend climbed aboard, Hank gave a quick glance at the brown pickup showing through the shattered windows and muttered beneath his breath, "To hell with the bastard."

Unaware of Hank's words, Jesse started the motorcycle. He thanked God he'd been blessed with the hardworking, loving people who were his parents and not cursed with a father like Hank's.

Thinking about his parents caused him to decide he'd better make a visit to their ranch that night while he could. Because after tomorrow, he had a hunch his life was going to be turned upside down for a while. It might be a good idea to prepare his mother and father for the next few weeks and what was bound to be a period of time that would upset them.

They were good people, and he loved them. He knew they were waiting patiently, hoping he would get this police work out of his system and return to the ranch, to the work they felt he was born to do. And right now he wasn't so sure but what they might just be right about that.

Chapter 4

Need some help?"

What the hell was she doing here? Jesse recognized the cap of cinnamon-colored hair almost as soon as he'd spoken. He wasn't ready for her yet; he needed time to figure just how he was going to handle winning her confidence, her friendship.

If Rand was responsible for this... Anger spread through him, and whether it was unreasonable or not, some of it was directed at the woman herself.

Lauren whirled around in surprise at the unexpected sound of his voice and stumbled back against the shelves in the middle of the aisle. The momentum of her fall caused the freestanding shelves to rock slightly, and the cans of flea and tick spray to totter, moving precariously toward the edge.

Without answering his question, she turned awkwardly and tried to prevent the aerosol cans from toppling.

What was he doing here? What was *she* doing here, she asked herself half-angrily. Was she fated to run across him every day for the rest of her life? Twice now in three days he'd managed to cross her path after years of hardly ever seeing him. And then she remembered that he'd said he was going to start work here today.

"Here, let me—" Jesse moved quickly and, reaching above her, spread large hands beside her own smaller, more feminine ones. He was unprepared for the abrupt jolt of feeling that her body plastered along the length of his generated as she started to back out of his way.

Lauren felt shock waves ripple down her spine as his chest, his whole body, seemed to enfold hers. Sensing the heat of a blush move up her neck and over her cheeks, wanting to sink into the floor in embarrassment, she was too tongue-tied to speak.

Two days ago she had literally bumped into him at the mall and now here she was jumping at the sound of his voice, nearly causing a disaster his first day on the job. He must think her the biggest klutz in the whole town.

Why had she agreed to come with Carrie today? The answer was simple, of course; her friend was getting quite big with her pregnancy, and Lauren worried about her going off alone shopping. Her time was getting close, but she refused to listen when Lauren or Rand told her to take it easy and get more rest.

Of course, none of that mattered at this moment; the only thing that did matter was to get away from Jesse, so she could breathe in a more even manner.

"I-I think it's safe now," she murmured a trifle breathlessly. "Everything seems to have steadied." Except for her nervous system, that is.

The edge of one shelf was making a permanent crease across the upper half of her chest, and she was sure her back must be steaming in the searing heat from his body.

Lifting both hands to rest beside hers, a hairsbreadth away, Jesse pressed closer, leaving an indelible imprint of male musculature down the quivering flesh of her body from shoulders to knees.

An untamed curl caressed his upper lip as he bent closer to breathe in the heady perfume of her hair. God, she smelled like no woman he'd ever known.

He'd spent the first day after their meeting in Del Rio attempting to get the scent of her out of his head. He could admit that to himself now.

"You smell delicious." The words slipped out unintentionally before he could bite them back.

Denying the sudden leap of her pulses, despising the way his husky voice scraped across her senses, she disregarded his words. "P-please. Will you move?"

His hands moved closer to hers, and like a frightened animal cornered by a snake, she couldn't move her eyes from them. They were wide-palmed, blunt-fingered hands, with large knuckles, the backs covered with a light dusting of freckles and a sprinkling of golden hair. A workingman's hands. Unbidden, the question of how those hands would feel on her body sneaked into her mind.

Jesse was tempted. That in itself wasn't unusual. Most good-looking women tempted him one way or another. The worrisome part was the fact that he wasn't acting on the temptation. He wanted to, all right, but she scared the hell out of him.

He could smell trouble a mile away; he'd been close to it often enough. And Miss Lauren Librarian reeked of trouble's alluring scent.

The sheriff wanted him to protect her. What he wanted to know was who was going to protect him from her. Even before agreeing to help Rand, he'd wondered what it would be like to be this close to her—and now he knew.

"That's fine, Mr. Tindle. I'll send Billy in tomorrow to pick it up." Carrie Slade and Sam Tindle moved into view mere seconds after Jesse had moved quickly away from Lauren.

The store proprietor looked up and smiled. "Jesse, the truck we've been waiting for just pulled up out back. How about helping them unload?"

Carrie looked at the tall young man leaning casually against the wall, ankles crossed, hands pushed into the pockets of the faded jeans stretched lovingly across his upper thighs and pelvis. She didn't know he'd started working here.

It probably wouldn't last long. According to town gossip Jesse didn't stay long in any one place. Trouble seemed to follow him like a shadow.

"You okay?" Carrie asked, her eyes moving over Lauren's pallid features in alarm.

Lauren was staring down at the wooden floor as though trying to memorize the myriad cracks and crevices. The side of her neck, just visible above the collar of her conservative white blouse, flamed where Jesse's lips had brushed against it only moments before the other two had appeared.

"I'm fine." Lauren glanced up, nodded in reply to Sam's greeting and asked Carrie, "Are you ready to leave?"

"There are a few things I need to discuss yet with Sam. If you want to wait in the car, I won't be a minute," Carrie replied, eyeing her curiously.

Keeping her eyes turned away from Jesse, Lauren nodded and made for the door.

Jesse, passing close beside her, stopped directly in her path, forcing her to meet his glance. She faltered a little under his cold blue stare, but moved around him and continued on out the door.

She hoped she never had to spend any time alone in his presence again. Everything she'd ever heard about him appeared to be true. He thought he was God's gift to women, that every female, regardless of age or interest was fair game.

Lauren exited the building and felt the sun beat down hotly on her bare head. As she stood by the car, rolling the three-quarter-length sleeves of the blouse above her elbows, she thought of the way Jesse's sleeves had shown off his muscular arms in the truck when she'd given him a ride.

Leaning against the side of her yellow car, she felt her breathing and pulse rate start to return to normal. Why had she let Jesse's nonsense affect her so strongly?

He was brash and cocky, and she had no time for someone like that. True, maybe she'd felt a minor attraction a couple of days ago. But Jesse was a good-looking man. What woman wouldn't find him attractive? That was all there was to it.

Besides, he was nothing like the type of man who interested her. Though, thinking back on it now, she had to admit she hadn't expected Raul to be her type, either. But that was different; Raul hadn't been a brash flirt, chasing every skirt in town. He didn't drink and start fights—especially fights over women, as she had heard Jesse did.

Disgusted with herself for attempting to justify her feelings for Raul, she pushed herself away from the car and checked her watch. She'd been waiting almost twenty minutes now in the hot sun. The hair around her forehead and cheeks had begun to curl tightly with perspiration, and a thirst had begun to build, sticking her tongue to the roof of her mouth.

Deciding that a nice cool drink was what she needed, she went to look for Carrie to let her know she'd be in the café down the street waiting for her.

But the store appeared to be empty. Lauren looked between the shelves, calling softly, but there was no answer. A doorway leading to another room, where sacks of feed were stacked against the walls, proved to be empty, too.

Lauren was about to give up and go back outside when she heard the sound of someone whistling. The off-key rendition of a popular tune was coming from beyond the door, where an open-roofed enclosure passed for the unloading dock.

Realizing that was where Jesse would be if he were unloading a truck, Lauren turned quickly, hoping to leave without drawing his attention.

"You looking for me?" Jesse asked from directly behind her, causing her to stop dead still and then turn slowly to face him.

"No."

Taking a step back, she shook her head, glancing past his broad, hair-covered chest. Why didn't he button his shirt? Men always thought they could get away with running around half-naked in public—but just let a woman try it and her reputation was ruined for life.

Against her will, she felt her eyes drawn to the blond hair sprinkled indiscriminately across the prominent pectoral muscles on display. She couldn't force her eyes away from the hypnotic movement of his Adam's apple as he swallowed, then felt them lifting slowly toward his face.

"I thought you were going to wait for me outside," Carrie asked a bit testily from behind her.

"I was. I did—I just came to tell you I was going for a drink and—" Motioning ineffectually with one hand, Lauren shook her head. "Let's go, I need some fresh air."

Even Jesse thought she looked a bit pale as she led the way outside. He hadn't handled things very well. After all his fine talk to Rand about not getting involved with the woman, he'd come on to her like a raunchy stud.

She probably figured he acted this way with every woman he met. But the truth of the matter was, he didn't. She affected him unlike any woman ever had, and he was doing his best to convince himself it was a thing left over from his frustrated teenage crush.

On the trip back from town to the ranch Lauren had to withstand Carrie's not so subtle questions. Normally she would have told her friend what had happened, all of it, but for some reason her lips remained sealed about Jesse Tyler. The subject of Kalan Holtzer and his much to be admired traits took up the remainder of the ride.

"Well, he's done it again."

Lauren was standing at the door to the library, key in hand, when Carrie spoke from behind.

"I beg your pardon." Lauren turned, recognized her friend and asked, "What are you doing in town so early?"

"It isn't that early. Besides, I have a doctor's appointment in a few minutes." Smoothing a hand over her rounded belly, Carrie smiled a beautiful smile and reminded her, "It's less than a month till Thumper here is due."

"I know." Lauren smiled back. "I'm the kid's only aunt, aren't I?"

Sobering, moving a few steps closer, Carrie said, "That's not why I stopped when I saw you here, Laurie. I wanted to give you the news before you heard it from someone else. It's about Jesse Tyler.''

''Jesse?''

''Yes, he's been fired from the feed store.'' Looking down at the porch, she paused for a moment. She didn't know how involved her friend's emotions were with Jesse—not deeply, she hoped—but she didn't want to hurt her.

''Fired? Well, that's too bad. Everything seemed fine when we were there yesterday.'' She caught the piercing look her friend turned on her and shrugged. ''It's nothing to me.''

''Good.'' Carrie smiled once more. ''I'm glad to hear that. I just wanted to tell you before you heard it from someone else. Yesterday the two of you seemed...'' She hesitated. ''...friendly.''

''I'm friendly to a lot of people. I'm supposed to be, it encourages them to come into the library and to read.''

Carrie nodded and started to turn away. Obviously she had been concerned over nothing. Lauren was too mature to be attracted to the flagrantly sexual charms of someone like Jesse Tyler.

''Why did he get fired?'' Lauren asked quickly as Carrie started to move away. She couldn't help herself, even after trying to convince herself that it wasn't her concern. She couldn't keep the words back.

Carrie turned, a speculative look in her green eyes. ''Does it matter?''

''Curiosity,'' Lauren answered. ''He has a knack for attracting...attention.''

''Trouble, you mean,'' Carrie insisted.

''Trouble,'' Lauren conceded. ''What did he do?''

''It hasn't been proved—that is, he hasn't been accused of anything, exactly. But the feed store was robbed last night.''

"Robbed! Is Sam all right?"

"It was after closing sometime. Sam wasn't there. Nothing was taken but the cash from the drawer. Sam had to let Jesse go, though, because he didn't feel he could trust him after that, even though Jesse claims he's innocent—of course."

"You said it hasn't been proved that Jesse did it." Lauren sprang to the man's defense. "Maybe he didn't."

"Maybe," Carrie agreed slowly. "But I don't suppose Sam was careless enough to let just anyone know he left cash in the drawer overnight. Look, I have to go." Again she turned away, but she was clearly not pleased with the conversation. She hesitated once more and then turned resolutely back.

"I'm going to tell you something that isn't exactly confidential, but it isn't common knowledge, either."

Lauren had no idea what it was, but all at once she didn't want to know. "Maybe you shouldn't—"

"No, I think you need to hear this," Carrie insisted. "Remember when Jesse left town so abruptly a few weeks ago. Why do you think he left?"

"I have no idea. I don't keep tabs on his comings and goings. I'm sorry," she apologized, seeing the hurt look on her friend's face. "I didn't mean to snap at you."

"It's okay, I know this is gossiping—just indulge me for a moment. And remember, I'm only thinking of your welfare. Jesse left town because he stole cattle from his father and their neighbor. His father refused to press charges and bought off the neighbor. Anyway, it was all hushed up, more or less, and Jesse left town for Brownsville."

A constriction in Lauren's chest kept her from replying immediately. Stealing? From his own father? It made her feel ill. How could a man steal from his own father? She felt something was wrong with the story. Jesse was bold and cocky, but she didn't think he was a thief.

Carrie nodded, "I overheard Rand and one of the deputies talking. Rand would have my hide if he knew I was spreading rumors. If it wasn't you, I wouldn't be. But I don't want to see you taken in by Jesse's false charm and cheeky swagger."

"It's all right, Carrie," Lauren hurried to assure the other woman. "I'm not angry with you, nor have I been captivated by Jesse's so-called charm. And I promise not to whisper a word of what you've told me to anyone, least of all Rand."

"Good." Carrie glanced down at her watch. "Oh, my gosh—I'm late, I've got to run. Call me," she instructed, as she grabbed the handrail and moved carefully down the steps. "We'll get together for dinner soon."

Lauren nodded absently and turned to enter the library, her mind full of unsettling thoughts.

Her day had hardly begun when Sheriff Slade paid her a visit. He had the equipment with him to put a trace on the library phone in case her attacker called. He'd had to requisition it, and it had only just arrived.

When he was finished hooking up the device that would allow them to record and trace the call, Rand took a seat across from where Lauren was working. He sat watching her make out new index cards in a neat precise hand for a few minutes before broaching the subject that was uppermost on his mind.

"I wonder, have you heard about the feed store being robbed?"

"I heard," she admitted. She couldn't imagine why he wanted to know.

"Folks around here seem to think Jesse is responsible for it, despite the fact there's no evidence to that effect."

"Maybe it's only to be expected, since he was working there at the time."

"Maybe," Rand agreed. "But it's a sad thing for his reputation if he's an innocent man." He surprised her by adding, "And I happen to think he is."

He knew damn good and well he was, because the missing money didn't exist. Sam was returning a debt Rand had called in. Jesse, Sam and the sheriff had cooked the whole thing up between them.

"Well, I'm sure you're right, but I fail to see what his guilt or innocence has to do with me."

"That's what I wanted to talk to you about. I thought maybe you could use someone to help you around here a bit."

"Jesse Tyler? You want me to hire *him* to work in the library?" She couldn't keep from laughing. "No." She shook her head decisively. "I'm sorry, but it's out of the question. There's nothing for him to do here. Look around you. What would you have him doing? Stamping books? Or reading stories to the preschoolers on story day?"

"I admit those things aren't exactly in Jesse's present line, but what about some fix-up work? Painting shelves? Uncrating books?"

At Lauren's skeptical look, he shrugged. "What about outside work, then? Surely there's something you could find for him to do here. All he needs is for someone to show the rest of the town they have some trust in him. It would be good for him, too—to know everyone isn't so quick to brand him a thief."

Lauren was well aware of the innovative ideas Rand Slade had for prisoners. In the normal course of things she usually agreed with his opinion that there were better ways for a man to work off his crimes than to sit in a jail cell twenty-four hours a day and let the taxpayers support him. But in this case, things were different.

"It just wouldn't work." She shook her head. "Why don't you just ask Sam to give Jesse another chance? Sam's a reasonable man—" She broke off, staring at the sheriff's face. "What is it?"

"I tried talking to Sam, but he won't budge. He isn't exactly accusing Jesse, but he can't account for the missing money, either."

"Does Mr. Tindle think Jesse took the money?" Lauren asked.

"There's no evidence to suggest Jesse had anything to do with the robbery."

"But that doesn't mean he *didn't* do it," Lauren said, her opinion swinging in the other direction.

"Maybe I should come back a little later, like when the two of you have finished discussing me and decided on my guilt—or innocence."

Lauren and Rand both twisted around to face the door, where Jesse stood with one blond brow raised and an impudent twist curving his full lips.

Giving Jesse a warning look from behind Lauren's back, Rand continued with his persuasive speech as though he hadn't been interrupted. "Look, it's only for a few weeks. By then the furor about the feed store will have died down, and Jesse will have a chance to find work somewhere else."

Lowering his voice and moving his head to the side, so Jesse couldn't read his lips, Rand added, "And I can keep an eye on him, just in case he has more money to spend than seems reasonable."

Lauren asked in a lowered voice, "You *do* think he took it, then?"

She had managed after that first glance to keep her eyes strictly away from the figure leaning nonchalantly, arms crossed, against the wall.

"I didn't say that," Rand put in hurriedly. "Just the opposite, in fact."

He'd only meant to gain sympathy for Jesse and pave the way for her seeing him speaking to Jesse periodically at the library so he could hear what progress he'd made. He hadn't intended for her to think he was convinced of Jesse's guilt.

"I'm sorry, sheriff." Her voice rose in agitation. She could feel the mocking eyes of the man they were discussing boring a hole in her back. "You know I'd be glad to help any way I can, but in this instance it just isn't possible. I have a responsibility to the library patrons—to the parents of the children who come in here every day. He isn't—it wouldn't create a proper...atmosphere for the kids."

"What she's trying to say, Sheriff, is that I'm a bad influence," Jesse put in, straightening. "I told you this was a bad idea to begin with, so can we just forget this whole thing and get out of here?"

He was more than half-serious about that. He still didn't like the idea of spending at least eight hours a day in close proximity with this particular woman and felt one of Rand's deputies would be better suited to the job of protecting Lauren Downing.

"All right," she said suddenly. Two pair of masculine eyes darted to her face. "I'll do it."

She wasn't quite certain why she was suddenly giving in. She still felt he was unsuited to working in and around the library. But something she saw in his blue eyes had caused her to relent.

"I'm sure I can find something for him to do for the next couple of weeks that will keep him out of trouble."

"Look, don't I have any say in the matter?" Jesse asked angrily.

The manner of her yielding irked him. It was true that a small part of him wanted to spend time in her company, but he was doing his best to deny that, especially to himself. Somehow he knew that any time they spent together was going to lead to trouble—for both of them.

"No," Sheriff Slade answered him shortly, grateful it was done. "I told you already, this is for your own good, and you agreed to give it a try. Besides, it will keep you within sight, in case anything else comes up."

"I didn't steal that damn money," Jesse muttered just loud enough for Lauren to hear, playing the part he'd been handed against his will.

When the sheriff had left, Lauren walked stiffly across the room to face her new employee. "I think there are a few ground rules we need to put into effect before we can work comfortably together."

"You think that's possible?" He raised a finely drawn, blond brow.

"I beg your pardon?"

"Our working *comfortably* together," he emphasized. Taking a step closer, crowding her, he continued in a deeper tone of voice. "When I'm around you, I feel a lot of different things. 'Comfortable' isn't one of them."

If his plan was to nip any attraction she felt for him from deepening by being a jerk, from the look on Lauren's face, it was working.

"Ground rules," Lauren stated determinedly, drawing herself up to her full stature, a little over five feet. "There will be nothing of a personal nature between us. We have no common ground. The only thing I wish to discuss with you is whatever work you happen to be doing for me at the moment."

She looked a bit uncomfortable now. "And I think it would be a good idea to confine your work to the back of the building during the hours the children are here from the grade school and preschool. I warn you, I won't tolerate any nonsense."

With that said, she led the way to the back rooms where the books coming into the library through donations or purchases were stored until they were readied for the shelves.

The one room she avoided, had avoided for over a week, was the storeroom at the very back of the building. The place where *he* had accosted her.

While Lauren explained what hours he would be expected to work and exactly what his job would entail, Jesse kept a rigid silence. She told him the position would be more ad lib than anything, with him doing whatever needed to be done at the moment.

She was rubbing him the wrong way, and Jesse had a feeling she was doing it deliberately. Did she think that if she showed him how disdainful she was of someone of his low moral character, that would protect her? Well, he would show her different. She expected a lecherous bastard, so he'd give her one.

It didn't occur to him at that moment how screwed up his thinking had become in the last hour. He'd behaved in a manner that was certain to keep them apart, and it had worked. She thought his level of thinking rose no higher than the level of his belt buckle. But he hadn't been satisfied with that; he'd had to push it.

"This must be rather an...unusual situation for you." She spoke unsteadily, her confidence shaken at his continued silence. He hadn't asked even one question about the work he would be doing, and his eyes had remained unwaveringly on her face the whole time she'd been talking.

"Unusual? How?" He asked, finally breaking his self-imposed silence.

"Working in a library, I mean. I imagine you're more used to ranching and the kind of work you were doing at the feed store."

"I'm not used to using my head, is that what you mean? I'm more suited to work involving brawn, not brain, right?" An angry gleam had taken the place of the blank stare in the blue eyes above hers.

Lauren backed unconsciously toward the door. "I didn't mean that—exactly."

"Then perhaps you meant it would be safe for me to work at a job where there was nothing to steal, unless you have a jar of overdue book fines hidden away somewhere."

He was enjoying this, he had to admit, and he narrowed his eyes to keep the gleam of anger from becoming a gleam of laughter. She was really buying the moody, angry stud bit.

Lauren felt an unwelcome wave of color invade her cheeks. "I didn't mean anything at all like that."

She was backed against the door. There was nowhere for her to go unless she made an undignified retreat into the hall. She looked up at him helplessly.

Stopping within a few feet of her, Jesse held her gaze, then let his eyes slowly travel the length of her. She was breathing in short uneven gasps, the rise and fall of her chest pulling the loose cotton blouse tightly across her small rounded breasts. All at once his pretense of anger became all too real.

He felt as though she *was* to be blamed for his present set of circumstances, for his being forced to work with her against his will. And he wanted to make her pay for it in some small way.

There she stood, cringing away from him like a frightened maiden, acting as though he was about to demand her virginity right there in that small, airless room. And for just a moment he wondered if the man who had attacked her had felt like this, as though she was asking for a man—a real man—to break down the barrier that kept her locked in her ivory tower, so calm, so serene, so out of touch with human feelings like need—and lust.

Lunging forward, he grasped her by the shoulders and hauled her into his arms. His mouth took hers forcefully, grinding her lips against her teeth. His hands seemed to move without thought, up across her shoulders and down over her hips and thighs.

She felt warm and soft, all woman in his arms. It had been a long time since he'd held a woman like this, and he felt the overpowering need to take her, regardless of the consequences.

Lauren was by turns shocked, frightened and excited. She felt his warm breath blow into her mouth, felt his heart kick against her breast as though it would burst from his chest, and was amazed that she could arouse him this way.

She tasted the salt of perspiration on his skin as he twisted his head and ran his lips over her cheek and along the side of her neck.

She was unprepared for the emotions that contact brought, and she had to grab hold of him to keep from falling. Her fingers dug into the thick biceps of his arms, and her lips moved whisper-lightly against the straining muscles of his jaw.

The touch of soft tentative lips gliding over the rough skin of his jaw and chin did what no angry protestations would have done. It brought Jesse to his senses and back into the real world.

Shoving her to arm's length, he held her away. "I'm sorry," he muttered, unable to meet her eyes.

Rand would have his hide if he knew what he was doing. He had hinted at it being all right to romance her, but he was positive the sheriff would draw the line at manhandling her.

It took a moment to get his emotions under control, and then, cocky attitude firmly in place once more, he met her confused glance and asked, "Is that the kind of nonsense you were referring to?"

Lauren was speechless. What had just happened between them? Was she the only one who had felt as though the earth had moved?

Obviously. She was a fool—and too old to play the kind of games this man was used to playing.

Ignoring his words, as she ignored what had just taken place between them, Lauren left without another word. Let him figure out for himself what he needed to do. She'd had all of Jesse Tyler's company she could take for one day.

His presence did achieve one good thing. For the rest of the day Lauren forgot to be frightened every time the phone rang.

Chapter 5

On Friday morning Lauren arrived at the library to find Jesse waiting for her. It was a beautiful day, with cloudless blue skies and warm temperatures. Jesse lay sprawled on the library steps, dressed in tight button-fly jeans, a pale blue western-style shirt and scarred brown boots. His wheat-blond hair had been parted and slicked back from his forehead and cheeks, but the wind had feathered it across his forehead, nearly hiding his fine brows.

Lauren felt disturbingly aware of his earthy attraction as she stood grappling with the lock on the door. He confused her at every turn; one moment he was warm and friendly, making her think the gossips were wrong about him, and the very next he did or said something to prove them right. She didn't know how to take him.

"Care to give me a try?"

Lauren froze, then felt her knees go weak and her mouth go dry. "I beg your pardon," she murmured without looking up.

"The lock. You want me to see if I can open it?" His shadow fell over her an instant before his warm fingers covered hers.

Lauren let go of the key instantly and jerked her hand away from his unsettling touch, then heard the keys clang loudly as they hit the porch. Jesse bent immediately to get them, and she stared down at the top of his head.

He had a cowlick. Right in the center of the crown of his head, a cluster of short, pale blond hair stood straight up without benefit of styling gel or mousse. There was something so heartening about the impudent, self-assured Jesse having something so homely that Lauren felt a sudden urge to lean over and plant a motherly kiss atop his golden head.

Jesse glanced up as his fingers closed over the dropped keys. "I got—" He encountered the warm look in her dark eyes, and swallowed in surprise. "—them."

She had been keeping her distance from him since the first day he'd come to work. He'd been puzzling over how he was going to win her confidence and get her to talk to him about the note she had found back in April. It was going to be pretty hard when she wouldn't even exchange a few words of greeting with him.

The incident at the feed store had left Lauren feeling bewildered, but the kiss he'd forced on her in the storeroom had her all at sea. Especially his reaction afterward.

One minute she'd been furious at him for taking unwarranted liberties, and the next—she remembered that breathless, pulse stirring excitement she'd felt when he'd held her in his arms....

"Lauren..." Jesse straightened, drawn to her by the look in her eyes. What was happening to him? All he wanted in the world at this moment was to feel her mouth beneath his.

It was with a sense of relief Lauren heard her name being called and turned to find Kalan making his way across the dusty street.

He joined her, and the two men sized each other up, Kalan with a calm demeanor, and Jesse with brows raised over insolent eyes.

Reaching for the doorknob, Kalan discovered that the door was still locked. After taking the keys from Jesse's unresisting fingers, he unlocked it and stood back to allow Lauren entrance, then followed closely on her heels. Neither paused to see if Jesse followed, only continued on into the small office behind the checkout desk.

"How is James Dean doing as a library assistant?" Kalan asked when they were alone.

"What?" She glanced up in confusion. She'd been miles away, lost in the memory of the uncertain look in Jesse's blue eyes just before he'd spoken her name so strangely. Her name had never sounded quite like that on anyone else's lips.

"The young rebel on the porch—I asked if you were having any problems there?"

He hadn't agreed with Rand's plans to help Jesse by throwing him into daily contact with Lauren. He knew Jesse by his womanizing reputation and brash demeanor. He had even voiced suspicions about Jesse being responsible for Lauren's attack, which Rand had promptly shot down by reminding him that Jesse hadn't even been in town at the time of the first incident.

"Oh, no," Lauren answered swiftly. "He keeps to himself, does his work and doesn't bother anyone." She tried to be fair to him. "Despite my reservations in the beginning, he's doing fine."

She knew Kalan was interested in her beyond the level of friendship, though he continued to maintain an undemanding air of cordiality. She wondered if he sensed something—the unrest Jesse caused in her, maybe—and was worried about it.

They'd had dinner together at the sheriff's house the evening before. It had been an enjoyable few hours, and when he'd risen to take her home she had braced herself to accept his token kiss, but he'd only taken her hand, given it a slight squeeze and stood waiting until she was safely inside the house, with the door locked, before leaving. Why, she asked herself, couldn't she have been attracted in that special way to him?

"Lauren, will you stop fiddling with that folder and come over here and sit down?"

Surprised at the authority in his tone, she did as he asked. But she didn't know what to say to him. She would like for them to be friends—she had a feeling he would make a very good friend to have in a bad spot—but she was afraid he wouldn't be satisfied with that.

"I know why you're so tense." Lauren glanced up quickly at that, but relaxed when he continued. "What with the attack here and the phone call at home, you have reason, but you need to relax."

Taking her taut shoulders in his big hands, he massaged them slowly, drawing her closer, between his knees. Lauren resisted at first, then leaned in toward the comfort and let his hands smooth some of the tension away.

"Are you getting any sleep? Maybe you should—"

Lauren looked up into his dark gray eyes. "I get enough," she answered before he could finish his suggestion.

"You should have gotten a dog, a big, mean watchdog. There's this man over off Radley Road who has German Shepherds—"

"No, I have Daniel. I don't need a dog," she insisted with a slight tilt to her chin.

"You're one stubborn lady, lady." He grinned. "Maybe that's why I'm so..." He paused, and his eyes roved her face for a long moment before he continued. "...fond of you."

"And I'm fond of you," she admitted, wishing he'd find that enough.

Before she could move away he leaned forward, clasped her in his arms and gave her a friendly hug. His mouth touched hers tenderly, and Lauren felt comforted by the kiss. There was no passion in the embrace, only caring and friendship. Placing her hands on his waist, she returned the gentle salute in kind.

A loud noise caused her to jump. Stepping abruptly away from Kalan, she looked up directly into furious blue eyes behind Kalan's shoulder. The daggers Jesse shot at the other man's back would have nailed him to the opposite wall if they had been real.

"Sorry," Jesse muttered arrogantly, stepping over the scattered pile of books Lauren suspected he'd deliberately knocked on the floor.

Indicating the colorful covers on the books, all of them science fiction, he murmured, "There's no accounting for taste."

But his real meaning was clear in the look he shot Lauren over his shoulder before strutting off down the hall.

Kalan followed Jesse's stiff retreat with narrowed eyes, then turned to face Lauren and saw her flushed cheeks and too bright eyes. "Lauren—"

A door slammed loudly in the back of the building.

"I think it's time I got to work," she interrupted him, turning quickly away.

Jesse didn't understand his reaction. What did it matter to him if the librarian was caught in a clinch with the dime-store cowboy? He'd christened the deputy with that name the first time he had showed up in Chance, months ago, fresh from some police department back east.

Kicking a box standing behind the door, he looked around for something to do. This job was boring. He needed to be doing something with more excitement, more challenge, to it. He needed to be back at his old job, gathering information in border towns, following up leads, not worrying about who the town librarian was currently playing footsie with behind the checkout desk.

After prying the lid off a can of paint, he stirred the thick liquid furiously, his mind on an inner vision. He could still see Lauren locked in the other man's hard arms.

"Damn it, this is a library," he muttered, "not Lover's Lane. She has no business conducting her love affairs in such a public place." Even *he* drew the line at that.

You're green with envy, Tyler, that irritating voice said, making itself known again. Why don't you just admit it? You wish it had been you in that clinch with her.

"Bull," he snarled.

She wasn't his type. He liked them taller, and more...fully developed up top. A picture of the busty Rosalita came to mind. Now, she was his type of woman, well-stacked, warm—and willing.

He looked down into the bucket of white paint he was whipping as though it were the batter for a cake. But instead of the thick, white liquid he saw Lauren, the wind blowing the dark curls back from her glowing face, the curve of her hip as she bent to retrieve a fallen book.

There was nothing wrong with the way she was made, he had to admit, remembering the feel of her well-rounded bottom backed up against his lap at the feed store. No indeed, nothing at all.

Come on, that little voice jeered, who're you kidding? Do you really think you have a chance with her? Jesse Tyler, the one voted most likely to do *anything*, as long as it was against the rules? All you're feeling is a leftover pubescent crush. If you had managed to take her out in high school you would have had her out of your system by now. She's just an itch that didn't get scratched.

"Kid stuff," he muttered in disgust.

Slopping a paint brush into the bucket, Jesse determined to put the whole thing from his mind. He was here to do a job, nothing else. And so far he hadn't done much toward that.

The phones were being monitored both here and at Lauren's home. But the man, whoever he was, appeared to be laying low. It was Jesse's opinion that he'd more than likely left town and forgotten all about Lauren.

He wanted to do the same. Get on with the work, the real work, Rand had kept him doing before calling him back to town. He wanted to find the man known as *El Personaje no Presente*. He wanted to find—and put away for good—the man who had cold-bloodedly murdered his friends, Sheriff Slade and Raul Estevez.

Rand should have done as Jesse had suggested and given this job of baby-sitting to someone more suited to it. Someone like Deputy Holtzer.

That afternoon Hank Benton stopped by the library to see Jesse, and Jesse put him to work. It eased the tension in the atmosphere whenever he and Lauren were in the same room. And it gave him an excuse not to have to be in her company overly much.

Whenever he needed to know something, he sent Hank to her with the question. He didn't notice the speculative looks his friend turned on him more than once when he was asked to relay information.

Lauren was glad to see the other man, too, and for much the same reason. Eventually she gave the men instructions for moving some things downstairs from the second floor and left them to it.

Later, a couple of hours before closing, feeling more in tune with her emotions, she bought cold drinks for the three of them, then suggested that the men take theirs outside to the picnic table. Surprisingly it was Hank who insisted that she join them for a few minutes' rest.

Giving in to his blandishment, she put a sign on the library door telling anyone who came looking for her, where she was, then led the way. She knew that anyone wanting a book would just come around to the back and find her.

Sitting at the table across from Hank, Lauren asked him what he'd been doing lately that had kept him so busy he'd given up coming in to get the mysteries he'd been so fond of reading.

Hank ducked his curly head shyly, embarrassed at having her attention focused solely on him, and shrugged his hefty shoulders. "I've just been busy—doing things for Dad. This is a busy time right now, at the ranch."

Jesse crossed one leg over the other and watched as his companions conversed. Lauren's face became animated as she discussed mysteries with Hank, whose face flushed at so much attention, though he managed to hold his own in the conversation.

Dropping his head back, feeling the sun warm his face, Jesse listened and thought with a feeling of surprise that this was nice. Sitting there with his best friend and Lauren, sharing a cold drink and a few minutes of relaxation, made him feel—good.

He began to pay more attention to the murmur of their voices and, with his eyes all but closed, focused his gaze on Lauren's face.

"I was hoping you'd be in to look through those new mysteries," Lauren was saying, unaware of Jesse's scrutiny. "One of them is by Bill Simmons. You've read all his other books, so I figured you'd be first in line to check this one out, too."

"I been pretty busy lately, like I told you. There ain't been time for me to read," Hank mumbled, staring at the red-and-white soft drink can.

"Yes, I know. I asked your brother, Paul, about you when you stopped coming in, and he said you had been away a lot of the time."

Jesse finished off his drink and reached down for a strand of grass, which he clenched between his teeth. He was trying not to watch the woman, trying to concentrate on his friend.

Hank was a real ladies' man—as long as there wasn't a lady anywhere around. He pretended he wasn't shy, but Jesse knew him pretty well. Hank wasn't much of a conversationalist, either, and Jesse was listening in case he needed to jump in and rescue the man, as he'd done many times in the past.

A brown-and-yellow butterfly landed on Lauren's dark curls, arresting his attention. It held perfectly still for a moment, and then, fluttering its wings, flew away without her ever having been aware of it.

She took a sip of her drink and licked her lips before answering something Hank had asked. The act was so natural, yet so sensual to the watching Jesse, that he nearly groaned out loud. He crossed his legs again to hide his growing awareness of her and tried once again to concentrate on their conversation.

They were discussing Paul and some of his habits, habits that would have been unusual in anyone but a boy of ten. Lauren threw her head back to laugh at something Hank said, and Jesse's glance was drawn to the delicate underside of her long, slender neck.

His glance shifted to Hank, and he surprised a look in his friend's gray eyes that he recognized. Lauren's charm was apparently not lost on the other man. She had a way about her that seemed to attract any man, whether he was a rancher, a deputy—or a screwup.

Jesse climbed abruptly to his feet, bringing the pleasant few minutes to a close. It was time to get back to work. Perhaps it wouldn't be good for Hank to spend too much time in Lauren's presence. Hank had enough trouble in his life, thanks to his father. An unrequited love for someone like Lauren would only bring him more pain and disillusionment.

Then he tried to convince himself that his concern for his friend had nothing at all to do with his own mixed-up feelings for the woman.

Lauren watched as Hank disposed of their soft drink cans, then gave a jaunty wave and loped off to his truck. He could be quite an amusing young man if you looked below his shy surface. She'd discovered that when he had started coming into the library a few months back. Today he'd really opened up once they began to discuss his half brother Paul.

"Hank is smitten." Jesse was watching her watch his friend. "It doesn't take much for a woman to knock a man for a loop, especially one like Hank. I imagine most women learn how to do it in their cradle."

Lauren faced him, a slight frown wrinkling her narrow brow. "Are you saying I deliberately led your friend on? That's the most absurd thing I've ever heard. Take a good, long look at me, Mr. Tyler. Do I look like your basic femme fatale?"

Without waiting for an answer, Lauren marched off to the front of the building, her back ramrod straight. The very idea of his accusing her of trying to...to vamp his friend was ridiculous. Laughable.

Her renewed anger at Jesse lasted the rest of the afternoon, and if he hadn't called her to the back of the building to ask where she wanted some boxes moved, she would have passed the rest of the day without speaking to him again.

An hour later, Lauren climbed the stairs slowly. The upstairs rooms were used only as storage areas. Someday she hoped to see them filled with shelves of books, but for now they were dark and dusty, a home for tiny creatures—like spiders.

"Jesse," she called at the head of the stairs. "Where are you?"

"Here."

The sound of his voice came from her left, and she turned toward it. Stepping through the doorway, she could barely make out Jesse's figure bent over a packing crate.

"Can you pull that blind and let a bit of sunlight in here?" she asked, her eyes adjusting to the shadows.

Her discomfiture in his company was forgotten for the moment as she glanced around the dim room full of cobwebs and dust motes. She hardly ever came up here, and now she realized she needed to give the whole upstairs a thorough cleaning, if for no other reason than safety's sake. She didn't need a fire hazard on the premises.

While Jesse struggled with the blind, Lauren poked around the room. There wasn't much of value in the place. There was some furniture dating back to when the building had been used as a home and not the town library. Most of that appeared beyond salvaging, and she decided that she would need to spend a whole day clearing the place out.

Stacked in one of the corners, she found a pile of magazines dating back to the early sixties. They appeared to be in good shape, and she began to leaf through them, becoming engrossed in the hair styles and fashions of twenty years ago. She was unaware of the small black spider slowly descending by a gossamer thread until it was almost on top of her head.

But Jesse, coming up beside her, saw it. "Don't do anything foolish, but there's a spider directly over your head. If you'll just move back, I'll get it out of your way."

Lauren had an abnormal fear of spiders, which she now admitted might have been a contributing factor to her having ignored the state of the rooms on this floor until now.

She backed away slowly, until she heard his murmur, "That's far enough."

She held her breath and closed her eyes. She didn't like spiders, but she didn't want to see one squashed, either.

"Okay, you can open them now." Jesse was standing beside her, a cheeky grin on his face. "In case you're interested, I didn't hurt the spider, I merely transferred it to another corner of the room."

"How did you know I wasn't looking?" she asked.

"If you had been, you would have seen me practically drop it on the end of your nose before I finally got hold of it."

Lauren answered his wide grin with one of her own. For the moment they were in perfect harmony. But of course that wouldn't last, she thought. Harmony and Jesse Tyler just didn't seem to go together.

The gleam of humor lighting Lauren's eyes drew Jesse like a magnet. Their glances met, and the air around them began to vibrate with tension. The silence stretched out, became brittle. Neither moved, neither seemed to breathe, and neither appeared able to break the diaphanous tie that was binding them closer together.

"Stop looking at me like that," Lauren managed to whisper at last; her vocal chords weren't working any better than her brain. All she could think of was how deep a blue Jesse's eyes were, and how much she liked seeing herself reflected back in them.

"Like what?" he asked gently. "How am I looking at you?" He moved closer, until only a few inches separated them.

Lauren breathed in unsteady gasps. She could feel the heat emanating from his body. She could see the dark emotions warring in his eyes. She could hear the rasping sound of his breathing.

The air filled with static around them, raising the fine hairs on the backs of her arms. The muscles at the base of her neck tightened as she continued to look up at him. Something warned her to run while she still could—and then he touched her.

With light, stroking movements his fingertips brushed wisps of hair back from her hot face. They didn't stop at that, but traveled on down her soft cheek, the contact gossamer light.

His touch became almost unbearable in its tenderness, and Lauren turned her face aside and made as though to turn away.

"No, don't run away—not this time," he pleaded softly.

His hands slipped up her arms, stopping her, bringing her closer. Lauren could feel the warmth of his uneven breath against her cheek.

"What is it about you?" he murmured against the silk of her hair, moving his face downward until his lips brushed gently against the shell-pink lobe of her ear. "What is it that makes me want to touch you every time we're in the same room?''

His hands were moving again; Lauren felt them pressing against her spine, molding her soft curves against the contours of his lean body. One large hand took her face and turned it up to his; the other was at her waist, pressing against her hip.

"P-please, don't—"

She was suddenly anxious to escape from his disconcerting presence. She strained back against his hold, every fiber in her body warning her against him. A sense of inadequacy rushed over her. She wasn't used to all this sexual tension, tension that appeared to be a part of the very air Jesse breathed.

Jesse closed his eyes tightly and rested his face against her hair. It was pointless to deny the attraction he felt for her. Breathing heavily, like a runner after an uphill climb, he waited for the clamor of his senses to die down, unable to release her just yet.

Lauren felt the kick of his heartbeat against her cheek and the strain of his hold, and misinterpreted the situation. Thinking he wouldn't give in to her request and let her go, she twisted furiously in his embrace.

Jesse opened his eyes and released her abruptly, watching as she backed toward the door as though afraid to take her eyes off him, in case he attacked her without warning. And when he expelled his pent-up breath in a long sigh, she started at the sound like a frightened gazelle.

Jesse raised his hands palm outward. "I'm sorry. I shouldn't have touched you. I guess I'm used to a more...accommodating kind of woman. I usually steer a wide berth around the more refined types, like you." He laughed without humor. "I'll stick to my own kind in the future. You needn't worry about that." Gesturing toward the boxes, he asked, "Now, what do you want me to do with these?"

"Take them downstairs," she answered slowly, once again at a loss as to how to handle him. "I'll go through them later."

Once downstairs, they proceeded to the back storeroom, where she instructed Jesse to stack the boxes. She stood back, unwilling to enter the room where the attack had taken place, but Jesse called to her from inside, and, swallowing her irrational fear of the place, she entered slowly.

"Is this yours?"

Lauren moved up beside him to peer at what rested in the center of his palm.

"No, I've never seen it before. Where did it come from?"

She reached toward the object, but instead of touching turquoise and silver, she touched skin—hard, callused skin. Electricity arched from his flesh to hers. The tension was back all at once, making it hard to breathe.

Before she could move away, long tapered fingers curled around her smaller, softer hand. Lauren felt the touch to the depths of her soul.

Something—fear, or perhaps self-preservation—came to her aid, and she jerked her hand from his hold. But her feet refused to move, and once again she stood looking up at him, a kind of fear laced with longing in her huge dark eyes.

What was it about him that affected her so? He could do with a look what no other man had ever come close to doing. Not even Raul, whom she had thought she might come to love. No one had ever caused her to feel such emotional highs and lows.

Sensing her turmoil and sympathizing with it, Jesse laid the medallion on a shelf behind and reached for her again.

Lauren saw a message in the sapphire eyes regarding her so intently, but was unable to decipher it. She was unaware of his intent until she felt his rough fingers take hers and lift them slowly to his face. He pressed her hand against his cheek, then continued to hold it there beneath his.

Lauren felt the stubble of his beard against her sensitive palm and thought how like his personality it was, uneven and abrasive one minute, then, when you least expected it, unbelievably gentle.

A sudden sound from the doorway drew them abruptly apart. Jesse was the first to move. He stepped aside and glanced over Lauren's right shoulder.

Kalan Holtzer was turning away as Lauren swung toward the door. For an instant she hesitated, and then she hurried out in the other man's wake.

Jesse stood staring at the empty doorway for a long time before picking up his tools and exiting the building by the back door without telling anyone he was leaving.

That evening, when Rand made his way to the room at the back of Pete's, Jesse was waiting for him.

"I want off this case," he stated baldly without explanation. "Nothing is happening. I feel like a teenager sent to watch the neighbor's kid. You don't need round-the-clock protection for her. No one is bothering her.

"Besides, you have her phone bugged at home as well as at work. If he calls, you can have someone out to her place before he hangs up the phone."

Jesse was pacing the small dingy room in a manner totally unlike his usual calm self. In fact, that was one of the things that made him invaluable undercover: he never lost his cool. Something told Rand there was more to Jesse's protestations than mere boredom with the assignment.

"What's the real reason for this all-out desire to drop the case?"

"If you remember, I didn't want to get involved in this to begin with."

"I know that, but this isn't something you can just walk away from. If we solve this one, we'll have *El Personaje no Presente*. I know it in my gut.

"Look, I'm sorry if the two of you clash. Personality conflicts are to be expected. Just remember, it's a job—and no one can do it like you can. Though I'm surprised at Lauren. I thought she got along with everybody."

Jesse thought he would have considered himself lucky if a personality conflict had been the only problem. What would Rand do if he suddenly explained that he didn't want to be Lauren's bodyguard because he wanted to get to know her on a much more personal level? He'd probably tell Jesse how lucky he was that he could do his job and court his woman all at the same time. He wouldn't understand the problem at all.

"Come on, man, nothing has changed. I still can't assign one of my deputies to her. It's you or nothing. You want it on your conscience if something happens to her?"

Jesse stood looking out at the night sky. It had clouded up at about four, and now the heavens let loose. Silver missiles darted past the window to land and be soaked up immediately by the hard, sunbaked earth. Standing guard outside Lauren's house would be no picnic tonight. He hoped this case would break soon, so he could get back to his usual undercover work. This case was causing him nothing but grief.

Rand came to stand beside him. "It's too bad I can't issue you a Blazer for tonight, but somehow I can't see the town council understanding a sheriff's vehicle being signed out to one Jesse Tyler.''

Jesse usually found it amusing that the men who professed to despise him would have to thank him and treat him with respect should they learn how hard he worked to protect them.

Tonight it hardly merited a grunt.

Chapter 6

The ride to Lauren's house was an uncomfortable one, both physically and emotionally. He was feeling guilty as hell. Though he'd been fighting it, he knew after the incident in the storeroom that he wanted to share something with Lauren. Something more than a few stolen kisses that had to be hidden away from the world. He wanted to come clean, to tell her honestly what he was doing in her life. To tell her that Rand had placed him in the library to protect her, but that in the interim he had come to feel something for her.

He steered around a puddle of water that stretched two-thirds of the way across the road. He was tired, and a headache was pounding away at his temples. Since he'd become Lauren's guardian angel, a few hours of sleep snatched here and there each day whenever possible was all he was getting. Fighting against a yawn, he wiped his faceplate clear of rain and slowed his speed down a hair.

Rand would have to assign someone else to relieve him on night duty once in a while, unless he wanted to give the game away. Lauren had already commented about how tired he was looking and intimated that he should curtail his night-life if he wanted to keep his job.

He had a pretty good idea what she thought he was up to after the library closed. But if she knew what he was really doing—keeping an eye on her, not only in the library, but after hours, too—there would be hell to pay.

That would put an end to any chance he had of making her understand the feelings growing inside of him for her. He knew there was no guarantee she would reciprocate those feelings, but he wanted the opportunity to find that out for himself, without all this subterfuge. He wanted to be up-front with her, to tell her the truth about his "reputation" as town stud and troublemaker.

It was true that at one time he had relished the idea of such a reputation; it got him women, along with a kind of admiration from the male population, even the ones who despised him as a blight on the town. But the time for enjoying that kind of notoriety was past. The thrill of living the lie of his undercover life was beginning to pall.

As strange as it sounded, even to himself, he wanted to be able to walk down the street with his head up and his shoulders back, and to feel respect from the people he met. The same kind of respect his father generated when he walked down the street.

In this fantasy picture someone was walking at his side, a woman, but for now he didn't let himself dwell on that. First there had to be an end to the guilt he was feeling, and complete honesty between them. After that, maybe he could make peace with himself and Lauren and really take a good hard look at the changes she was responsible for making in him.

* * *

Lauren had been bone-weary when she finally climbed into her little yellow car and drove away from the library that evening. The unsettling incident with Jesse, and then Kalan's coming in unexpectedly and finding them that way, had left her feeling depressed. The rainy weather matched her low spirits perfectly. All she wanted was to go home, climb into bed and pull the covers over her head.

She didn't want to have to think about Jesse *or* Kalan, because then she would have to admit to the fact that Jesse's entrance into her life had turned it upside down. At the moment she simply wasn't capable of sorting through her feelings and coming to a decision as to how she really felt about him.

She drove through the deep puddles in her drive and, instead of parking at the side of the house as usual, stopped parallel to the porch. As she was making a dash through the rain for the steps, she slipped in the mud, caught herself, then made a leap onto the porch. She slid her key into the lock, wiping the rain from her cheeks and chin with one hand, then entered the house and breathed a sigh of relief.

She was shaking the water from her skirt when Daniel called, "Hello—awk! Damned bad weather—awk! What?"

Lauren grinned halfheartedly and agreed that the rain wasn't to her liking, either. After hanging her damp sweater over a chair in the kitchen, she took an apple from the refrigerator. She pared it quickly and was feeding it to the bird, a piece at a time, when a sound from somewhere in her bedroom caused her to pause, then turn around.

Lauren placed the apple in the bottom of the cage and went to investigate. As she entered the darkened bedroom and reached toward the light switch, an indistinct figure darted from the bathroom, hurling itself at her. They both crashed back across the bed, Lauren buried under her attacker's greater bulk.

She opened her mouth to scream, but a hand clamped over her face, squeezing her jaws together and muffling the sound. Momentarily too frightened to attempt an escape, Lauren lay beneath the man, barely able to breathe, his weight like a heavy rock crushing her chest. The large metal tongue of the zipper on the dark jacket he wore dug into her stomach, and the rough material of his jeans chafed her bare legs where her skirt was hiked almost to the tops of her thighs.

"Are you alone?" The sibilant whisper vibrated against her ear, sending chills racing across her skin where the wool of his black ski mask made contact.

Unable to speak, she blinked her eyes and gave her head a slight jerk.

"Do you know why I'm here?" He appeared to be grinning beneath the mask.

Lauren moved her head to the side, and his bruising grip tightened painfully on her chin. Evil eyes locked hypnotically onto hers, burning into her soul, branding her with an unspeakable horror.

He read her fear and pain and seemed to gain strength from them. Rubbing his other hand up her chest, gripping her throat in a powerful stranglehold, he began to squeeze slowly, watching panic dilate the pupils of her eyes.

Lauren choked, heard the surge of blood pounding against her eardrums, and, feeling sick at the contact, felt him harden against her stomach.

"You owe me for all the trouble you've put me through. And I'm here to collect—tonight!"

The fingers at her throat tightened even more, causing her eyes to bulge and her lungs to burn. She tried pulling her arms from between them to rip his hands from her throat, but he dug his pelvis into hers, locking them in place.

"It's just you and me, baby, here in this great big bed. And I'm going to make the most of it."

Leaning closer, pressing his mouth against her skin, he whispered a question in her ear and ground himself against her suggestively.

Nearly unconscious from lack of oxygen, she only half heard the repugnant details of his plans for her before he finally put an end to her life.

Lauren felt the sharp prick of a knife at her throat, then felt it move slowly across her jaw to the neck of her blouse. There it snagged beneath the material and began to slice downward, parting the delicate cloth as it descended. Goose bumps rose on her pale creamy skin as it was exposed to the damp chill air—and his burning gaze. With the pressure gone from her throat she could take in small draughts of air, and she could hear the hard panting sounds of his breathing. His eyes began to glow as her breasts, beneath the lace of her bra, were revealed to his hungry gaze. She could imagine him licking his lips beneath the mask.

Lauren felt sick; what little she had eaten that day heaved in her stomach. He was going to rape her. And there was nothing she could do to stop him—not with the threat of the cold steel lying against her bare, quivering flesh. Please, dear God, she prayed silently, let me pass out—right away.

Suddenly his eyes darted toward the bedroom door, and his body freezing, like an animal scenting danger, he cocked his head in a listening attitude. He'd heard a sound, one Lauren hadn't. The sound of an approaching vehicle. A motorcycle. Cursing beneath his breath, he shoved her away and leapt for the window.

Lauren had no idea what had caused him to let her go and run. The only thing she could think of was that he must have heard someone approaching the house. She fell off the bed in a hurry and lurched toward the door. By the time she reached the front door, the air fully restored to her lungs, she was screaming bloody murder.

Jesse, hearing her cries, made no attempt to hide his presence and hurtled down the drive and up onto the porch. He was met at the door by a disheveled Lauren whose dark eyes looked too big for her pale face.

"Quickly—the back of the house," she croaked. "He's gone out the window—catch him—he tried to kill me." One hand rubbed at her throat while she pointed with the other.

Without stopping, Jesse changed directions and headed into the rain-blackened night. He was in time to glimpse a dark figure disappearing through the trees a few yards from the house.

In seconds he had caught up with the figure and they fought, tearing at each other's clothing. Jesse got hold of the man's jacket and managed to pull him off his feet. They both crashed to the ground and into the mud, but Jesse came out on top. Straddling his foe, he tightened his knees around the man's ribs, one strong hand at the man's throat. As he exerted pressure against the larynx, he reached with the other hand to lift the edge of the black ski mask.

Jesse thought he had him. But when he touched the mask, the only barrier against his knowledge of the man's true identity, the figure suddenly appeared to be filled with re-newed strength. He began to fight like a wild thing, buck-ing and twisting, kicking and jerking.

In seconds Jesse was the one on the muddy ground being subdued by the man above. Attempting to shake the mud from his eyes, he glanced up in time to see a black-gloved hand lift a rock high. It came crashing down onto the side of his head, and Jesse knew nothing more.

Sometime later, he had no way of knowing how long, Jesse sat up and shook his head groggily. When he raised a hand to his temple, he wasn't surprised to find blood.

Stumbling to his feet, slowly getting his bearings, he weaved his way back to the house. Upon entering, he found Lauren sitting on a loveseat in the living room with a shotgun across her lap, staring at him.

"Are you all right?" he asked quickly, eyeing the gun with surprise. He'd always thought her too mild, too timid, to even contemplate handling a gun.

"Y-yes," she answered vaguely, her eyes remaining fixed on the empty doorway. "He must have heard you coming—" She stopped, as though she didn't know what else to say.

"What happened? Can you tell me?"

She was looking up at him now, her head back at an awkward angle. "H-he tried to—" She couldn't bring herself to say the word rape. "S-strangle me," she whispered. "He m-meant to k-kill me." With dazed eyes, she suddenly looked around the room. "He must have h-heard you c-coming," she repeated.

He could see that she was barely holding her emotions in check. Her lower lip was trembling, and the hands clutching the shotgun were jerking spasmodically.

"P-please, I don't want to be alone. D-don't leave me alone." A tear slipped across her lower lashes and slid slowly down her pallid cheek.

"I'm not going anywhere," he assured her huskily.

He found her bedroom quickly and pulled an apple-green robe from its hanger. He hurried back to her and draped the robe around her shoulders, pulling it snugly beneath her quivering chin.

He wanted to drop to his knees and haul her into his arms, where he knew she would be safe. He wanted to give vent to his own fear and anger, to curse the bastard responsible for putting that lost, blank look in her eyes. But giving in to his own emotions would only make it harder for her to keep the tentative grip she had on her own.

"I'm going to call the sheriff. Can you tell me where the phone is?" he asked gently.

"Yes." She nodded her head like a child, but made no further answer.

Shock. He recognized the symptoms. "The phone, Lauren, where is it?"

"What?" she asked nebulously, her eyes once again darting around the room.

Knowing it would only upset her more to insist on an answer, he moved about the room looking for the phone himself. As he passed the bird cage, Daniel hopped up onto the tree-like perch and whistled.

"Oh—oh—awk! There's-going-to-be-hell-to-pay." He whistled again. "Trouble tonight—damned-rain."

Jesse stopped for a moment and looked curiously at the bird. He knew the bird was only repeating phrases he had been taught, or had heard frequently enough to pick up, but the accuracy of his comments was uncanny.

Jesse finally found the wall extension inside the kitchen and made his call. When he turned to go back into the living room, Lauren was standing behind him, not more than a foot away, still gripping the shotgun.

"Lauren, the sheriff is on his way. Why don't you let me take that?" He touched the stock of the gun. But she resisted his attempt to remove the weapon, and he desisted.

"You said you wouldn't leave," she accused, her eyes over-bright, with too much white showing.

"I'm sorry," he apologized quickly. "I had to make that call. Come on, we'll wait in here." He led her back to the living room.

When Sheriff Slade and Deputy Holtzer arrived a few minutes later, it was to find Jesse sitting across the room from her watching her uneasily. Lauren sat staring down at the floor, the single-barrel, twelve-gauge shotgun lying across her lap.

"Lauren?" Rand moved to her side. "What happened?"

Lauren recounted the night's events slowly and hesitantly, her eyes darting frequently in Jesse's direction, as though for reassurance. When she got to the part about the knife, she gripped the front of the green terry cloth robe in both hands. The numbness was beginning to wear off, and her lower lip began to tremble.

"That's all I can remember," she said, ending her narrative abruptly. The things the man had said, the things he'd threatened to do to her, his seeing her nakedness, were too personal for her to go into detail about them with the three men. She felt ashamed, as though she were somehow to blame for what he'd done. And she was terrified that the next time nothing, no one, would be able to save her from his vile purpose.

"Can you describe the man for me?" Rand asked gently.

"It was dark. I didn't have a chance to t-turn on the l-light." Lauren hugged the robe closer about her quaking shoulders.

"Black jacket, jeans, gloves and a ski mask," Jesse put in softly.

Rand glanced up from his seat beside Lauren on the couch, but made no comment.

"Was there anything about him that seemed familiar?" Rand once again directed his question to Lauren. "His way of speaking? Anything?"

"H-he whispers," she answered slowly, staring down at the gun on her lap. "He always whispers."

"What else did he say?" Rand probed carefully.

Lauren shook her head, swallowing tightly. She couldn't repeat his awful words. She saw the compassionate look in Rand's hazel eyes and whispered, "Sick things." She shook her head again, harder this time. "I can't—I can't repeat them. H-he said ... vile ... disgusting things."

Rand patted her hand. "It's all right, Laurie, I'm just trying to get the facts. I understand. Did he mention anything more about what he's afraid you can reveal about him?"

"He asked if I was a-alone. He asked if I knew why he was h-here." She looked up at Rand with tears drowning her big brown eyes. "He s-said I had put him through a l-lot of t-trouble—" Her voice broke off suddenly, and she raised her hands to her face. The gun fell from her lap, but Rand caught it before it hit the floor.

"Now, now," he began awkwardly, touching her shoulder clumsily. He handed the shotgun to a hovering Deputy Holtzer. "I think you should let me take you to see Doc Stillwell. Just to make sure you're really okay," he suggested gently.

But the suggestion met with unexpected stubbornness on her part. "No, I'm fine." Wiping the tears from her cheeks with the backs of her hands, she announced with no uncertainty, "I don't want to go anywhere."

After looking helplessly at Kalan, Rand then turned toward Jesse and asked, "How did you happen to be here when all this was taking place?"

He had to pretend to question the man's presence, something Lauren would do later, anyway. But the message in his eyes was a demand for an explanation of how he could have let this happen.

"I don't know. Just luck, I guess. I was out riding and remembered Miss Downing lived around here." He shrugged. "I just decided to drive by, you know..." He glanced over at the sheriff, slid his eyes to Lauren and then shrugged again.

"Anyway, I was riding by—"

"In the pouring rain," the deputy, silent until now, added in a challenging voice.

Jesse winced mentally, but let the man's skeptical words pass without comment. "I was riding by and I heard Laur— Miss Downing yell. I came as fast as I could to see what was wrong, and she said someone had tried to kill her. I took off after him, and we fought."

The reddish brown stain in the matted blond hair at the side of his head attested to that.

"He got away," Jesse finished with an apologetic look at Lauren. He shifted his glance to the sheriff. "What's going on? What was the guy after?"

"Maybe you can tell us," Kalan murmured suggestively, as he moved to stand beside Lauren, blocking Jesse's view of the woman. "You sure seem to be in the right place at the right time a lot lately."

A not altogether false militant light blazed from Jesse's blue eyes. He was used to this kind of suspicious innuendo from men like the deputy, who believed he could be guilty of anything.

"You got something to say, Holtzer, spit it out." Jesse gained his feet and took a threatening step forward, his hands knotted into fists.

The deputy straightened to his full height, a good six inches more than the younger man. He didn't back down from any man, and especially not this one.

"That's enough, deputy. We're here to assess the facts, not antagonize the witnesses." Rand motioned for the other man to keep quiet. "There was a previous attack on Lauren, Jesse. It happened a couple of weeks ago."

"I didn't know," Jesse murmured, pretending shock.

"No reason why you should," Rand told him in a stern voice, then directed his attention to the woman at his side. "Why don't I call Carrie and have her fix up the spare room for you, Lauren? It might be safer if you didn't stay out here alone the next few nights."

"No." She surprised them all by refusing. "I appreciate the offer, and I don't doubt you're right about it being safer. But I have Daniel to think about, and besides, how can I let this—this maniac, run me out of my own home?"

"Then I'll send one of my men over for a few days. I know Carrie would have my hide if I was to leave you here alone."

"I—" Lauren started to protest.

"I'll stay—if you want me to." Jesse spoke abruptly, looking past the deputy to Lauren. "I mean, if you think there's a chance the guy might come back—"

Three pairs of astonished eyes focused on Jesse's uncertain face.

"You will?" Lauren asked softly.

"I've just been hanging around town lately anyway, staying a night here and a night there with friends," Jesse explained. Lauren wondered if Rosalita Mendez qualified as one of those friends.

"I don't think—" Kalan offered a protest since no one else appeared to be going to.

"It sounds like a good idea to me. You can have the spare room," Lauren agreed readily, amazing even herself.

"It's settled, then," Rand said, and hoped he didn't sound too enthusiastic. The more he thought about it, the better he liked the idea. Jesse would be around to keep an eye on Lauren, and while he was about it, he could concentrate on ferreting out any information Lauren might have unwittingly hidden in the recesses of her subconscious,

something that might be easier in this more intimate setting. And that would leave *him* free to figure out a way to
use her to trap the man.

Deputy Holtzer wasn't nearly so happy about the outcome of Jesse's suggestion, and he was very vocal about it
as he and the sheriff left a few minutes later.

"Kalan, you're a good man, but you haven't yet learned
to judge a man by what you see, not by what you hear about
his character. In fact, there's something I think I'd better tell
you about Jesse Tyler. Something I think will put your mind
to rest about his staying with Lauren tonight."

After the sheriff and his deputy left, Jesse picked up the
shotgun he'd taken from the deputy and placed it in the wall
mounts above the fireplace, where it belonged. Then, finding the bathroom, he wet a washcloth and offered it to
Lauren to soothe the angry-looking bruises forming on her
throat.

She glanced from the cloth in his big hands, dripping water onto the floor, to his sympathetic expression. Tears
welled up in her eyes and spilled silently onto her cheeks.

In the grip of a new and powerful emotion, Jesse groaned
helplessly, dropped the cloth to the floor and, going down
on one knee in front of the couch, gathered her into his
arms. With his face buried against her shoulder, he rocked
slowly back and forth.

"Don't cry, baby," he whispered deeply. "Please don't
cry. It will be all right, I promise. Whoever did this will
pay."

Pressing his lips against her tender skin, he comforted her
as best he could. She felt so small and helpless in his arms,
so fragile and defenseless. How could anyone want to harm
her?

Closing her eyes, Lauren felt the surprisingly light touch of his lips and the scrape of his whiskers on the delicate skin below her ear. Catching her breath, she drew slowly back. Then she gave a tentative smile, and it was like sunshine breaking through the clouds on a rainy day.

She laid a gentle finger on a spot just below Jesse's bottom lip and sent his pulses careening wildly out of control. Get hold of yourself, he urged silently. Remember your purpose in being here.

Capturing her face in his hands, he asked, "Are you hurt anywhere else?"

"No, but this time..." She hesitated, quaking at the remembered look in the man's eyes. "He really frightened me this time, Jesse. I think he really would have k-killed me if you hadn't shown up."

"What does he want?" Jesse demanded angrily, his body unconsciously drawing closer to hers. "What the hell does he want?"

Lauren almost told him then about the accusations the man had made the first time and the derogatory mention of Raul. But then she would have had to tell him about the man's threats of rape, and she couldn't bring herself to speak of it to Jesse. Not to a man she felt such a strong attraction for. It was different talking to the sheriff, and even then she hadn't been able to mention it. But with Jesse—it was impossible.

"Do you have any idea who he is?" Jesse tried to remember that it was his job to learn anything he could concerning the man, about what Lauren might know—or have sensed—about him. "Did you recognize his voice, or anything about him?"

Lauren shook her head and seemed to shrink down deeper into the robe she wore. "I think of him as *the whisperer*, because he always speaks in a high, whispery voice. He

threatens to kill me and says a lot of disgusting things—''
Turning her face away, eyes on the floor, she couldn't continue.

"The bastard!" He couldn't hold it back.

Such fierce anger colored his voice that Lauren drew back in alarm, her eyes darting to his face. Jesse bolted to his feet and began to pace the floor. God, how he wanted the man—for more than one reason.

"Please." Lauren stood beside him, touching his arm, stilling his agitated movements. "I just want to forget about what happened tonight."

Rubbing her hands up her own arms, she shivered and continued, "I want to wash his touch from my skin. And go to sleep and forget."

A good thirty minutes later, wrapped in a bathsheet and feeling as though she'd scrubbed the first two layers of skin from her body, Lauren left the bathroom filled with steam. The linens she'd dumped in the corner after removing them from her bed, were gone, and her bed was freshly, if not neatly, made with clean sheets.

Jesse.

After everything that had gone before, this one simple act of caring broke through the shell she'd begun to construct to protect her sensibilities after the horror of the unnamed man's brutal attack.

Dry shuddering sobs began deep in her chest, choking the breath from her lungs as effectively as the whisperer's large hands had done. Her throat aching, shoulders heaving and knees trembling, Lauren hurled herself across the bed, burying her face among the pillows.

Standing with his back against the door, out of her line of vision, Jesse had just decided to leave her in peace. When she bolted abruptly toward the bed, he took an involuntary step in her direction, then hesitated, on the brink of turning away. Perhaps a good cry was what she needed at a time like this.

But he found he couldn't go, not and leave her like this. Every sound, every soft gasp, every despairing whimper, every tremor racking her small frame, found its way inside him, to a part of him he hadn't known existed. He felt her pain as though it was his own.

This new and unfamiliar feeling frightened him, made him want to turn tail and run as far and as fast as his legs would take him. He didn't want the complications involved in caring so deeply for someone else, even though he had already begun to admit his feelings for Lauren.

He didn't want to be responsible for someone else and their emotions. He had always sought distance and variety in his love life. He needed the rush a new conquest could bring, and the sight of a new face in his bed at night.

Right. That nosy voice was at it again. *Then how come the only face you've been seeing for a mighty long time now is right over there on that bed, crying its eyes out?*

Instead of making a self-preserving bolt for the door, Jesse ended up beside her on the bed. In an instant she was curled against his chest, her head on his shoulder, her hair against his lips.

Grasping his shirt in both hands, Lauren, for the moment aware only of a warm comforting body, moved her wet face against his neck. Racking sobs shook her body, hurting her bruised throat.

"I was so s-scared, s-so scared—" She hiccuped. "I thought h-he was g-going to k-kill me th-this time, and he laughed—he laughed—" Unconsciously she pounded his chest. "He was g-getting a big ch-charge out of it."

When the blows got harder, Jesse caught her wrist in one hand and, despite her struggles, raised it to his lips.

Lauren looked startled. She met his soft blue gaze, a wild look still in the depths of her own dark eyes. He held her glance, letting her see only the tenderness and caring in his own. The doubt and uncertainty he was feeling about what he was doing were kept buried deep inside.

All at once the very air around them seemed to shimmer with electricity. Lauren couldn't tear her eyes from his face, and she wondered if she was the only one feeling the change. Then she saw him swallow tightly, his Adam's apple bobbing jerkily.

Her body began to feel heavy and warm, and she could feel the uneven tenor of his breathing. His heat scorched the length of her. A spark of some indefinable emotion lit in the blue eyes holding hers, and the hand holding her wrist moved once more toward his lips.

At his slight urging, Lauren opened her fingers and watched as he pressed a slow, hot, wet, kiss against the skin of her palm. A shudder passed through her, and she took a quick, uneven breath.

The sweetly intoxicating, musky scent of his body overwhelmed her. All at once she became aware of an unfamiliar ache low in her body, just as it grew to demanding proportions. Unconsciously trying to relieve the ache, she rubbed against Jesse's hard thigh and felt his muscles draw tight.

This was it, he thought with a groan. He had to put a stop to things before they got out of hand. Admittedly he wanted to allow things to progress to their natural conclusion, but he couldn't. He was here to act as her bodyguard, to keep her safe from anyone who wanted to hurt her. And right now, he knew that someone was himself. As much as he wanted it, he couldn't make love to her. It would be unethical. Unethical, hell. It would be devastating—as much to him as to her.

"I think it's time I found the spare room—"

He pulled away, putting a small distance between them on the bed. His voice was deeper, huskier, than he would have liked, but she made no move to stop him. He figured he was home free.

"He was going to rape me," she stated bluntly, all at once, coming to a decision. "He told me all the different ways he was going to do it."

Jesse stilled instantly.

"He doesn't just want to kill me—he wants to rape me first."

"The sheriff won't let anything like that happen," he assured her quickly, once again moving toward the edge of the bed. The bastard. If he got his hands on him again, he'd be dead meat.

"I've never—I—there's never been anyone before...." The words were hard to say. She couldn't just come right out and say, I'm a twenty-six-year-old virgin.

Was she saying what he thought she was saying? he thought in wonder.

"Please." She touched the bunched muscles of his shoulder. "I don't want the f-first time to be—rape."

Chapter 7

Jesse shifted in measured movements until he was facing Lauren. Was she asking him to make love to her?

"Please," she repeated in faint tones, her eyes begging him not to make her go into detail. "I don't want the first time to be rape."

"That's ridiculous!" Jesse almost snarled, pulling away from her touch. "No one is going to rape you. We—the sheriff will see to that." He'd already been fighting his own demons, and her invitation—no, her plea—had thrown him off balance.

Lauren held the blue bathsheet to her breasts and came up onto her knees beside him in the wide double bed.

"You don't understand. You don't know what it's like to be in my position." Her whole manner became agitated, and she grasped the front of his shirt with one determined fist.

"There's supposed to be something . . . special about the first time. Rape is devastating at any time, but—oh, God, please understand. If it *should* happen, if Rand can't stop him, I don't want it to be the first time for me." Her hand tightened in the knot she'd made of his shirt. "Please..." she whispered.

What should he do? Tell her that he couldn't, and why? It would be just as bad for her if he made love to her under these circumstances, only to have her later learn of his true purpose in being with her. She would hate him then, and perhaps herself, too, for encouraging him.

"Look, Lauren, I appreciate the honor, but I—"

"Honor!" Cold fingers covered his lips. "It's *my* body, and I want to have a say—a choice—in what happens to it. And my choice is you."

The words were a faint, velvety whisper spreading softly across his skin as she slowly leaned forward. First her sweet breath and then her warm mouth replaced the cold fingers stilling his lips against words of denial. She was a little surprised to feel his mouth tremble beneath hers before she coaxed him into kissing her back.

Jesse made no attempt to disguise the effect she was having on him. He hauled her closer and took the kisses she offered, drawing deeply on her sweetness.

At last he drew back, the taste of her still on his lips, and looked closely at her wide eyes. "Still feel the same? Or has this dampened your thirst for knowledge?"

In answer she pulled his shirt from his belt and began to unfasten it with determined fingers. Sensing her fear, but also her indomitable will to go on with what she had started, he captured her fingers in his and said, "Not yet. Things like this take time, and right now, time is all we have."

But nowhere near enough of that to satisfy him, he realized. He knew that she was in a highly emotional state tonight, and he was only a temporary port in a storm for her. But for him, she was a distant dream come true. Lauren would gain experience from their lovemaking and reassur-

ance against her fears—but he would be left with the bitter-
sweet memory of their one night together before she learned
of his deception.

Jesse's hands slipped up her arms, and Lauren thought it
was to bring her closer. But instead he pushed her away.

This was not the time, nor the place, to make love to her,
he knew. He had to make her understand his decision without understanding his reasons. "You're upset—that's natural. But I can't take advantage of the situation, of you—"

"But I want you to," Lauren broke in, pressing against
his restraining hands. Her hands moved up the front of his
chest. "I won't be...assaulted," she whispered desperately.

"I told you, we won't let that happen—"

"Make love to me, Jesse—I want you to." Her eyes met
and held his, telling him in every way she knew that she was
serious.

"Lauren, think about what you're asking—"

"I have—I've thought about nothing else since the first
time he attacked me, when I thought I was going to die
without it. Without ever knowing a man. I've sat up nights
thinking about it, talking to Daniel, frightened half out of
my wits at every tiny sound I heard. And the horror of it
doesn't get any better with time."

"This isn't the answer," Jesse protested.

"No? Then what is? To let that—that monster have his
way?" With her head thrown back, she challenged him. "I
won't be raped!"

Jesse opened his mouth to respond, but before he could,
she asked, "Are you afraid of me? Is it that you've never
before been to bed with someone you didn't have to
pay—"

His grip tightened on her arms as anger darkened the
sapphire eyes locked on hers. He caught his breath to hold

back the words of fury on the tip of his tongue. And instead of speaking, a change began to take place somewhere in the backs of his eyes. The hands at Lauren's shoulders moved, and she felt the towel slide slowly down over her shoulders and chest an inch at a time.

"If this is what you really want—" he laughed tightly, "—who am I to object."

"No!" Lauren changed her mind all at once, making a grab for the disappearing bathsheet. Pulling it back up to her neck, she turned her eyes aside in shame.

"I'm sorry—I didn't mean what I said—I—"

Understanding without her having to explain, Jesse covered her to her neck and held her against his chest.

"It's all right—forget it. I understand." And for a while he just held her, neither of them speaking, while her trembling subsided.

"I . . . really am sorry," she murmured in a faint whisper. "He was . . . brutal. . . ."

"Sh-h-h, it's okay. You don't have to talk about it. Close your eyes and go to sleep if you want. I'll be here when you wake up."

For a little while she seemed to follow his advice and closed her eyes. He heard her breathing become slow and even, and he chanced a look at her face. Twin fans of thick brown lashes rested against her cheeks. The small dark mole to the left of her mouth, he discovered with surprise on closer inspection, appeared to be in the shape of a half-moon.

But then, Lauren was full of surprises. He hadn't expected her to know how to handle a gun, but she did, and he certainly hadn't expected her to ask him to make love to her.

"Jesse?"

"What?" he'd thought she was asleep.

"I meant what I said a few minutes ago. I want you to make love to me."

Twisting in his arms, she slid an arm up around his neck and planted a shy kiss against his chin. The bathsheet slipped down to the tips of her breasts, and this time Lauren did nothing to stop it as Jesse's eyes followed its line of descent.

What was wrong with her? Didn't she know better than to tempt a man in this way? And in the back of his mind the question of whether she had tempted the other man, the man who had attacked her, in some similar way, surfaced. But Jesse beat it down; Lauren wasn't a tease.

Was she ugly, or too bold? Lauren was asking herself, wanting to cringe under Jesse's hollow-eyed stare. She felt gauche and stupid and too embarrassed to go one step further.

Sensing her feelings of inadequacy and feeling guilty for his thoughts about her being in some way responsible for the attacks, Jesse smoothed a comforting hand down one shoulder and dropped a soft kiss at her temple. The clean smell of soap radiating from her skin, more sensuous than any perfume he'd ever known, caused his hands to suddenly shake, his fingers to linger on her skin against his will.

"Do you have any idea what seeing you like this, holding you like this, is doing to me? I'm supposed to be protecting you." He shook his head in protest, as much for what he was feeling as what she had asked.

Feeling his resistance weakening, he determined to leave her, and quickly.

"I know what it's doing to *me*." Rubbing her chin against the brawny forearm beside her, she gazed dreamily up into his worried blue eyes and smiled.

"You know," he found himself saying, "I used to dream about you when we were in school together."

"No," she remonstrated. "You were only a child back then."

"Child? I was fifteen when you were a senior, plenty old enough to think about making love to you. The first day of school, my freshman year, I saw you sitting in the back of the bus, and I didn't see anything else the whole ride."

Lauren had long forgotten that incident. But now she remembered. Carrie had been home with a sore throat and missed the first three days of school. The tall, tow-headed, gangly youth had stepped onto the bus, looked directly at her and headed straight for her seat at the back of the bus. She'd felt sympathy for his inability to articulate a response to her friendly overtures.

"I remember."

"I thought you were in my class. You were so pretty, you took my breath away. And when you tried to talk to me, I couldn't speak over the lump in my throat. You must have thought I was a real dummy."

"No, I didn't," she protested in embarrassment. "I thought you were shy—and sweet."

The difference in their ages, which back then had made him seem so much younger, didn't seem so great at the moment. Not nearly as great, even, as it had seemed a few days ago.

"Did I put you off by asking you to—to make love to me? Are you thinking I'm too brazen?" she asked with lowered eyes. And then, before he could answer, she continued. "You have the experience I lack. You know what to do to make it good—for the both of us—that's why..."

Her words twisted a knife somewhere in Jesse's gut. At no other time in his whole life had he felt as honored as this— or as angry—or as inadequate. Once again his reputation had won him something he desired—and once again it was the same reputation that was keeping him from taking it.

Never in his adult life, not with any other woman, had he wanted things to be so perfect, as perfect as he could make them.

Lifting her head, Lauren looked at him, so close she could see the fine pores in the tanned skin stretched over his cheeks and chin, the tiny laugh lines that would one day become age lines at the corner of his suddenly vulnerable eyes.

"Maybe you should be asking this of the deputy, Holtzer. I know the two of you are friends."

"My choice, remember?" she asked slowly.

Looking uncomfortable, he replied, "I'm not the right person for what you're asking."

"Is that so? Well, who saved my life tonight? The saying goes that when you save a life, after that you're responsible for it, right?" Noting the guarded look in his wary blue eyes, she whispered, grinning, "Don't worry. It won't hurt *you*, a bit."

Oh, yeah? If she thought that, he realized, she really was an innocent.

"Your experience isn't the only reason I chose you, Jesse. I like you. I'd like to think we've become friends in the last couple of weeks. And friends help each other out, don't they?" She waited for his reluctant nod. "Then be my friend, Jesse. Help me out in this situation."

"Is that what we are—friends?" He locked eyes with her, an unreadable expression on his unusually serious countenance.

"I'd like for us to be."

"If I *were* your friend, what would you want from me right now?" he asked abruptly. At her raised brow, he added, "Besides that."

Lauren paused to give serious contemplation to his words before answering. "Comfort, understanding, a shoulder to lean on."

She asked so little, when he wanted to give her everything. Pulling her close, fitting her small soft curves against his longer, harder angles, he settled her head against his shoulder. And with his chin resting against her hair, he sat gazing into the dimness.

This was a woman worth fighting for, a woman worth any effort it took to gain her love. But was *he* a man worthy of her? He couldn't match her in either gentleness or learning. He was a rancher's son, a man of the hard, rough land his ancestors had for generations both fought and loved. She was a woman of delicate sensibilities, and he felt outclassed at every turn.

Lauren snuggled close, curled a hand onto his chest, where she could feel the steady, rhythmic beat of his heart, and closed her eyes. She hadn't felt this safe in years, not since before her parents' deaths. When she was a child, her father had held her close just this way, and she would fall asleep with an ear pressed to his heart.

It didn't make sense, feeling this safe and serene after what she'd been through such a short time ago. Not to mention the fact Jesse was hardly a father figure.

As a matter of fact, most fathers around town kept their daughters well away from the wild young man. Lauren yawned and burrowed closer, allowing her fingers to drift upward, idly sifting through the blond chest hair spilling from the unbuttoned neck of Jesse's shirt. In a moment she was breathing softly and evenly in sleep.

Aware of stirrings that, amazingly enough, embarrassed him, Jesse captured her fingers and held them clasped warmly beneath his while she clung trustingly to him in sleep. Eyes on their joined hands, he marveled at how small and fine the bones felt beneath his hard fingers.

As he gazed down the length of her supple body cloaked in the blue bathsheet, seeing the gently sloping shoulders and softly rounded hips, a strangely fierce, protective emotion stole over him.

At the same time he wanted to shove her aside and spring from the bed. What was she doing to him, this librarian, this quiet, mousy, unexpectedly sexy woman? She made him feel weak, afraid, confused; yet at the same time he felt as though there wasn't anything he couldn't do. She was able to reach a part of him no one had breached since young adulthood, when he'd taken on the macho image so admired by his friends. She awakened a need in him for things he'd never wanted—she made him feel. And that was the whole of it; she just plain made him *feel*.

For a moment his body tensed in panic. What was he doing here? This wasn't his style at all; he was much more at home with the type of men—and women—he associated with in the taverns and cantinas both above and below the border. There were plenty of women, like Rosalita, who didn't have "ball and chain" printed on their foreheads, for him to spend time with. All they were interested in was a good time, and who provided it, or for how long a time, was unimportant.

Lauren whimpered in her sleep; the hand clasped in his tensed, her knees jerking upward. Releasing her hand, he smoothed the hair from her restless face. Murmuring soft gentling sounds, he was once more overcome by a need to stay beside her, to keep her safe. With careful stroking movements he smoothed a hand downward in a reassuring manner over her shoulder, side and hip.

After a brief time Lauren relaxed, breathed a sigh into the side of his neck and slept on.

It wasn't that easy for Jesse, though. The hand at her hip wanted to continue its journey, exploring curves as an explorer charts new, never before traveled, territory. He forcibly restrained himself, and his eyes wandered about the room, seeking something to distract him from the tempting warmth radiating along his right side and draped so trustingly across his chest.

Idly, his glance roved over the furniture and across the shelves lining one of the walls. They held a varied assortment of books, pictures and mementos. Leisurely he explored their contents, and by the time his eyes drowsed shut, he felt as though he knew her intimately.

Lauren was dreaming. She was sitting on her father's lap, curled against his chest, half dozing, the TV droning in the background. She felt her father touch her hair with a gentle hand, sliding down her cheek to her chin. The hand curved lovingly beneath her jaw, curling slowly around her neck. Lauren moved restlessly beneath the caress. "Too tight, Daddy," the little girl whimpered. "Too tight. Hurting. Hurting me."

All at once the hard fingers bit into the delicate skin of her neck, choking her. Eyes wide, she stared up into her father's face and tried to scream. Her father was wearing a mask—a black ski mask—and he was laughing—laughing—as his fingers tightened on her throat.

Eyes bulging, heart pounding, she tried to fight him. "You're not my daddy," she tried to scream. "Who are you?"

"You know me," he whispered, then laughed, squeezing harder. "You know who I am."

Her hands in fists, she pounded his chest, his words striking terror into her heart. He wasn't her father—but he was someone she knew. Someone she had met before. Someone who terrified her.

"Lauren. Lauren!"

Jerking upright, Lauren stared down at the man lying at her side with her nails gouging into his chest.

Tearing her hand from his shirt, she murmured, "Oh—I'm sorry. I thought—I dreamed—" Shaking her head, she muttered again, "I'm sorry."

It was only a dream—a nightmare, she realized with relief, brought on by the latest attack. She was safe in her own room, in her own bed, held close by the man who'd saved her life—the man she was clawing like a wild animal.

"Except for some missing skin on my chest," he was saying with a wry grin, "I think I'll survive. What are you doing?"

Lauren was bent over him busily unbuttoning his shirt.

"I want to see how much damage I've done," she answered. Head lowered, she revealed an ever-widening expanse of chest as button followed button from its anchor.

Despite his protests, she laid the shirt back, revealing four red scratches starting just below his left nipple and extending downward to his navel.

"Oh!" Meeting his glance, she bit her lip in contrition. "I'm really sorry."

On impulse, she leaned over and touched consoling lips to his flesh, trailing soft kisses along the line of scratches to where they ended. Her warm breath blew across the susceptible skin of his chest, causing him to shiver.

Jesse sucked in quivering stomach muscles as warm, moist lips drew close to his belly. Lifting a hand to push her away, instead he pressed her closer.

"Oh, Lauren, you don't know what you're doing."

Brown eyes peered up at him over the swell of his chest, the glance affecting him like a match to tinder. With a hand placed at either side of her head, he drew her forward, her body sliding up his, the bath sheet caught between them.

Warm, naked breasts glided smoothly along the rugged muscular length of hair-roughened chest, the scratches forgotten.

Eyes brimming with tenderness and passion, and a glint of wonder, he brought her inexorably closer. And then, angling his head, he breathed one word against her waiting lips. "Lauren."

Relaxing slowly, her pliable lips met his eager ones, and kiss was returned for kiss with reckless abandon. Their bodies fused together as one, accommodating each other. Feminine fingers passionately massaged muscular shoulders. Masculine fingers tenderly cupped delicate breasts, eagerly tangled in silky hair and lovingly touched soft cheeks. Pleasure radiated from every point of contact; emotions whirled and skidded; thoughts spun, until neither knew where one ended and the other began.

Lauren had never dreamed hands could be so gentle, nor lips so warm and persuasive. A tremor starting deep within her spread outward, traveling the length of her body. Yearning for something unnamed, something she sought blindly in the depths of her inexperience, she locked liquid black eyes on the burning blue ones watching her so closely and rode the tide of feeling to its magical end.

Experiencing similar sensations, sensations that were wondrous and new to him, Jesse leaned forward and captured her full bottom lip between both of his. Rubbing the tip of his tongue against the sensitive skin of her mouth, he drew an added response from her.

For the first time in his life Jesse wanted more from making love with a woman than sexual gratification. Gone was his desire to protect her from himself. She had asked him to make love to her, and that was exactly what he was going to do. He was going to love her as she'd never been loved, and never would be again. She had been so right when she'd told him that the first time was special, and he had never been the first with anyone before.

Trailing kisses along the delicate line of her jaw to below one ear, he nibbled on an earlobe, touching the moist tip of his tongue to the sensitive inside of her ear, and felt her shiver in response.

Careful not to frighten her, he moved his gentle onslaught to her mouth and confined the expression of his passion to the touch of his hands. Hands that smoothed and stroked, explored and caressed, bringing him as much pleasure in their wanderings as they brought to Lauren.

With achingly tender lips he touched the bruises marring the pale skin of her neck and shoulder, negating the pain and terror of their source, leaving only a trembling awareness in its place. His lips sought the small mole above her lip that had always fascinated him, and he caressed it, feeling its slight velvety softness with his tongue.

Again and again his mouth swooped down on hers, drinking in her sweetness, but always with the care her earlier fright demanded. Never had he given so much, cared so much, about the comfort and pleasure of his partner. With each moan of delight, every sigh of ecstasy, she drove him to new heights of desire.

Lauren, caught up in her own needs, basked in his slow, thorough lovemaking. Capturing his face with trembling hands, pressing open lips to his, she quenched a thirst the magnitude of which, until now, she'd never known.

Rolling Lauren onto her back, fitting her slight curves neatly to his, he thrust a leg between both of hers. Body to body, he showed her the extent of his arousal.

Lauren breathed sharply, eyes widening at the contact. Her eager hands kneaded the inflexible muscles from shoulder to hip. She wanted him with an intensity that defied reason.

Jesse nuzzled her ear with unsteady lips and whispered in an uneven tone, "Are you sure about this? Beyond any doubt?"

Speech was almost beyond her, but with her face against the corded muscles of his neck, she managed to whisper, "Yes."

"We—can still stop—"

There was no way she could understand the homage he paid her with those words. He who took a woman to bed on a whim, intent only on the outcome of the act, caring little for finer feelings, or sensibilities, was offering her the choice.

But the choice had already been made. Her answer was a slight shake of the head, a moist kiss planted on hot skin, while trembling limbs wound themselves tighter around his.

Jesse's insides knotted. Lowering his head to one breast, he traced its soft fullness in a smooth caress.

Lauren shivered and, twisting her head, captured his mouth with hers, slipping her tongue inside, tasting him. He tasted sweet and salty and all the ways a man should taste when his kisses were burning a woman up inside with the need to know it all. To know the truth and beauty of man and woman.

Jesse disposed of his clothing as expediently as he had the bath sheet Lauren had worn. They were together at last, the fierce heat of his naked flesh glorying in the feel of her silken skin.

She slid a leg up the inside of his thigh, feeling tissue and tendon quiver at the contact, the wiry prick of the hair tickling her skin as her knee drew close to the source of his desire. And higher yet she moved, until the round curve of her knee lay against a heat so intense it flared against her skin. Ever so gently she pressed daringly onward, gliding back

and forth, mystified and intrigued by the feel of such softness, and hardness, confined to one small area.

The blood pounded in Jesse's brain, leaped through his
veins, and he thought he might explode at any minute from
his need of her. Breathing like a man undergoing physical
strain, he pressed her leg to him, rubbing back and forth
against it. Lauren gasped at the thrill, and Jesse strained
forward, taking the sound wildly from her lips with his.

No one had ever aroused him to the heights upon which
he now trembled. And yet he knew her to be a virgin, un-
loved and untouched. The thought both excited and frightened him. He wanted to give her a memory to look back on
with delight, not regret.

Forgetting his own passion, he pleasured her with kisses,
readying her for the final act in this play of the senses. His
tongue made a path down her ribs to her stomach, while his
hands searched for pleasure points. One hand caressed her
taut stomach, then slid down to the swell of her hip.

Lauren lay beneath him, alive to his touch, her body
swept away by waves of new experiences. Her breasts thrust
toward him, feeling full and heavy, aching for relief.

Jesse took one of her hands in his and began to run his
thumb lightly up and down her palm, while taking one of
her taut breasts into his mouth. As he drew deeply on the
flowered bud, her body arched instinctively toward his.
Jesse placed the hand he held against his throbbing hardness, encouraging her participation.

For a moment, breath suspended, Lauren lay still, his
body pulsing against her rigid palm.

"It's all right," he breathed against her ear. "You don't
have to do anything you don't want to." He drew slightly
away from her touch.

Suddenly she wanted to touch him, and going on pure in-
stinct, her hands responded to his needs. Jesse flowed into

her, their bodies slick with sweat. The hot musky scent of their lovemaking filled the air as they moved together as one.

Hands caressing the length of his slick back, Lauren gasped in sweet agony as his body breached her body's defenses. Then suddenly she withdrew from the flare of discomfort. Jesse lay without moving, waiting to see if she would reject him or finally, willingly, accept his invasion.

In a few moments, the discomfort minimal, Lauren became aware of an awakened response deep within her. Lips against his damp skin, she nipped impatiently with her teeth and felt his jerk of surprise. Pulling back, he eyed her curiously and seeing the blaze of hunger glowing once more in her dark eyes, released his breath in a sigh.

Blue eyes scorching brown, he began to move, the flames of passion once more burning brightly, consuming them both. With each deepening thrust she quivered, and, wrapping her legs around him, she pulled him more deeply into her. Their bodies came together in an interlocking rhythm as they made love with a hungry intensity.

With long, surrendering moans, they both soared to an awesome, shuddering height. Patiently he had brought her to the brink of climax, and now his own fevered groan could not be stilled as he jerked inside her, filling her, taking her to a shuddering world of fulfillment.

Wrapped in each other's arms, the afterglow still drawing them close, Jesse rolled over onto one elbow to get a better look at Lauren's face. The last vestiges of wonder still sparked in his deep sapphire eyes.

"What is it?" Lauren asked uncertainly. Had she done something wrong?

There was so much he wanted to say to her. Things like, "It's never been like that for me before." Or, "I've never felt this way." But the words all sounded trite, and this was a moment beyond such expressions.

Shaking his head, drawing closer, he brushed her kiss-swollen lips tenderly. The gentleness of the gesture sent the pit of her stomach in a frenzied dash to her toes, and she lowered her glance in confusion, surprised that she could feel this way so soon after their lovemaking.

Jesse grinned in understanding and laid a finger against her pink cheek. "It's okay, you know, to feel it again so soon."

Eyes darting to his face, she asked, "It is?"

"Yes." He grinned and brushed back a curl stuck to her hot forehead.

"Have you—I mean—" Feeling the heat travel down the length of her body, she stammered, "I-I mean—have you before? Is it—always—like this?" Her eyes watched his expression intently.

"No, I've never felt the need again so soon."

Her expression changed, and her glance shifted hurriedly away, then darted back at his next words.

"Not until now."

"Oh," she breathed, a smile lighting her eyes.

He took the word from her lips, but only that and nothing more. "It's too soon for you. We still have time."

Snuggling close, she spread the big bath sheet over them and settled back into his embrace. She was filled with an amazing sense of completeness and knew she had been right to choose Jesse as the instrument to bring her on her journey from chastity to womanhood. Because somehow, somewhere along the line, in the last couple of weeks, Lauren Downing had fallen in love with Jesse Tyler.

Chapter 8

Lauren stood in the doorway to the bathroom, staring at Jesse in the mirror above the sink. From behind, she noted how the faded jeans, splattered with mud from the rain last night, fitted him like a second skin, emphasizing the powerful muscles of his buttocks and thighs. He was bare from the waist up, his broad shoulders narrowing to a slender waist spanned by the thick leather belt with its heavy brass Texas buckle.

Setting down the can of fragrant-smelling shaving cream, embossed with pink-and-blue flowers, he picked up a curved, lavender-colored razor with long narrow fingers and eyed it disparagingly. This wasn't the first time he'd used a woman's shaving gear after a night spent in her bed. Glancing up, his eyes locked with Lauren's in the mirror.

She felt that glance like a bolt of lightning spearing into her. She could feel heat travel down the length of each limb, seep into tissue and bone, melting away everything, until all that stood before him was a warm mass of sensual need in the shape of a woman.

A drop of moisture clinging to a strand of blond hair on his forehead captured her attention. The drop lingered there for a heart-stopping moment, looking like a small glistening diamond before it fell. Her eyes followed its descent over one bruised cheekbone to the golden beard-shadowed chin. She had the strongest urge to close in on that drop of water and take it onto her tongue.

"We're a pair." Her voice sounded rusty, and she winced as she swallowed.

Jesse glanced from her mirror-image to his own. The bruise along his cheekbone, from his fight with the intruder the night before, was nothing compared to the trophies he'd gotten in past fights. Rolling his eyes in her direction, he gave a slight shrug and shook his head at the sight she presented. Purple-and-green streaks on her jaw radiated toward her cheeks and chin. Blue marks spotted her throat.

"We look like the losing contenders for a boxing championship," was Jesse's wry comment.

He tried to ignore the message he saw in her eyes each time they met. Damn, she looked as though she'd like to devour him. She looked like a woman in love....

Shifting away from the sink, Jesse sat down on the closed lid of the toilet and folded his hands between his knees. As he stared down at them in a cold sweat, a trapped, panicky feeling began to enfold him. Last night had been great. Better than great—it had been stupendous. But he was feeling the burden of his actions.

He felt guilty as hell. Somehow he would have to get their relationship back on the level it had been before he'd taken advantage of her. Later, when the man had been apprehended, and his own ardor had a chance to cool down, then, when he had explained things to Lauren, when he was certain of his own feelings—when he could look into her eyes and not feel as though a noose was tightening around his neck...

"What is it?" she asked, sensing his unease.

When he failed to answer but only sat staring at his clasped hands, she crossed the small space separating them and knelt at his knees. Placing a hand on his inflexible thigh, feeling the muscles tense at her touch, she looked up questioningly into his strained face.

"What is it, Jesse? We're friends, remember?" She gave a tentative smile and continued. "Can't you tell me about it—whatever it is?"

"Last night—" He spoke abruptly, but couldn't meet her eyes. "It should never have happened. Not like that—not at all. Any...relationship between you and me... It just wouldn't work—not now. The town librarian—" he tried to laugh "—and the town troublemaker. What kind of a bad joke is that?"

Lauren's heart skipped a beat, then continued out of sync. She couldn't seem to breathe properly; both hands had become cold and clammy. Could he feel the ice forming between the skin of her shaking palm and the rough material of his jeans?

"Bad joke?" She withdrew and climbed to her feet. "Is that how you see it?" she asked in choked tones, turning away.

Her eyes caught her own image in the mirror. Was that her face, the eyes like huge black holes in a stark white cloth?

"You aren't under any obligation to me, just because we—went to bed together, Jesse."

Why did it sound like that? Such an unremarkable and unimportant thing to have done, yet it had been a monumental moment in her life.

His denouncement of it dealt her a crippling blow, both to her self-respect and to her femininity. Never mind that she herself had had a few bad moments upon first awakening that morning. She'd gotten through the discomfort of knowing she had begged a man to relieve her of the burden of her innocence and come to the realization of her deep feelings for the man involved. And now his words boiled down to one unpalatable fact: Jesse Tyler was rejecting her.

"It was all wrong for us—for you. Can't you see that? Can you imagine what the people in town would say? I can't do that to you. I think it's best if we forget last night—pretend it never happened." Jesse was floundering, trying to make a bad situation better, but his eyes on her taut fingers, held twisted before her at waist level, told him he was only making it worse.

Why was *he* feeling so damned reprehensible for taking her innocence? She had begged him to do so. And why did he feel even more of a heel for trying to slow things down, trying to keep a level head about what had happened? Trying, for once in his life, to do what was best for the other person.

"I understand," Lauren answered slowly. And without another word, or a backward glance, she left the room.

He wanted to go after her. His heart, that strangely sentimental organ he'd recently discovered he possessed, told him to find her and explain, really explain, what was going on in his mind, his uncertainty—and own up to the truth about why he was in her life.

But the cool-thinking part of him, the part that had kept him alive in places most men, even the tough ones, shunned, told him to leave it alone for now. The most important item in his life at the moment was the job he was doing to guard her against the man who had tried to kill her last night.

Jesse knew that after this Lauren would think he was a cold, unfeeling bastard, and that was okay with him. As long as she was angry with him she wouldn't think too much about the passion they had shared, or the impression he'd given that it was something special for him, too.

A few moments later the sound of the telephone ringing in the kitchen caught his attention. Jesse entered the room in time to hear Lauren scream, "Leave me alone!" before banging the phone against the wall in frustrated fear and anger.

He crossed the room swiftly and took the receiver from her shaking fingers, then held it to his own ear.

"Who is this?" he asked sharply.

There was silence from the other end, but he could hear the hissing sound made by an open line. And then a voice spoke jeeringly.

"Still there, are you? Got some of what I was after last night, I'll bet. Well, it doesn't matter. She's mine! Body and soul, she belongs to me!"

"I don't know who the hell you are, fella', but let me tell you one thing. If I get my hands on you, there won't be anything left for the sheriff to put behind bars. You got my meaning? You're dead meat—dead meat!"

"Don't be too sure. Ask your girlfriend what happens when someone interferes with my plans. She got away, thanks to you, but someone else took her place, took her punishment. Ask her how many more dead men she wants to carry on her conscience."

"What the hell are you babbling about?" Jesse looked at Lauren's profile.

She was staring fixedly at the far wall, her whole face tense, the sound of the man's whispered words still ringing inside her head.

The only answer from the phone was a long hissing laugh that sent a cold chill down his spine. And then the sound quit abruptly, and he was left holding a dead line. Replacing the receiver slowly, he turned toward the shaken woman.

"Lauren? What did he say to you?"

She continued to stare straight ahead, as though she hadn't heard his words, her lower lip quivering.

Taking her by the shoulders, he shook her slightly. "Talk to me, damn it. What did that bastard say?" He shook her again, harder this time.

Lauren blinked, and transferred her dead gaze to his face. "He k-killed someone last night. He s-said—it was my f-fault—" she answered dully.

"Oh, God! Who? Where?" He gave her shoulders a squeeze. "Who did he kill?" Squeezing harder, he repeated, "Who? Did he say who it was?"

"S-someone in town—a convenience store worker—oh, God—not again. Please!" she cried. "Not again! I can't take any more of this—no more threats." She shook her head wildly. "No more of this—no more!"

"Stop it! Lauren! Stop it right now. You had nothing to do with this. The man's crazy! You can't be responsible for his actions. Besides, he could be lying."

Lauren closed her mouth abruptly, hopefully, and looked with over-bright eyes from him to the telephone and back. Jesse made the call.

Kalan Holtzer answered on the second ring. Yes, he admitted reluctantly, there had been a death the night before; a man had been shot at a convenience store in town. He asked Jesse how he'd come to hear of it; it hadn't even been on the news yet.

Rand came on the line then, and Jesse told him about the phone call from the killer. And killer he was for certain now, and by his own admission.

"Did you remember to punch the button to trace the call?" the sheriff asked quickly.

Jesse felt his spirits sink even lower as he admitted that neither he nor Lauren had thought to do so. He didn't mention the cause of their preoccupation.

Rand wanted to shout at the man, to ask him where his brain had been. He hadn't forgotten the killer's threats against his own wife. He knew with a certainty that this wouldn't end here. Their attacker had a taste for killing. If he was *El Personaje no Presente*, the smuggler, he'd killed in the past, but only, to Rand's knowledge, to protect his identity.

Now it appeared as though he had developed a taste for it. Now he killed out of frustration. He was becoming more dangerous with every passing day. Lauren's life was in grave danger, and before Rand hung up, he cautioned Jesse to stay close to her, to take every precaution.

The instructions couldn't have come at a less propitious time, Jesse realized. Lauren would want to see as little of him as possible after this morning. But he would do his job. He'd protect her with his very life.

Jesse did his best to try to talk Lauren out of going in to work that morning, but to no avail. He had no way of knowing that to her way of thinking, the only safe and sane thing in her life at the moment was her work.

So he followed her to her room, where he got the door slammed in his face, leaving him to try to convince her through its panels that it would be prudent to stay at home that day. But all he actually did was get under her feet, making her more nervous and more determined than ever not to do as he asked.

And all the while Jesse toyed with the idea of telling her that his job at the library was a farce, that he was trying to save her life. What would she say if he told her the sheriff suspected the notorious smuggler and killer, *El Personaje no Presente*, of being the man who was pursuing her?

But he knew he couldn't tell her, because then he would have to explain how he had come by the information. And in her present mood, with that knowledge, there was no way, he knew, that she would allow him to stay near her. She would be convinced he had used his position to get close to her—to get her into bed.

Ready at last, Lauren stood at the front door, her cold eyes on his unhappy face. "I would appreciate it if you wouldn't follow me too closely into town. I don't want the townspeople to get any wrong ideas about the two of us—and our relationship.

"And let me say now that I appreciate your staying with me last night, when I was so...upset, but it won't be necessary for you to stay again tonight. I'll be fine alone. I have Daniel to keep me company, and I won't hesitate to use the shotgun if I have to."

With a toss of her head, she descended the steps carefully, climbed into her car and, spinning the tires on the gravel, drove off in a rush.

Jesse watched her leave with narrowed eyes. She'd paid him back in full with her cool, unemotional voice and icy demeanor. He began to wonder if he had only imagined the look he'd thought was one of love on her face that morning.

After making certain the house was thoroughly locked, Jesse took off after her on his motorcycle as fast as the muddy, deeply rutted road would allow. Ignoring her request, he caught up with her about a mile past her driveway and rode sedately along behind, knowing she was no doubt more furious each time she looked up and spied him in her rearview mirror.

It was midmorning when Deputy Holtzer dropped by to speak to Lauren. He wanted to add his own personal assurances that she had nothing to do with the death of the convenience store attendant, and also to reassure her that the sheriff was doing all he could to find the man who was responsible for it.

Lauren stopped what she was doing and invited Kalan to sit for a while and talk. She had put a tight rein on her emotions and was able to converse calmly, even smiling once or twice at an amusing bit of conversation. The deputy had the good sense not to notice that the smile looked a bit shaky around the edges.

Lauren was attentive to his every word, but when their conversation was finished and he went to find Jesse, she knew, beyond a shadow of a doubt, that there was no place in Lauren's life for him as anything more than a friend. But he would be that for her, whenever she needed him.

Jesse was bent over, unpacking a box of books, when Kalan interrupted him.

"I've been wanting to speak to you since the sheriff let me into his confidence last night. I know all about your secret."

Jesse stiffened.

Kalan went on. "I think the work you've been doing for the sheriff's department, and the work you're doing to protect Lauren, is admirable." There, it was said, even if the words had stuck in his craw.

Jesse relaxed only slightly. Rand Slade had no business telling anyone about him or his work. They had a deal. Couldn't anyone be trusted to keep his word these days?

"Look, I admit I had you figured all wrong," Kalan went on when Jesse made no immediate response. "But you've done one heck of a job convincing the whole town, including me, that you are what you pretend to be. You can't blame us all for taking you at face value, can you?''

Jesse thought that over for a moment and had to agree with the man. If you convince someone a rock is an egg, can you then resent him for trying to make an omelet with it?

Still kneeling by the box of books, Jesse looked up at the man towering over him. Kalan looked as though he didn't know whether to offer his hand in friendship or belt him upside the head.

''It's okay.'' Jesse smiled. ''I guess I'm a pretty good actor at that.''

A dark gleam entered his eyes as he spoke, and his smile faded a shade. Just how much understanding, he wondered, could he expect from Lauren when she learned his guilty secret?

Sensing more behind the man's words than he let on, Kalan took a step forward and held out his hand. ''Friends?''

Jesse stared at the man's hand for a long moment. He wasn't used to anyone offering him a hand in friendship. It was a milestone, testimony to the changes taking place in his life. He realized it meant a great deal to him—especially now.

Climbing to his feet, he gripped Kalan's hand and pumped it slowly, and then, meeting the other man's glance, pumped faster, a grin spreading across his handsome features.

''Friends,'' he agreed deeply.

It was Thursday, three days since the last attack on Lauren had taken place. Jesse was back spending his nights hidden outside her house, keeping close watch. Only now, twice a week, he had some relief; Rand had assigned one of the other deputies to spell him, and a patrol car made the rounds frequently during the long night hours. Sometimes one of the men even thought to bring Jesse a cup of hot coffee. Jesse's secret was out, but only among the close-mouthed sheriff's department.

Now Jesse stopped work long enough to watch the single line of fifth-graders file into the library. He spotted a familiar face among the group and waved. Paul Benton, Hank's younger half brother, made his way across the room in Jesse's direction.

Advancing slowly to where Jesse was setting up some new bookshelves, keeping one eye on the teacher, he pretended an interest in a book across from where the man was working.

In whispered undertones, Jesse and Paul carried on a conversation that had nothing to do with books. Knowing about the mistreatment Hank had suffered over the years at the hands of his father, Jesse had kept a kindly eye on the younger boy. He was determined to step in, if necessary, and keep Paul from the same kind of punishment that was still being meted out to his older brother. But Hank doted on the boy and protected him from their father's wrath.

Lauren moved into view from the back office, and Paul's eyes followed her as she moved about the room. Jesse watched the boy's interest for a moment and then asked him if he liked Miss Downing.

"She is so beautiful," the boy said softly. "I like her very much. She is very kind to me—to everyone—and she always smells so good, like flowers."

Paul's huge dark eyes glowed beneath the fringe of black hair falling over his forehead as he smiled up at the older man.

After a moment Paul left the man's side and moved to where Lauren stood. He reached into the small black-and-red bag he carried over his shoulder, then withdrew a bright red rose and offered it to her.

Jesse saw her blush and smile prettily as she accepted the token of the small boy's affection. He couldn't hear their conversation, but he could imagine Paul telling her how its beauty reminded him of her. Despite his youth, Paul had the courtly ways of a Spanish *grandee*.

Jesse's eyes lingered not on the flower but on the woman. He knew that her fragrance was the kind that remained in the senses long after the actual perfume had vanished. It had been a cold three days in the library, bereft of smiles and friendly conversations. Not that Lauren had sought him out before, but now she kept her distance religiously. And he missed her.

Lauren praised the small silk rose and thanked Paul sincerely for it.

"I'll keep it on my dresser, where I can see it every morning when I get up and every night before I go to bed," she assured him.

Paul flushed darkly and dropped the book he'd been carrying. Backing up a step, he bent over to pick it up. In his embarrassment, feeling clumsy under the stare of the woman he liked so much, he fell against the corner of one of the reading tables.

The necklace he wore spilled out of the collar of his shirt and caught the edge of the table. As he withdrew, the book in his grasp, the necklace jerked him back.

Lauren, hiding a smile at his predicament, leaned over to assist him. The necklace consisted of a unique design of beaten silver and turquoise. She detached it from the corner of the desk and held it, turning it over in her hands and admiring its intricate beauty. Somewhere she had seen something, a painting, perhaps, or another piece of jewelry, that reminded her of the unusual design.

"It was a birthday present," Paul told her proudly, "It came from Mexico."

"All right, boys and girls," the fifth-grade teacher announced all at once. "Make your selections and take them to the desk. Our time is up and we must leave."

Lauren glanced up at the woman's words, the medallion sliding through her fingers. The thought of it was chased from her mind as she faced twenty fifth-graders clamoring for her assistance in checking out their books.

After the children had left the library, a few regulars, who liked to do some quiet reading, came in, and the afternoon passed sedately. Lauren began work on carding the new acquisitions.

Jesse observed her unobtrusively for a while, enjoying the way she tucked a strand of dark hair impatiently behind one small ear, frowned, then bit her lip in concentration over the work she was doing.

There was something so fine, so demure, about her. There was real beauty in the dark, shiny-silk hair that barely brushed her chin when she bent over, in the liquid sparkle of her huge brown eyes, and in the pale creaminess of her skin. But unlike the other women he'd known, Lauren did nothing to enhance what nature had given her. She didn't need to, and she was either intelligent enough to know that, or she was oblivious to her own charms. He suspected it was the latter, and that attracted him as much as anything else about her.

"I've finished with the new shelves. If you'll tell me what you want on them, I'll get started filling them."

Lauren looked up. "What?"

A faraway look of bewilderment widened her large eyes, making them look like those of a startled doe. Held by the look, fascinated by everything about her, Jesse found himself leaning slowly toward her, drawn almost against his will.

She shifted abruptly, and the spell was broken. Jesse straightened quickly and glanced away. Clearing his throat, his eyes coming to rest on the red silk rose lying on her desk, he said the first thing that came to mind.

"Paul is a great fan of yours."

Her eyes moved to the flower. "Yes, well, I'm a great fan of his, as well."

"You like kids."

"Very much," she admitted. "Some day I hope to have some of my own."

"Were you and Raul talking marriage before—"

How stupid, he realized before the sentence was completed. Speaking about a dead man, especially about one whose death she felt in some way guilty, was not a brilliant conversational gambit.

"We hadn't gotten around to discussing anything as permanent as marriage," Lauren answered softly, unaware of his self-castigation.

Propping a hip against the corner of the desk where she worked, he asked, "What is all this really about?"

Rand had been pushing him to talk to her about the note, to probe her memory about the night she had found it, to try to discover if there was more to the story than she had told him. So long as they were speaking again, he figured he'd better get on with his job.

Besides, the sooner this was finished, the sooner a way might present itself for him to straighten things out between the two of them. More and more he wanted an opportunity to get below the surface of his feelings for her and learn how deep, how lasting, they really were.

"I beg your pardon?"

"This whole thing," Jesse said, professing ignorance. "Why is someone after you? Why did whoever that was the other night want to hurt you? You said it wasn't the first time he'd tried something. Do you know why?"

Lauren's glance fell on the doorway leading to the storeroom where the first attack had taken place. Should she discuss that first attack with him? The sheriff hadn't told her not to discuss the situation with anyone. And he had allowed Jesse to stay with her that night after she'd been throttled by the maniac. Perhaps it would help her to talk things over with someone else.

She had locked their night of love away in her mind, buried it behind her insecurities, and was striving to forget about it. She had been a fool to let herself become emotionally involved with him in the first place. No one was to blame but herself. Not even Jesse; he'd only been acting in character. How could she expect him to be thrilled about taking an inexperienced woman to bed? He was used to a different kind of woman, one who knew the score.

Returning her gaze to his face, she delved beyond the curious expression in his eyes and sought the reason for his interest. And there, far back in the blue eyes, she saw a very real concern.

Their personal conflict had nothing to do with the threats against her life. Jesse had proved himself to be the kind of man who was good to have around in a bad situation. He'd saved her life. Besides, she needed to talk to someone about that night six months ago, and despite their differences, she felt more easily able to do that with Jesse than anyone else, even Carrie.

"To answer your question," she said at last, "I'm not quite certain what he's after, or what I've done to deserve his . . . attentions." She swallowed, dry-mouthed, at the remembered terror, then continued. "It may have something to do with the deaths of Raul, Sheriff Slade and the grade-school custodian.'' She darted a glance around the nearly empty room and lowered her voice before she spoke again.

"It wasn't common knowledge—I mean, it wasn't broadcast about, though several people knew about it—but I found a note here in the library the night the three men were killed.

"It was there.'' She pointed to a long table practically centered in the room. "It was a Thursday, like today, and the fourth-grade class had just left. I was straightening up—you've seen what it's like after a group of nine- and ten-year-olds have spent an hour looking through the books. Anyway, I was picking up books and straightening chairs, and I found a folded piece of paper beside one of them. Thinking one of the children must have dropped it, I unfolded it to see if there was a name on it.

"I can't remember exactly what it said now, but there was a time, and a place, at the bottom. I didn't think too much about it. I guess I should have. But I was getting ready to leave, and who would expect a note found here to be taken seriously? Raul was picking me up for dinner that night, and when he came in, he saw the paper. He read it and asked where it had come from. I explained about finding it and thinking one of the boys had dropped it.

"He agreed with me, but—'' She frowned. "There was something about his manner...'' She shrugged. "I don't know, I can't explain it. But that evening he seemed almost impatient for dinner to end. I asked him several times if he was all right, and he said yes, then changed the subject. When he brought me back here, so I could get my car and go on home, instead of waiting the way he usually did, he kissed me, told me he'd call me the next day and left. I never saw him again—not alive.'' Lauren paused before continuing.

"I had left some books I wanted on the counter here, so I unlocked the door and came inside. That's when I discovered the note was gone. At first I didn't think anything about it. I took the books, went home and got ready for bed. But while I lay there, I kept thinking about the note. Something in the back of my mind kept asking, what if it was somehow important? What if it wasn't just a schoolboy's prank? At the time I really didn't think it was..." She faltered.

"I never suspected," she continued in a lower tone of voice, "that it would lead to murder."

Unconsciously she reached out to him. "I would have torn the damn thing up and thrown it away if I'd even come close to guessing what finding it would lead to."

Jesse squeezed her hand in sympathy. There was no doubt that she felt somehow responsible for the murder of the men, but Rand was wrong if he believed she knew anything more than she had already told him about their deaths.

"I had no idea Raul would take the note," she said a bit wildly. "How was I to know he would take it seriously—it was just a scrap of paper." Tugging at his hand, she asked, "Would you have believed something you read on a piece of paper left on the floor of a library?"

Without waiting for a reply, she continued. "I called the sheriff, and he told me not to worry. He said he'd take care of it. He said the note had probably blown off the desk and gotten lost. He said if I could remember the time and place written on it he'd just check things out and everything would be all right.

"I allowed him to calm my fears. I wanted it all to be my imagination. But when I hung up I called Raul's number—and there was no answer. It wasn't until the next morning—" she was gripping his hand now "—that I learned the three men were—dead."

"Why do you suppose Raul didn't go to the sheriff if he thought the information in the note was legitimate?" Jesse asked gently.

"You knew Raul. He was a quiet, soft-spoken man. But there was one thing that really made him mad, and that was his people being lied to and brought across the border into the U.S. to be used as underpaid slaves. He must have thought he could put an end to it himself."

Hoping to take her mind off the remembered pain of the men's deaths, he asked, "What made you think the note had been lost by one of the children?"

Lauren blinked damp lashes and looked down at their clasped hands, as if only then realizing they were joined. Gently removing her fingers from his, she folded her hands on the marred surface of the desk and stared down at them.

"There had been a fight between two of the boys that afternoon, over a book. It started with a few names being exchanged, then they were throwing books at each other, and finally the fists began to fly."

"It doesn't make much sense, does it?" Jesse reasoned, shoving both hands in the pockets of his jeans as he straightened away from the desk. The hand Lauren had been grasping tingled, and he wanted to get it out of sight.

"What would a child be doing with a note that actually *was* from a smuggler?"

"I have no idea," Lauren responded.

"Did anyone speak to the children that were here that morning?"

"I don't know," Lauren answered somewhat vaguely. "Everything was so—" She lifted her hands helplessly. "The sheriff had been murdered, along with the other two men. The town was in an uproar."

"Yeah, so I heard. I wasn't here at the time."

Jesse had been in Mexico following a lead for Grant Slade at the time of the murders. He'd been stunned to learn of the man's death from Rand, when he'd called in to make a report.

"Do you think one of the children might be able to shed some light on where the note originated?" Lauren asked Jesse with a frown.

"I don't know," he responded slowly. "Maybe one of them found it on the school premises. I've heard the sheriff had proof of Hernandez Aguilar's involvement in the smuggling. He could have dropped it, I guess."

"Or maybe," Lauren put in thoughtfully, "maybe one of the boys saw the person who wrote it hiding it, then stole it before Aguilar could get to it.

"Jesse," Lauren breathed in excitement, "that would mean one of the boys might know who the man behind everything really is!"

Chapter 9

The next day at the library, during the lunch hour, Jesse was having a sandwich out back at the picnic table when Sanchez, the son of one of the Mexican waitresses at Pete's, brought a message to him. Rosalita Mendez wanted to see him; it was urgent.

There was a time when Rosalita and he had had a pretty good thing going, but Jesse wasn't the marrying kind, and Rosalita planned to be a good-time girl only until she found the right man to settle down with. When she realized it would never be Jesse, they became friends and had remained so.

He made a call to Rand that afternoon to let him know someone would have to keep an eye on Lauren's house that night for a few hours until he could get there.

He also told him they needed to talk, because he had a hunch that someone needed to follow up on. Rand told him that he couldn't get away that night but would meet him at his room behind Pete's late the next evening.

Lauren was spending the day with Carrie, doing woman things, she had explained, when she gave him his instructions for work the next day. A volunteer would be taking her place.

Jesse had had the devil's own time convincing her that she should talk to the sheriff concerning their idea that one of the fifth-grade boys might know something important involving the note she had found. He couldn't tell her that *he* would be talking to the man about it, so she was all for going to the school and questioning each and every one of them right there and then.

About two that afternoon Hank came by to see if Jesse could use his help. He also invited Jesse to a motorcycle race that weekend. Since Jesse didn't know what stage the investigation would be at by then, he told him he'd get back to him on that.

"Hank," Jesse said as he filled boxes with useless items Lauren had removed from the upstairs rooms, "you ever hear Paul mention Aguilar, the guy that was killed a while back along with the sheriff?"

Hank was lifting a large box of trash into the green Dumpster and almost dropped it. Jesse moved up beside him and helped him to steady it. Wiping his hands on his pants legs, Hank screwed his face up in concentration, then shook his head.

"Don't remember him saying anything about the man. I know he worked at the school—janitor or something, wasn't he?"

"Yeah, he was the janitor."

"What you want to know about him?"

"Nothing much. I just wondered if Paul knew him, that's all."

"Well, I don't think he did, but you can ask him, if you want."

Jesse shrugged. "It doesn't matter—maybe I will."

Hank helped him dispose of the rest of the boxes and then left, after reminding Jesse to let him know about the race as soon as possible.

About an hour before closing Lauren returned, looking hot and disheveled. She had brought cold drinks for both Jesse and the woman who'd been working in her place. She also offered them each some fudge she and Carrie had made that afternoon.

"Marie said Hank was here for a while today. Did he come for that book I told him about?" Lauren asked Jesse later, loosening the white ribbon holding her hair back from her face. The volunteer had left, and the two of them were alone, putting the last of the day's returned books onto the shelves.

"No, he didn't."

"Oh, I guess he came by to talk to you. Did you put him to work like you usually do?" she asked with a grin. "Don't think I haven't noticed how you use your friend shamelessly whenever he stops by."

Jesse had unbuttoned his shirt while he'd been working outside that afternoon and had only fastened the last two buttons when he came back inside. He ran a tired hand down the hair on his chest and grinned back at her teasing observation.

The careless gesture drew her eyes, and suddenly Lauren found it difficult to concentrate on what she was doing. The sight of his tanned muscles rippling beneath the opened shirt quickened her pulse. She had no difficulty in remembering the weight of him pressed against her breasts.

"I think this about finishes it for the day," she murmured briskly, when she'd been caught staring at a streak of dirt across one collarbone for too long.

"Lauren..." Jesse moved to block her exit. He'd been fully aware of her scrutiny, and his blood ran hot in his veins at the thought of her wanting him as much as he wanted her—right this minute. It had been too long since he'd held her, kissed her.

Lauren met his questioning glance for only a moment before looking away; its meaning had been all too obvious.

"It's time to go home." She stepped around him resolutely.

"Lauren," he whispered as he moved up behind her, his breath stirring the short hairs at her neck.

"No," she almost moaned.

"You're so lovely." He breathed deeply. "And you smell like heaven—"

"No," she repeated again, weakening despite herself. She mustn't let him do this to her. She was mired in enough confusion as it was; Jesse was a complication she had already put aside.

"I can't help thinking about the other night, can you? I can still feel you in my arms." His hands slid up her bare arms to her shoulders. "When I close my eyes, I can see you, and every time I breathe your perfume, I can taste you."

Lauren jerked away from his touch and flew out of reach. She was going home; she couldn't trust herself alone with him. As she gathered her things, informing Jesse that it was time to leave so she could lock up for the day, she kept her face and voice expressionless.

That evening Jesse made his way to the entrance of Pete's place. At the door he caught sight of Buck Gonzales. Buck worked as a part-time bouncer for Pete; it was also said that he kept company with Rosalita, when she wasn't busy with someone else.

Motioning for Buck, Jesse gazed around the smoke-filled room. He spotted Hank in one corner quietly getting drunk, if the glasses lined up across the table were any indication. Jesse was of a mind to get him out of there while he could still walk. But first he had to find out what Rosalita had to tell him that was so important.

After a moment's whispered conversation with Buck, Jesse backed out of the cantina's dark entrance and made his way around the back to Rosalita's room. He was lighting the large white candle in the center of the small round table when the woman entered, slightly out of breath.

"Jesse, it is good to see you again. You have not been to see me in over a week."

Lifting both hands to him, she raised her cheek for his kiss.

Jesse obliged her, squeezing her small fingers before letting them go. Gesturing toward a place at the rough wooden table, he pulled a seat out for her, then took one across from her.

"I've been busy. I came by once, but you were gone. I would have made a point of seeing you sooner or later. I'll be staying in my old room here for a few days. So, Sanchez said you wanted to talk to me."

"That is correct. I have been visiting relatives a few miles south of here. That is what I want to talk to you about."

Scooting closer, she placed her elbows on the table and gave a slight, cautious glance over her left shoulder toward the door.

"I was called to my Aunt Carmen's house a few days ago because two of my cousins from Mexico had arrived. They are looking for a man, someone who they say will hire them to work for him." Rosalita paused as if to give dramatic impact to her next words.

"The man they are looking for is *El Personaje no Presente*." Jesse tensed visibly but remained silent. "It is said this man lives near here. Pedro was told that he could find work with him, smuggling other Mexicans across the border for pay.

"I told him he should be ashamed to even think of doing such a thing. I told him he would burn in hell for selling his family and friends like goats. But Pedro said it was better to be a slave in the United States, to have a roof over your head and food in your belly, than to starve like a dog in the streets of your village," Rosalita said, repeating her cousin's words.

"I know it is a bad thing to go hungry in your homeland, but, Rosie, it's even worse to be sold like cattle to wealthy men who would treat you no better than animals. Some of your people are being sold to work as prostitutes in big cities, women—and children. And despite what your cousin has been told, many of those brought across the border are dying from starvation and beatings.

"And the man they are looking for is a killer," Jesse added darkly.

"What am I going to do, Jesse?" Rosalita asked, wringing her hands. "How can I stop my cousins from working for such a man? They will not listen to me. In their eyes I am only a woman, good for just two things."

Jesse stood and paced the floor. He wanted to tell her that he was on the trail of the man, and that if he could find him, her worries would be over. But he was sworn to secrecy, so all he could do was try to reassure her that someday the man would be stopped.

Rosalita listened as Jesse did his best to comfort her without giving anything away. She knew him better, perhaps, than even his parents did, and she knew about the meetings he and the sheriff sometimes had in Jesse's room here behind Pete's. She didn't know what went on in those meetings—she had never violated their friendship by eavesdropping—but she knew Jesse must be working with the law.

Jesse was a good man, despite what the foolish people of the town thought. He was kind to his friends—just look at the way he treated Hank Benton, a man who was, in her opinion, undeserving of Jesse's care.

"I will try to be patient, and I will continue to talk to Pedro, and to Emilio, and pray that they come to their senses before it is too late."

The hour was growing late, and Rosalita knew Jesse would be leaving shortly, but she didn't want him to go—not just yet. There were things she wanted to know about him. She had heard rumors about him and the town librarian, and though she knew there was no chance that she could make him happy herself, she wanted him to find happiness with a woman who deserved him.

"Is it true that you are sleeping with the librarian?"

Jesse whirled around and stared at the dark young woman in shock before demanding angrily, "What are you talking about?"

"It is being said." She shrugged shapely shoulders bared by a black-and-green lace-trimmed peasant blouse.

"Well, don't listen too closely to gossip."

"It is not gossip. You care for her."

When he raised one blond eyebrow, she gave a little smile and continued.

"You do not have to say the words. It is there in your eyes, in your face. You care for the woman. I pray she is good for you, worthy of such a man as you."

"Don't make me into a saint, Rosie," he told her sternly. "And don't repeat gossip."

"No saint." She shook her head firmly, a twinkle in her dark eyes. "But *muy hombre*."

"I have to go." Jesse straightened and prepared to leave.

He wondered whether Lauren had heard the gossip. Obviously not, or he wouldn't still be working at the library, he was certain of that.

"No, wait!" the young woman protested. Though she knew he was not for her, she needed to know a little about the woman he *had* chosen, the woman who had managed to capture his heart.

"This librarian—she is in trouble?"

"Where do you get these ideas?" Jesse asked disparagingly. But Rosalita only shrugged, and he conceded the point. "I'm . . . helping her out of a bad situation," was all he would admit to.

The Mexican woman wasn't stupid; she knew that if the sheriff was involved it was more than a "bad situation." And she determined silently that if she could be of assistance to Jesse in any way, even if it meant helping his woman, she would.

"I have to go," Jesse repeated, moving toward the door.

"Jesse!" She stopped him. "There is more—about this *El Personaje no Presente*. It is said that he is a *norteamericano*."

Until now he hadn't been certain whether he was looking for an American or a Mexican. But he didn't doubt her word. If he trusted anyone to keep her facts straight, it was Rosalita.

"Is that all? Do you know who he is?" he asked her earnestly.

There was a brief hesitation, but then she pressed her ruby red lips tight and shook her head. She had only suspicions drawn from conversations she had overheard, sights she had seen by keeping her eyes open, by looking deeper where others only saw the surface. She would not point the finger of accusation without first being positive of the man's guilt.

"I know nothing more," she answered firmly. "You go now—to her?"

"No, I'm going to go get Hank and take him home before his father comes looking for him. I saw him in the bar when I was searching for you. He was getting plastered."

Jesse spotted his friend in exactly the same place where he'd seen him earlier, only now there were twice as many glasses set before him. Personally he saw nothing wrong in his friend belting down a few too many sometimes to let off a little steam. Hank had had one hell of a life. His mother had died when he was a kid, and his father was a real bastard.

He was the reason Hank hadn't been able to get into the military, why he hadn't been able to shake the dust of Chance off his feet, even for a few years.

Due to an old injury at the hands of his father, Hank hadn't been able to pass the physical for entrance into the Marine Corps.

Jesse cursed the man every chance he got, and he knew Hank hated him with a deep abiding hate. But he had stayed around instead of leaving, as Jesse would have done in his place.

No, perhaps he wouldn't have, if he'd had a younger half-brother like Paul to take into consideration. Hank didn't discuss his vigilance over his brother's welfare with Jesse, beyond saying he would kill the old man if he ever laid a hand on the boy. Jesse guessed that was what had kept Hank around, taking the abuse, so none of it would be heaped on his brother's head.

Straddling a chair across from his friend, Jesse noted the bruises on Hank's face, but he didn't say anything. He'd gotten used to seeing the marks of his father's brutality on Hank over the years.

But that didn't stop the anger from coursing through him every time. And if the elder Benton had been within hitting distance, Jesse would have landed a few blows of his own. At that moment he would have liked nothing better than to give the bullying bastard some of his own back.

Once, just after they had learned Hank had failed the physical and wouldn't be going into the Marines, Jesse had wanted to take a poke at the man. But Hank had physically restrained him.

When they were kids, Jesse had tried to talk Hank into telling the school counselor, or Jesse's father, about the abuse, but Hank had refused. He'd said they would probably figure he deserved it, or that he was lying. And then his father would only beat him harder for bringing trouble around.

In later years, when Jesse asked him why he didn't give the man back a taste of his own medicine, Hank had assured him that the old man wasn't worth it. Even though his own mother was gone and could no longer be abused there was still Paul to worry about. Occasionally the elder Benton took some of his frustration out on Paul's mother, but the woman didn't seem to mind. Presumably she was too terrified to complain.

Hank caught a glimpse of Rosalita out of the corner of his eye and recalled Jesse to the present by suggesting that the woman had been missing him lately. Jesse shrugged and made no comment.

"You've been spending a lot of time with Lauren Downing these days. Is there something going on there I don't know about?" Hank asked in slurred tones.

Again Jesse shrugged and signaled one of the waitresses for a drink.

He had never told Hank about his second life, the one he led while working undercover for the sheriff. One of the reasons was that he was afraid Hank would, in some way, see it as a betrayal. They had always flouted authority while growing into manhood. Though they had never done anything really bad, they had skated close until their senior year.

The work he'd done with the former sheriff on busting the drug ring at school was the first thing he'd ever kept from Hank. He'd never told him any part of it, because he knew Hank wouldn't understand. And that was why he'd kept his work in the military, as an MP, to himself as well.

"Have you thought any more about leaving town?" he asked Hank now.

"I think about it all the time." His head nodded forward, and he jerked it up before continuing. "But until I can save enough money, thinking's all I can do. When I go, I'm taking Paul with me, and for that I need a whole lot more money than I got now."

Hank signaled for another drink and burped loudly, then grinned. Jesse wondered if he was already too far gone to get home by himself without mishap. And if he would be able to comprehend what Jesse was about to ask him.

Jesse had decided to ask Hank to speak to Paul about Hernandez Aguilar. Hank would be able to get something out of the boy if anyone could.

Paul was bright, and very little appeared to get past him. If he'd been at the library the day the note was dropped, perhaps he knew something. And, too, since Aguilar had worked at his school, Paul might know something about the man, as well. If Hank asked the right questions, maybe Paul would be able to tell them something useful.

"Hank?"

"Hmm?" He tried to focus gray eyes on his friend's face.

"I was working at the library the other day when Paul came in with his class. That's one heck of a kid there. Did you know he has a crush on Lauren?"

"No—really?"

"Yeah." Jesse moved his glass of beer around on the scarred table. "I was wondering, you know when those three men were killed a while back? Well, I was wondering if any of the school kids had been questioned about that man, Aguilar. He worked at the school, and kids see a lot more than you'd suspect."

"Yeah," Hank agreed groggily. "A w-h-whole losh—lot more."

It was no use, Jesse realized, as he kept his friend from sliding off the chair and onto the floor. Hank was over the limit. The best thing he could do for him now was to get him home and in bed.

"Come on, buddy," Jesse murmured, lifting the other man with an arm around his waist. "I think you've had enough."

"Who—you—think you are? My muvver?" Hank protested halfheartedly.

Jesse led the man out the door. After getting Hank settled in front of him on the motorcycle, Jesse headed west, out of town, toward Hank's father's ranch. There would be hell to pay, he knew, if the elder Benton was awake and sober himself.

When they arrived the house was dark, and Jesse, knowing which room was Paul's, threw gravel at his window until the boy appeared. Paul was fully dressed and immediately took in the situation at a glance.

In a few minutes he had the front door open and, carrying a flashlight, led the way upstairs to Hank's room. Between the two of them, they had Hank ready for bed in minutes. His loud snores followed them from the room.

"Thank you for bringing him home, Jesse. You are truly my brother's good friend."

Jesse mussed the boy's hair and descended the stairs quietly. Once outside on the porch, he paused long enough to tell Paul that at the first opportunity, he'd like to have a few words with him.

Though somewhat puzzled, the boy asked no questions, only told him he would be staying in town after school the next day. He agreed to meet Jesse at about four, out behind the library.

Jesse left the Benton ranch mulling over the many things he'd learned that night. Perhaps he wasn't so far from solving the mystery of *El Personaje no Presente*'s identity after all. And, in so doing, he would remove the threat to Lauren's safety, which to him had become the most important part of the solution.

Chapter 10

The drive to Lauren's house didn't take long. After walking his motorcycle the last five hundred yards, Jesse stashed it in some bushes. He was surprised to find Kalan Holtzer on the stakeout. This was the first time, to his knowledge, that the man had drawn the job. Rand had generally assigned one of the younger, less experienced, deputies to share the stakeout with him. Kalan, he guessed, was more valuable in the field.

"Been quiet?" Jesse greeted the other man.

"Nothing stirring but a few night creatures," was the man's ready reply.

Jesse studied the other man under the guise of asking questions about the ongoing investigation into the murder of the convenience store operator. Kalan told him the place had been robbed, and then the man had been shot, point-blank, between the eyes.

Jesse listened with part of his mind, while with the other he speculated about the man and his relationship with Lauren. Holtzer was an all right guy. Jesse recalled how he'd offered his hand in friendship a few days back, despite the fact that he must have been envious of all the time Jesse was spending with Lauren.

It was quite apparent—to Jesse, at any rate—that the man was in love with Lauren. What he couldn't figure out was why Holtzer hadn't made his move before now.

He decided he wasn't jealous of the man any longer. Truthfully, he thought Kalan was probably the better man for Lauren. Jesse knew that if he was half the man his father was, he would step aside now, while nothing had been settled between him and Lauren, and give the other man a clear field.

He also knew he wouldn't do it—he wasn't that noble. The thought of the deputy touching her—making love to her—made him want to tear the other man apart. So much for noble thoughts and sentiments—and an end to jealousy.

Somewhat reluctantly Kalan took his leave, and Jesse settled down to a long night of watching the house. Resting his back against one of the broader mesquite trees, making a pillow of his jacket, he thought back to the conversation he and Lauren had had earlier that day.

She was of the opinion that at least one of the boys from last year's fourth-grade class could shed some light onto the deaths back in April. But what she hadn't done in her thinking was apply it on a more personal level. If her theory was correct, then that meant that somehow her own danger sprang from something she knew—about one of the boys?

The question was, what? What did she know? And which boy—or boys—was involved?

He hoped that when he and Paul got together the next afternoon, they would be able to work something out between them. If Paul suspected Lauren's safety was involved, Jesse was positive the boy would strive to remember anything that might help.

Jesse's problem was in how much to involve the boy, and how to talk to him without upsetting him. That was why he had wanted Hank to do it for him—even if it meant letting Hank know something about what he was doing with the sheriff's department. Sooner or later, Jesse knew, his secret would come out—it was already beginning to happen.

What was that? A slight noise to the right caused him to whip around, but not swiftly enough. There was a blur of movement, and then the world exploded in pain, a shower of blinding light and the silence of darkness.

Sometime later, Jesse began to stir, one hand moving slowly toward the side of his head. The place had hardly had time to heal from the blow he'd received when he had chased after the man who'd tried to strangle Lauren.

Lauren!

Trying to focus his eyes, he looked toward the house. All at once he became aware of a strange scent in the night air. Raising his head and sniffing like an animal scenting danger, he was even more puzzled. The odor was unfamiliar—whatever it was, it didn't belong to the area—to the night. Then, suddenly, he realized what it was. The smell of smoke.

The house! Dear God! The house was on fire!

Lauren!

In the distance Jesse heard sirens, and as he stumbled to his feet, a tan Blazer skidded onto the gravel drive. Kalan Holtzer jumped from the vehicle almost before it came to a complete stop, turning to face Jesse as he half staggered, half ran up the drive.

"What happened?" Kalan yelled. "I saw the smoke and flames, so I called in the alarm."

"I don't know what happened. You left and something—someone—hit me. I just came to—I don't know how long I've been out. Where's Lauren?"

Jesse moved his head from side to side and rubbed the back of his neck. A pounding headache was blurring his vision and making sounds come and go.

"Lauren?" Kalan repeated dumbly.

Both men stared at the house in sudden fear.

"No!" Jesse cried and made a desperate leap for the steps. Kalan grabbed at his shirt, stopping him as another car, the sheriff's vehicle, slammed to a halt in the drive.

Jerking a look back over his shoulder, Jesse saw Rand practically fall from his vehicle and head in their direction. Fire trucks were pulling up into the yard, divulging men in yellow-and-black slickers, who began unfurling a heavy water hose. Cars and trucks followed in their wake as men dressed in jeans and boots descended on the scene.

Jesse took in all the activity and confusion at a glance, but the only thing on his mind was a name. Lauren. She must still be in the house. Pulling loose from Kalan's hands, he darted through the forming crowd and hurtled up the porch steps.

Before the sound of the raging fire drowned every other sound, Jesse heard someone yell that the firemen would get Lauren out if she were still inside. But he wasn't about to wait for that. It was his responsibility to see to her safety, and he'd failed her. He'd get her out alive—or die trying.

Inside, the house was filled with thick, gray smoke. In seconds he was coughing and choking, his eyes burning and tearing. Close to blind in the darkness and smoke, already nauseated from the blow on his head, he stumbled against something trying to find Lauren's bedroom door.

Whatever the object was, it wobbled, tipped back and then swung forward, hitting him in the chest. Fitting his hands around it, he realized it was Daniel's cage. Poor Daniel, he had squawked his last squawk.

At last he found the handle to Lauren's door and pushed it open. Everywhere he looked there was smoke, and flames were climbing the curtains, the walls. Even the ceiling appeared to be smoking. And there was an odor, something other than the smell of burning furniture. It was strong here, in Lauren's room. Turpentine? Paint thinner? He couldn't be certain.

All that mattered right now was to get Lauren out of the room, and out of danger, as speedily as possible. He could see her figure in the light of the flames, sprawled out on the bed. Thank God the fire hadn't reached the bedcovers yet.

Dropping to his knees, where the smoke was less thick, he tugged the top sheet from the bed, crawled to the bathroom and wet it in the tub. Pulling a towel from the shelf, he wet that, too, and tied it over his nose and mouth. And then, still on hands and knees, he moved toward the bed. The carpet was smoldering in several places, and the ceiling was beginning to fall down in big patches.

After wrapping Lauren in the damp sheet, Jesse lifted her inert form into his arms and lurched toward the doorway. It, too, was aflame now, and he hesitated for a moment before plunging through it into the hallway.

Finding the front door proved to be harder than he'd expected; there wasn't much left that wasn't at least smoking. A fireman entered the room and, spotting Jesse's figure through the haze of smoke, gestured for him to follow.

In a short time he was standing on the porch, surrounded by people. One of the firemen reached for the sheet-enshrouded bundle, but Jesse pulled back. Rand touched him on the shoulder and told him to let the man takc her. She needed help Jesse couldn't give. Reluctantly Jesse placed his precious burden in the stranger's arms, but his eyes stayed on the still, white figure until it disappeared inside the orange-and-white ambulance.

The fire chief asked Jesse if there was anyone else left inside. "Daniel," he murmured between coughing bouts. "Only Daniel—and it's too late for him."

Rand shook his head at the man when he made as though to enter the burning shell.

"Daniel is a bird. And it sounds like he's beyond help."

A member of the Emergency Medical Team tried to examine the burns on Jesse's shoulder and neck, but he jerked away, telling the man he was all right. Then the abrupt cadence of the ambulance's siren and the intermittent flash of the red lights drew everyone's attention.

Jesse bounded from the porch and raced toward the fast disappearing taillights. Rand came up behind him and caught his arm. Thinking of Carrie, he understood Jesse's feelings.

"Come on," he said. "I'll take you. And while we're there, someone can give you a going-over, too."

In the car on the way to the hospital Rand explained more about Kalan calling in the alarm.

"He answered a call from one of the locals about a domestic disturbance, and on the way back he decided to make another pass by Lauren's house. It's a good thing he did, too. What happened to you?"

"I wasn't paying as much attention as I should have been," he admitted angrily. "If I had, I'd have heard the bastard before he hit me from behind."

"Well, like I said, it's a good thing Kalan doubled back. With you out of commission, by the time you came to and turned in an alarm, there wouldn't have been anything left of the . . . house but a pile of ashes."

Though neither man mentioned Lauren's fate in such an event, they were both seeing the same picture. Lauren with her head dangling over the attendant's arm, her limbs drooping flaccidly as he carried her to the ambulance. Without any encouragement from Jesse, Rand stepped down harder on the gas pedal.

"I should have been paying more attention!" Slamming his fist against his thigh, Jesse turned to face the window, biting back self-accusatory expletives. Lauren had to be all right. She had to! He wouldn't even consider any other possibility.

At the local hospital, a small, twenty-bed facility more used to dealing with tonsillectomies and appendectomies than accident victims, Rand and Jesse pulled to a screeching halt. Almost as one they descended on the emergency room.

The smell of smoke and burned clothing captured a nurse's attention immediately. In seconds a protesting Jesse was being led away to have his burns cleaned and treated. All during the procedure he made objections and inquiries that went unanswered about Lauren's condition and the sheriff's present whereabouts.

After they had finished with him, and he'd refused both pain medication and an offer to spend the night in the hospital for observation, Jesse was turned loose. He lost no time in finding Rand Slade. He and Carrie were standing before the double doors to the operating room with their arms wrapped around each other.

"What's the word?" Jesse asked before either one of them was aware of his presence.

They both turned, but it was the sheriff who answered. "She's still unconscious, but her vital signs are good. And she doesn't appear to be burned."

"Then why the hell isn't she awake?" Jesse asked impatiently, pacing the small hallway in agitation.

Carrie eyed Jesse curiously but refrained from speaking. She, too, was feeling the strain of waiting and worrying. Drawing closer to her husband, she looked up into his face and tried to understand the expression of profound compassion in the hazel eyes directed toward the younger man's figure.

Twenty minutes later, after Jesse drank a cup of bitter black coffee brought by one of the nurses, the dark green double doors finally parted to emit a lone figure.

Dressed in surgical greens and a white lab coat opened down the front, with a stethoscope around his neck, the doctor stopped before the sheriff.

"Rand..." He spoke to the man first, then turned to look at Carrie. "You should be home in bed." He gestured to her protruding stomach. "How's the little one taking all this late night activity?"

"I'm all right, Dr. Stillwell. But, please, how is Laurie? Is she going to be okay?"

"She's probably feeling better than you do right now, or will be soon. She's conscious, and except for some discomfort from breathing so much smoke, she's fine. We have her on oxygen right now, just to make things easier for her, but in a few minutes we're going to take her to a room. I want her to spend the night so we can keep an eye on her, and then I would suggest she stay with someone for a day or two, just for safety's sake."

Jesse had remained quiet during the doctor's monologue, but he spoke up now.

"When can I—" He glanced at Rand and Carrie, and amended it to, "When can we see her?"

Dr. Stillwell, a native of the town, was well acquainted with Jesse Tyler. He had removed his tonsils at the tender age of ten and treated him for various childhood ailments and accidents. He was surprised to see him here in conjunction with Lauren.

''I've given her a sedative, and she'll probably fall asleep any minute.'' He saw the objection building in the blue eyes and added, ''If you want to wait a little while, until we get her settled into her room, you can see her for five minutes, no longer.'' His gaze encompassed the sheriff and his wife, as well.

Jesse elected to go in to see Lauren last, and when it was his turn, he stood in the doorway for long moments and simply stared at the unmoving figure on the bed. A dark green tank with gauges at the top and a thin, clear-green piece of plastic tubing leading from it to Lauren sat beside the head of the bed.

Seeing her here, so silent and still, almost made him disbelieve the doctor's reassurances that she was going to be fine. Going closer to the bed, a step at a time, he could see how pale and waxy the skin of her face and neck looked. The dark hair had been pushed carelessly back from her forehead, and the elastic band securing the plastic tubing to her nostrils dug a ridge in the skin of both cheeks.

Someone had turned the sheet and blanket back to her waist and folded her hands across her chest. The sight made him angry. It was the pose always used to denote death in movies.

Adjusting the elastic band across her face so that it wouldn't leave a red welt, he then considered the folded hands. After pulling the blanket further down, he rested her arms at her sides and covered her to her chin.

Standing back, he contemplated her new position. Yes, he decided, she looked more natural, and more comfortable, too. His time was almost up, but he couldn't leave without one last thing.

Bending close, he placed a soft kiss on each closed eyelid, one on her forehead, and one on her cool lips.

"I'm sorry, Laurie," he whispered sincerely, using the nickname he'd heard the Slades use. That was how he thought of her now, as his Laurie. "I didn't do a very good job of protecting you, did I?"

He should have been more alert. The guilt weighed heavily on his shoulders. He'd been negligent, and it had almost cost Lauren her life. He was more determined now than ever to discover the identity of the man responsible for tonight's piece of work.

A question had been buzzing around inside his head, but he was only now becoming aware of it. Why hadn't the man killed him? Twice now, he'd had the chance, and both times he'd only stunned him. Yet he had killed an innocent man, the convenience store attendant, someone who had no contact with Lauren. Why? Somehow, he felt that if he could solve that puzzle, he'd know the identity of the killer.

"Laurie, please, this isn't the time for your stubborn pride to rear its ugly head." Carrie stood with feet slightly spread and her hands on her belly.

Lauren had left the hospital the day before and gone directly to Carrie's house. Rand had increased the security on his own house before picking her up at the hospital, but she didn't know that. He'd done it without telling either woman, because he hadn't wanted to alarm them any more than necessary. She was supposed to spend at least a couple of days there, but she was already making plans to leave.

She was set on the idea of moving into two of the upstairs rooms at the library until she could make other arrangements. She had already contacted the town board and gotten permission.

"Carrie, I appreciate your offer of a place to live until I get something else. But you know you don't really have the space." Before her friend could protest, she continued, "And besides, I refuse to cower behind anyone else's skirts." She couldn't explain that she was putting her friend in danger by staying there, and that was the real reason why she was leaving so soon.

Sitting on the bed, Lauren smoothed her skirt with unsteady fingers. She was still feeling a bit weak from her ordeal, but the weakness only firmed her resolve to see the man responsible for her plight caught and punished.

He had taken everything from her now. Her home, her possessions, her past—even Daniel, her pet. She would *not* let him take her independence, her self-esteem. She would not be forced to run, to hide, to cower before him. How could she explain her feelings so that her friend would understand?

"Come here." Lauren held her hand out to the other woman. Carrie took it and lowered her bulk beside her.

"Do you remember how when we were kids sometimes we got into trouble for things we didn't do? Like at school when the teacher wasn't sure who was responsible for putting glue on her chair that time, and I got blamed?"

Carrie nodded, but frowned.

"Well, I wouldn't cry then, no matter how hard Mrs. McKnight spanked me, because I knew I hadn't done anything wrong. And I wouldn't give her the satisfaction of seeing me in tears."

Carrie nodded again, the light of understanding dawning in her crystal-green eyes.

"Well, this situation is sort of like that. I wouldn't give in then, and I won't give in now. No matter what that maniac does, I won't let him see that he's got me scared, and I won't run.

"If I could figure out whatever it is that he thinks I know about him, I'd have it printed across the front page of every newspaper from here to New York City," Lauren said.

"I understand." Carrie squeezed her hand. "I just want you to be careful. You're special to me, and I want you around to help me love this one." She patted her protruding belly gently.

"I will. I'll be careful, but I won't let him make me hide. I'm tired of being frightened out of my wits every time I hear a sound I can't immediately identify. I'm tired of being stalked like an animal in the woods. I think it's time for me to fight back."

"Just don't do anything foolish, okay?" Carrie asked gravely. Lauren nodded, and they both went back to what they had been doing.

Friends and neighbors had been bringing clothing, household furnishings and food to Lauren at the Slade ranch ever since learning of the fire. While the two women packed the gifts in boxes, Carrie decided to sound her friend out about Jesse.

"I know Jesse Tyler has been working for you the last few weeks, but I didn't realize you had become . . . so close."

Lauren stood, with her back to the other woman until she had managed to get her emotions under control. Jesse hadn't been near her since before the fire. He hadn't even called to inquire about her health. And it hurt.

"We aren't close." She folded the blanket she was holding and placed it in the box.

"Really?"

There was an unfamiliar note of hurt in the other woman's voice, and Lauren turned to face her with a question in her eyes.

Carrie met her glance. "If you don't want to talk to me about it . . ." She shrugged and looked away.

"Carrie, there isn't anything to talk about."

She couldn't bring herself to tell her friend that she had been susceptible enough to Jesse's flagrant charm to sleep with him—worse yet, beg him to sleep with her—and then to fall in love with him.

"Okay, if that's the way you want it. But you'd better tell Jesse to tone it down a bit if you want to keep things a secret."

"I don't understand," Lauren replied with a puzzled frown.

"The other night, the night of the fire, he was like a caged lion while we were waiting for the doctor to tell us how badly you'd been hurt."

"Jesse was there?"

"There! Honey, he saved your life."

Lauren looked dazed. "He did?"

"Yes, didn't anyone explain what happened? Jesse plunged into the blazing house and carried you to safety."

Regarding her friend with amazement, Lauren murmured softly, "I didn't know. No one said anything. I thought it was one of the firemen, or Rand."

Carrie shook her head until her red hair flew out around her face. "It was Jesse. And, honey, he was so worried, he wouldn't let them touch you at first. And he refused help for his own burns at the scene. Rand said they had to shanghai him at the hospital to treat him—"

"He's hurt?"

"Nothing major," her friend rushed to assure her. "Only a few superficial burns on his shoulder and neck. He's fine. Really.

"You know, I suspected the two of you—" She glanced down at her hands folded on her belly. "Well, you know.

But until the other night I wasn't too thrilled about it.'' Meeting Lauren's eyes, she confessed, ''I always kind of hoped you and Kalan—well, it doesn't matter now. I just want you to know I've changed my opinion about Jesse Tyler. He could have died in that fire, but according to Rand and Kalan, he didn't even hesitate. That takes a special kind of man in my mind. And I want you to know that whatever makes you happy is all right with me,'' she finished in a self-conscious rush.

''Has he been to the house since I've been here?'' Lauren asked slowly.

Carrie shook her head. ''But I'm sure he's talked with Rand or Kalan.'' She couldn't bear to see the light die out of her friend's brown eyes, or to see that pinched look once more take over Lauren's wide mouth.

Lauren had no difficulty in finding strong backs willing to assist her in moving her things into the two rooms she and Jesse had already cleared upstairs in the library.

She didn't see Jesse until that evening, when he arrived to help move the heavier furniture up the stairs. He made polite inquiries about how she was feeling, listened to her answers, then gave a cool nod and went on about his business. She felt chilled to the marrow every time he looked at her in that new impersonal way.

The long-sleeved shirt he wore covered the dressing on his shoulder, and for the first time since he'd begun working at the library his shirt was buttoned to the neck.

Lauren wanted to ask how he was faring, too, but since he hadn't been around, she didn't want him to know she'd been talking about him. Apparently he didn't want her to know about his part in saving her.

The library was closed for the next couple of days to allow Lauren to regain her strength and get settled into her quarters. Jesse spent the time helping her, but it was a silent, morose man who moved to do her bidding.

When Hank Benton showed up to offer his assistance Lauren was more than happy for his presence. She hoped he would help to relieve some of the tension that thickened the air whenever she and Jesse were in the same vicinity.

But Jesse's behavior toward his friend was almost as constrained as it was toward her, and she caught a few of the sidelong glances Hank threw Jesse's way. After a little while Hank made an excuse and left.

Lauren's bedroom was finally ready. All she had to do was to make up the bed. She knew she was feeling more tired than the physical activity called for and realized she must still be suffering from the aftereffects of smoke inhalation.

Jesse was somewhere downstairs working in one of the storerooms. He seemed able to find plenty to do to keep out of her way. Lauren decided a rest in the recliner some kind soul had donated was just what she needed. Slipping off her shoes, she sat back with a long, drawn-out sigh and closed her eyes.

The next thing she knew she was being awakened by someone calling her name. Opening her eyes, she looked up into Jesse's face, so close she could see darker, almost black specks in his sapphire eyes.

"What is it?" she asked anxiously. Jesse was leaning over her, a hand on either arm of the chair.

"You were having a bad dream. I figured I'd better wake you up before you started screaming and someone decided I was trying to murder you."

It was the wrong thing to say; he knew that almost before the words had left his mouth. It had just been something to keep her from realizing how much he wanted to pull her into his arms.

"I'm sorry, that was insensitive."

Lauren looked away, trying to hide the tears filling her eyes. Her chin quivered, and she bit her lower lip to try to ease the strain. She was *not* going to act silly about all this. Hadn't she told Carrie she wasn't going to let herself be frightened any longer? Well, she wouldn't let this man turn her into a crybaby either.

"It's all right." She got herself under control and asked in a careful voice, "Will you let me get up, please?"

Jesse loosened his hands and stepped away from the chair. He watched as Lauren brought her feet to the floor, stood and moved across the room toward the unmade bed.

She picked up a cotton sheet covered in red-and-yellow rosebuds, flapped it in the air to remove the wrinkles and began to make the bed. She had to do something to stay busy or else she was afraid she would hurl herself into Jesse's arms. She was of two minds; she wanted him to leave— yet she longed for him to stay.

"Here, let me do that." Moving up behind her, he reached around and took the sheet from her fingers.

"No—"

Whirling, she found herself within the circle of his strong arms. And she couldn't speak past the sudden lump in her throat. Her feelings for him, which she had thought she had under control, all at once overwhelmed her.

Their eyes met and locked, hers filled with a kind of desperation, his with an unchained need.

He intended only to offer her comfort, to remove the signs of strain in her face. It was a diversionary tactic, he told himself, an act of kindness from one friend to another; he would stay uninvolved beyond that.

And then his lips touched hers and nothing else mattered.

As his mouth moved over hers, Lauren parted her lips in protest. Her arms, trapped between them, pushed against his chest. This was all wrong; they shouldn't be doing this.

The kiss was surprisingly gentle, and she could hardly withstand its tender persuasion. His hands rested at her waist, and he pulled her slowly into him, crushing her breasts flat against his chest. One hand slid up to the back of her head, the other pressed lower.

As the kiss intensified, Lauren no longer strained against his hold. Her hands crawled up his chest and around to the back of his head. There they became entangled in the strands of blond hair at his neck.

With a lazy, sensuous move, Jesse slipped a leg between hers and felt her tremble in response. At the same time his tongue pressed against her lips, seeking entrance. Emitting a small whimper, Lauren opened her mouth and clung to him more tightly. Gliding over the smooth wetness of her teeth, his hot tongue caressed the inner walls of her mouth. She tasted so sweet, and how he'd missed her sweetness.

The blood pounded in her veins, leapt from her heart and made her knees tremble. She felt transported on a soft wispy cloud where no one existed but herself and Jesse. She wanted this moment, this kiss, to go on forever.

The soft sounds she uttered twisted Jesse's insides into knots and at the same time drove him on to a deeper level of passion. She confused and confounded him, at times infuriated him, but she belonged to him. He'd made her his that first night they had made love, and no one, nothing, could ever take that away from him.

Twisting his body, he maneuvered the two of them to the bed. Lowering her carefully, he came down beside her. The pile of blankets and pillows slid unnoticed to the floor.

Lauren moved against him, her hands touching his face, his shoulders. She loved the feel of him, the raw masculine scent of him, the sweet weight of his body crushing hers. Lost to everything except this man, this moment, she rose onto her elbow and moved half over him. Her skirt rode up her shapely thigh as she teasingly moved a heel up the muscles of her calf.

Jesse's hand followed the path of her skirt up the smooth supple flesh at the back of her thigh and settled on her hip. Groaning aloud at the pressure building in his lower belly, he fastened his lips on hers, taking her mouth in desperation.

His hands were drawing the blouse from her skirt when he realized she was not trying to help, but to stop him instead. He pulled his mouth from hers and looked up.

"No." She spoke softly, regretfully. "We can't." Smoothing her clothes down over her body, she got off the bed. "I'm sorry," she murmured with her back to him, tucking her blouse back inside her skirt. "I'm sorry, but I can't."

She hoped he would understand that the timing was all wrong. Their...association, had begun in desperation, in fear on her part. She wanted it to be different the next time—if there was ever to be a next time. She wanted him to make love to her because he loved her, not to comfort her.

Jesse lay there for long moments, the sound of his breathing filling the room. And then, when he had his emotions under control, he got off the bed and left the room. She was right to have called a halt before things got out of control. Things needed to be put right between them before they again shared a bed.

And he knew where to start. Jesse had a hunch—one that, if it was correct, could give him the name of the man trying to kill Lauren.

Chapter 11

The next morning was Saturday, and the library was only open until noon. Jesse planned to find Paul and talk with him again. There were still some things bothering him that he thought the boy might be able to help him get straight in his mind, and he'd been unable to keep their previous appointment because of the fire.

He continued to stay in his room behind Pete's on the nights when he wasn't keeping an eye on Lauren, and he hadn't gotten much sleep the night before, even though he hadn't been stationed outside the library all night. The noise from Pete's had kept him awake until the small hours of the morning. And if that wasn't enough, his thoughts hadn't made very comfortable bedfellows, either.

Lauren opened the library the same as usual, but with a distracted air about her. She made a wide berth around Jesse; in fact, she spent so much time avoiding him that she began to grow nervous and irritable.

Many people stopped by just to see for themselves that she was really all right. And then there were those curious souls who only wanted a peek at someone the whole town was talking about. If any of them suffered from the librarian's unusually short-temper, they put it down to the fire and immediately forgave her.

After a while Lauren managed to get back on an even keel and took the curious in her stride along with the regular library patrons. It wasn't until about eleven-forty-five that something happened to shake her, once again reminding her of the mess her life had become.

It was close to closing time, and the library had cleared out. She was checking in the last of the books, preparing to return them to their shelves, when the doors suddenly burst open and Paul Benton rushed inside, panting.

Jesse was coming down from upstairs, where he'd been fixing an electrical outlet in one of Lauren's rooms. He glanced up at the commotion and saw Lauren move around the counter toward the boy.

Paul caught sight of Lauren immediately and headed straight for her. Throwing skinny arms around her waist, he hugged her tightly, sobbing.

Stunned, she looked up and met Jesse's eyes, all the while squeezing the distraught boy's shoulders soothingly.

"Paul? Honey, what is it? Are you ill?"

But he only moved his head back and forth against her skirt and continued to sob.

Jesse descended the last of the stairs and joined the two. Pulling out a chair, he sat down and took the boy's shoulders in his hands, turning him around. Paul transferred his wet face to Jesse's chest.

"Okay. It's okay. Come on, fella', tell us what's wrong. If you aren't hurt, what's all the fuss about?" Jesse asked.

"Is it your family?" Lauren asked softly, kneeling beside the distressed boy.

Jesse felt Paul stiffen at her words, and the sobs suddenly increased in force. "Come on, Paul. Dry up the waterworks and tell us what's wrong. Whatever it is, Miss Downing and I will help."

"You can't," Paul mumbled against Jesse's shirtfront. "You cannot help."

"Are you sure about that?" Pushing the boy back, Jesse caught his dark tearful glance and smiled. "Nothing is ever hopeless. Tell us. We'll decide if we can do anything or not."

"It is too late. It is done," the boy murmured sadly.

"It's never too late—" Jesse began, only to be cut off.

"Yes, yes—it is. It is too late now. What has been done cannot be changed," Paul insisted heartbrokenly.

"Where are your parents?" Lauren asked abruptly.

"Home. I came to town alone. I had to see you." He turned his huge, liquid black eyes to Lauren's face. "I had to make certain you were all right."

"Is that what this is all about? Were you afraid I had been hurt in the fire?" Lauren smiled gently and cupped a hand to Paul's smooth cheek.

"I..." He hesitated, glancing first at Jesse, and then away.

Jesse spoke first. "Paul, what's wrong? Why are you so upset? I can understand being worried about Lauren, but—"

"I must go." The boy pulled away from Jesse's hands. "I must get home before I am missed."

"How did you get to town?" Jesse asked.

"I rode my bicycle," he replied, hurrying toward the door.

"Your bicycle!" Lauren exclaimed. "But that must be a ten-mile ride!"

"It is nothing. I am strong," Paul assured her proudly. "I have ridden farther than that."

"Wait," Jesse said, stopping him. "I want to talk to you. I'll give you a ride home on my bike." He knew how much the boy loved to ride on the back of his motorcycle.

A wary look came into the dark eyes peeking out from beneath the black fringe across Paul's forehead. "I must go," he repeated quickly. "I must go." And before either adult could stop him, he was out the door and gone.

Jesse's eyes narrowed on the closed door. Refusing a ride on his motorcycle was totally unlike Paul. In fact, the whole episode was unlike him. Something more than worry for Lauren's safety had prompted the boy's display of anguish, and he intended to discover its cause.

"What do you suppose has gotten into him?" Lauren asked in a baffled tone.

"It's hard to say," Jesse replied noncommittally.

Taking a seat at the table beside him, she asked, "Jesse, do you suppose he could be the boy we've been looking for?"

Jesse's head swiveled sharply in her direction. "What do you mean?"

"Well, I've been thinking. Paul was here the day I found that note. He was one of the boys in the fight I told you about. Do you suppose he could know something about that man, Aguilar? Or worse yet, what if he saw him with this *El Personaje no Presente* character? His life could be in danger. What should we do?"

For the moment her ban on being close to him, and the reasons for it, were forgotten as she leaned toward him, concerned only for the safety of the boy for whom they both felt so much affection. It didn't even seem strange to her that she was discussing this with the town "bad-boy." Jesse was someone she had learned she could count on, could trust, in a bad situation. Looking to him for comfort and reassurance in time of trouble was becoming natural to her.

"Don't you think you're jumping to a lot of conclusions here, just because Paul was upset—"

"But *why* was he upset? Something more than worry over my health sent him here today. And I think it could be danger—fear—for himself and his family."

Jesse hadn't thought of that. He hadn't considered the possibility that Paul might be in danger.

Grabbing his arm in her agitation, Lauren said, "Jesse, what if Paul knows who this smuggler is? What if he can identify him? What if he saw him hide the note and picked it up—and that's how the note came to be in the library?"

Getting up from the table, Lauren moved around the room, working the possible sequence of events out in her mind. "Paul must have been curious about what was on the piece of paper and taken it after the other man left—"

"You're forgetting one important fact," Jesse interrupted her. "If Paul saw the note being hidden, and took it and read it, he would have gone to the sheriff afterward."

"Oh, I never thought of that. You're right." Deflated, she sat back down, shoulders slumped. "Unless," she straightened up, "he didn't read the note. Maybe the bell rang for class, or a friend came up, and he just put it in his pocket and forgot all about it."

Jesse gave her a disbelieving look and shook his head. "I still think you're counting on a lot of 'what ifs' being facts. And if he didn't read the note, then how could he know it had anything to do with what's been happening to you?"

That was a valid point. Paul wouldn't know the note had any bearing on the threats on her life. In fact, except for the fire, which had been labeled an accident for the benefit of the town, no one except the sheriff's department, Carrie and Jesse, knew about the attacks on Lauren.

"But what if I'm right?" She refused to give up the idea. "Paul could be in real danger," she insisted.

"I guess it's a possibility we shouldn't ignore," Jesse agreed reluctantly.

"Then we should warn him." She made as if to jump from the chair and dash after the boy. Jesse stayed her with a hand on her wrist.

"If what you suggest is true, whether he found and read the note or not—he *is* frightened. And if today is an example of how much, don't you think we should tread lightly and not make it any worse?"

"Yes, of course," she agreed, sinking back onto her seat. "I just don't want him to get hurt. And I want this whole mess to be over with. I want life to become normal again— normal and dull." She looked up and gave him a small, constrained grin.

"I know." He touched the back of her hand. "I know.... Do you trust me?" he asked all at once.

Though it bothered him to ask the question, he felt that he had to be completely honest with her, at least about this.

Lauren met his clear blue gaze head-on, the slow rhythmic caress of his thumb against her skin pushing all thoughts from her mind. She wanted with her whole being to trust him—and she did.

"Yes," she answered without hesitation.

"Then let me talk to Paul. We've been friends for a long time. He knows I'm only interested in his safety—and the truth. I'll find out what he knows, if he knows anything. Okay?"

And in the meantime he planned to have a few words with the sheriff, as well. He was ready to come out into the open with his own part in things. The town be damned. He wanted Lauren to know who and what he really was. He wanted to stand before her as a man, no hidden motives, no lies.

Jesse wanted her to see *him*—a man who had fallen desperately in love with a woman. A woman, some might say, he was too young for. A woman, most would say, he wasn't good enough for. And maybe they were right, but the time had come to find out if *she* felt that way about it.

"Okay?" he repeated.

"Yes," she readily agreed.

Jesse didn't know it, but Lauren had a few ideas of her own. She, too, wanted things to be out in the open between them, with all the misunderstandings and misconceptions cleared away.

She needed to see Rand, needed to discuss a plan with him. Her plan, a plan to end the terror of the last few weeks—and, possibly, the mystery of the murders six months back.

That evening Lauren waited for Rand with nervous anticipation. She was ready and willing to be a decoy, the instrument of her attacker's destruction, but she was frightened all the same. She did her best to keep her thoughts from dwelling on what would happen if Rand agreed with the idea and if they misjudged the man—or the situation. She could end up dead, as dead as the whisperer had been planning since that first attack.

But when Rand finally arrived he wasn't alone. Jesse and Kalan were with him. Lauren kept her questions to herself for the moment and led the way upstairs into the room she had made into a sort of parlor.

When everyone was seated Lauren started right in on her idea, despite her curiosity about the presence of the other two men. "I want you to use me as bait to draw the killer out—"

"What!"

"No!"

Jesse and Kalan protested at the same time. Jesse rose from his seat and crossed to stand before her.

"You can't do that. I won't let you."

"You have nothing to say about it—"

"Damned if I don't—" he began furiously. "I didn't pull you from that burning house and stand guard over you for the last few weeks just to have you do something stupid like this and get yourself killed!"

The room roared with silence at the end of his words. The cold, hard glitter freezing Lauren's dark eyes sent shafts of ice down Jesse's spine. He'd wanted her to know the truth, well, there it was.

"Is that true, sheriff?" Her gaze remained fixed on Jesse's pale but determined features. "Has Jesse been guarding me?"

"Ah . . . yes . . . we . . ."

"Since when?" she asked in a neutral tone. When no one answered, she asked Jesse, "When?"

"From the first," he admitted reluctantly.

"The robbery at Mr. Tindle's—the whole thing was a farce? You came to work for me so you could spy on me?"

"It wasn't spying. I was trying to protect you," he insisted.

She looked at him as though he was something distasteful that had crawled into the room. He'd made love to her as part of his job. What a conscientious employee, she thought scathingly.

"You were working for the sheriff the night you saved me from being strangled." She dared him to meet her eyes.

"Yes." His voice was so low she could barely hear it. He knew what she was thinking, but he couldn't explain his feelings to her now, not in front of the other men.

So that accounted for the sudden interest he'd taken in her. It was more believable than the idea that Jesse Tyler, the man who could get any woman he wanted by merely lifting a finger, had become suddenly enthralled with Lauren Downing, the mousy town librarian who'd never been to bed with a man.

What a laugh! No doubt the whole town would find it worth a good chuckle, if they hadn't already. And she had fallen for it. Fallen for *him*, a voice she didn't want to acknowledge whispered. *Hook, line and sinker.* He'd reeled her in like a prize fish—prize fool was more like it!

"I didn't hear you." She made him repeat it in a louder voice.

"I said *yes*!" he all but shouted. "Yes! Damn it! Yes, even then!"

Looking at Rand, then Kalan, she asked, "This was your idea? You were both in on it?"

The other two nodded uncomfortably and found something in the far corner of the room to study intently.

There was no easy way out of this. Jesse had known all along that she would see his having made love to her as part of the role he was playing. He'd been prepared to accept her anger—or had he?

There was, he knew, no use in trying to offer explanations or reassurances right now. She wasn't ready to listen—and he couldn't blame her. Things looked bad. Perhaps if he'd had a few more years on him, he might know more about what to say, what to do, to reduce the sense of betrayal he knew she must be feeling.

"Did you file a report every time you were with me? And did you remember to include *everything*?"

"I made my reports concerning what I observed during my surveillance," Jesse answered with tight lips and a furrowed brow.

The other men heard the cold anger in Lauren's question and the frustration in Jesse's answer. Whatever was going on here should be discussed in private. It made the sheriff and his deputy uncomfortable to be within hearing distance of something so personal.

Standing abruptly and moving around Jesse's taut figure, Lauren stood facing the man she had always thought of as her friend, the sheriff.

"I make my own decisions. I have for several years now. I don't need to ask anyone's permission to offer myself as bait—unless it's yours. I'm over twenty-one—and have been for a while," she added significantly.

Jesse made a sound in the back of his throat, knowing her words were a slur because he was younger than she was—only a couple of years past twenty-one, in fact. Without a word to anyone, he strode from the room.

She was a fool, and if she wanted to get herself killed and the sheriff was going to let her do it, then so be it! He washed his hands of her—of all of them.

After he'd left the silence stretched until finally Kalan cleared his throat noisily.

"I'm afraid I have to agree with Jesse on this, Lauren. I think it's too dangerous a thing for you to do. The man has attacked you physically three times—"

"I'm waiting for your answer, sheriff." Lauren overrode Kalan's opinion. "I'm the one being threatened here, and I'm tired of living in fear. I want to see this crazy man brought to justice. I'm willing to bet my life he can be caught—what are *you* willing to bet?"

"When do you want to get started?" Rand asked after a long moment of silent contemplation.

"Soon. As soon as possible," was her quick reply.

Rand nodded. "We'll discuss this and come up with something—"

"One condition," Lauren said. "I don't want Jesse Tyler anywhere near me."

Standing, his back ramrod straight, a hard glint in his hazel eyes, Rand answered her sternly. "I don't know what the problem is between the two of you—it isn't any business of mine—but that boy—*that man*—has saved your life more than once. It would seem to me that you owe him a debt of gratitude.

"You may offer yourself willingly as bait, but I'm still running the show. Jesse has been doing a fine job of protecting your skin so far. He stays—and that's *my* condition."

Lauren looked from one man to the other; she could see they were both in agreement about this. So be it. She didn't have to talk to him, or spend any time in his presence. With a brittle nod she turned her back on the two men as they made their way out of the room.

The next few days passed slowly. Nothing of much note happened, except that there was less open contact between the sheriff's department and the library. Kalan had been given other duties to perform, and Lauren's safety was left solely in the capable hands of Jesse Tyler.

To the public, nothing appeared to be any different. But if you were the killer, you would, so Rand hoped, feel as though things had cooled down some since the fire. Jesse was only the town screwup, surprisingly maintaining a job at the library. And Lauren was going on with her life. She went more places after work and was seen on the street alone, even after dark if you cared to look—if you were someone interested in how easy it would be to get to her.

What no one saw, or so they all hoped, was that Jesse was always somewhere close by, hidden, but watching Lauren nevertheless. Keeping an eye on her as she met with her friends and carried on with her normal activities.

The days began to pass by in a blur for Lauren. Rain had settled on the area, and that meant real danger from flash floods in low-lying areas. She was glad to be in residence at the library in town and not to have to worry about traveling the unpaved roads to her house.

Nothing had been done about her house as of yet; the insurance claim had been filed, and now she was in a period of waiting. There was the question of arson to contend with. The evidence pointed to the fire being deliberately set by person or persons unknown. Kerosene had been used to start it, in the hallway outside Lauren's bedroom.

Carrie was in and out of the library as usual, but she could see that Lauren was distracted and didn't stay long. She noticed that though Jesse was still working there, he was rarely in evidence. She was still in the dark about what was going on there.

Rand had not discussed with her the part Jesse was playing in Lauren's life, nor the fact that Lauren had openly volunteered to draw out the killer. He knew she wouldn't have approved, and he didn't want her burdened with needless worry over her friend's safety, not with the birth of their child so close.

Lauren stood on the porch one afternoon, hugging her shoulders and staring at the sky. It wasn't raining at the moment, but a chill wind had blown up, and gray clouds were scudding across the horizon.

Hank Benton drove by in his father's old brown truck, and she raised a hand to wave, but dropped it when he turned his head without responding and the truck picked up speed.

Seeing Hank brought his younger brother Paul to mind. She wondered if Jesse had talked with the boy yet. Or maybe he didn't intend to do so now.

Jesse's attitude had become one of polite deference. He spoke to her only when necessary and kept strictly to his own part of the building. As far as the town knew, he was staying in a room at Pete's. But in reality, after the library officially closed, he sneaked inside through the back door, where Lauren waited to let him in each night.

There were two hours each night when Lauren felt particularly defenseless: the hours between nine and eleven. That was the time Jesse spent in his room at Pete's waiting for darkness, for the streets to quiet down. Then he returned to the library by a circuitous route and spent the night in one of the downstairs storage rooms.

There were four hours in the morning, too, when she was alone. Jesse left at five a.m. to return to his room to shower and dress so he could reappear at nine. But those hours didn't bother her; it was the darkness she feared.

An alarm had been rigged to go off in the sheriff's office any time Lauren punched it, and she carried a small black signal box in her pocket. Even at night, when Jesse was with her, the alarm stayed within her reach.

A swift gust of wind carrying rain with it lashed out at Lauren, and she drew her pink sweater closer around her. It was time to go back inside and get on with her work.

At five she was ready to close the library for her dinner hour. She would reopen at six and stay open until nine. The chilly weather made her long for a hot bowl of soup. She put the closed sign in the window and went to find Jesse to let him know he could take his dinner break.

After all this time it wasn't really necessary to tell him when to break for a meal, but all at once she was feeling lonely; she just wanted to speak to someone for a few moments.

He was repairing some ceiling tiles where they had discovered a leak since the rains had started, and she stood for a moment watching him work without speaking.

He was dressed in a tight black T-shirt and jeans, and the play of the muscles in his shoulders and forearms, knotting and flexing with each new square of tile he stapled into place, drew her eyes. A small pink scar was visible on the right side of his neck, reminding her of his heroics in saving her from the fire.

He laid the staple gun on the top of the ladder, folded his arms over his chest and turned his head in Lauren's direction. "You wanted something?"

"I just wanted to know if you would like to share a bowl of soup with me instead of going out for something." She surprised even herself with the offer. "It's raining again," she said by way of an explanation for the invitation.

He looked as though he was about to decline, but then, meeting her glance, he changed his mind and nodded his acceptance. If he was surprised at the invitation, he kept it to himself. "Thanks. Hot soup sounds good."

Feeling unaccountably nervous now that he'd agreed to share a meal with her, Lauren clasped her hands together and backed out of the room. "Give me ten minutes and then come up."

It was more like fifteen when he knocked on the open door of the sitting room, and Lauren noticed he'd washed up and slicked his hair back from his forehead and cheeks.

"It's chili beef; I hope you like it." She fluttered her hands to indicate the table spread with their meal.

"I like any kind of chili, except Yankee chili. I had some when I was stationed in the east, and I don't think macaroni has any place in chili.'' He wrinkled his nose at the thought.

Lauren laughed and said, ''Well, this is canned, but I haven't seen anything that looks like macaroni floating around in it.''

''Good.''

When they were seated at the table, a steaming bowl of soup before each of them, along with a cold glass of milk, and a plate of chicken sandwiches sitting in the center of the table, Lauren cleared her throat and prepared to ask him a question.

''I was wondering—'' she kept her eyes on the spoon she was dragging through the bowl of soup, ''—if you'd had a chance to talk to Paul yet.''

Jesse laid his spoon down without ever having placed it in the bowl. Scraping his chair back from the table, he stood towering over her. She looked up at him in surprise.

''You didn't need to bribe me with food to find out if I'd talked with Paul.'' Shoulders stiff, he paced to the door. ''All you had to do was to ask,'' he threw over his shoulder as he disappeared. ''And the answer is no, I've been too busy with *other duties* to get out to the ranch,'' he called back.

Lauren sat staring dejectedly at his empty place. He had thought her invitation was issued for the sake of learning something about his talk with Paul. He didn't realize what she really wanted: a little time spent in Jesse's company.

It was ten minutes until eleven, and Lauren was making her way downstairs with a flashlight. She couldn't turn on any lights in the building, because that would give away the fact she was awake and moving about. The whole idea was to make the killer think he had an unobstructed chance at getting her. With that in mind, her lights went off upstairs every night at precisely ten p.m.

Keeping the beam of the flashlight directed toward her feet, she moved quickly through the dark hallway to the back entrance. Two new locks and a bolt had been added since she had taken up residence, and still, when she was alone at night before Jesse arrived, she didn't feel safe. Once he was inside, though, all but the flimsiest of locks were left unfastened to allow the killer an opportunity to enter.

The wind that had started that day hadn't died down during the evening, and it howled mournfully around the building and rattled in the rafters. Lauren pulled her housecoat closer about her neck and stopped to lean against the wall beside the door.

Come on, Jesse, she kept thinking. She felt more unsettled than usual tonight. It was probably nothing more than an uneasy conscience because of their misunderstanding at dinner. But the ten minutes continued to drag until she was positive she'd stood leaning against that particular spot for hours.

A rattle at the door that might or might not be Jesse alerted her. She came away from the wall in one swift movement.

"Is that you?" she hissed, leaning against the door. She was waiting for him to identify himself, as he always did before she unlocked the door.

Mindful of the need to keep his staying here at night a secret, she didn't want to call out his name in case it wasn't him. Then the thought of who it might be if it wasn't him had her backing away from the door in fear.

Something crashed against the outside of the door. Lauren gave a startled yelp and leapt back. Oh, God, it was him! The killer!

Her fingers hovered over the alarm button in the pocket of her housecoat. Should she push it? What if it wasn't the killer? What if it was only a dog or a cat, looking for food? What if it was Jesse, and he'd been hurt?

There was a sudden waiting stillness from outside, and she moved closer to the door, then leaned slowly against it and pressed her ear to the wood.

All she could hear was the sounds of the night, the wind rustling in the bushes at the sides of the building, the intermittent patter of rain on the windows and roof.

And then, abruptly, there was the sound of a fist on the wood. Lauren screamed and darted back, her hand diving unhesitatingly into her pocket. Grabbing the alarm, she felt for the button just as the words, "It's me. Jesse," were spoken.

Just for a moment they didn't truly sink in, and she kept fumbling for the small red button.

"Lauren, are you there? Open the damn door. I'm getting soaked out here."

Lauren dropped the alarm back into her pocket and nearly dropped the flashlight as well. Clutching it under one arm, she began to unfasten the dead bolt and locks.

Pulling the door back, without even waiting for him to come inside, she threw herself into his unprepared arms, almost knocking him off his feet.

"It's you! Thank God! He was here! Oh, Jesse, he was at the door, trying to get in." Wrapping her arms around his neck and burying her face against his cold neck, Lauren clung to him tightly.

Chapter 12

"Who? Lauren, who was here?"

Jesse clasped her straining arms and withdrew them from around his neck. He walked the two of them out of the pouring rain and into the dark, silent building.

"Him!" she whispered urgently. "The man who's been stalking me. He was here!"

Jesse put her aside and turned to close and fasten the door. The top lock, as per routine procedure, was the only one he snicked into place. The flashlight Lauren had been carrying lay on the floor at their feet.

Bending to retrieve it, Jesse flashed the light on her drenched figure huddled in the corner behind the door and asked, "Are you certain it was a somebody and not the wind? It's pretty strong out there tonight."

"Yes—I mean, no—no, it wasn't the wind."

"Then an animal perhaps?"

"No—no, not an animal—at least, I don't think it was," she qualified after a moment's hesitation. "I heard something beat against the door. I thought it was you—but when I called out, there was no answer. I was afraid to call your name.''

"It wasn't me. Could you have mistaken the slap of the rain for someone's fists?'' Jesse asked keenly, one hand gripping her shoulder.

"I don't know—maybe.''

Lauren fell back a step and pulled her arm from his grasp. He was hurting her, and making her more uncertain of her facts by the moment. "I don't know,'' she repeated slowly. "I just don't know. I thought it was someone—I had this feeling of a presence.'' She shook her head.

"All right.'' Jesse sighed heavily. "If it will make you feel any better, I'll take a look around outside—''

"No! Please, don't leave me! It doesn't matter now. Whoever it was, is gone. And you can't see anything in the dark, anyway.''

"I thought you were set on catching this man. Isn't that why we're putting on this little farce every night?'' Jesse asked sharply. "Our quarry likes to play with fire,'' Jesse reminded her. "I'll be back in a minute. Lock the door after me and don't let anyone in. I'll call your name twice and identify myself when I get back.''

In a moment he was gone, leaving Lauren shivering beside the locked door, shivering, but not from the cold. His voice had dripped with ice, and he hadn't put any stock in her insistence that there had been someone else at the door before he had arrived. He thought she was only imagining it.

But that wasn't the foremost reason for her trying to dissuade him from going outside. Not only had *she* been attacked by the maniac, but Jesse, too, had been injured by him. He'd been lucky so far; the physical damage had been minor, but . . .

A knock reverberated beneath her cheek. Lauren jerked back as she heard the familiar deep tones call her name twice. Grappling with the lock, she threw open the door and tugged him inside before he ever had a chance to identify himself. He was soaked from head to foot.

Pushing wet rattails from his eyes, Jesse secured the door once more and told her that the only thing he'd seen was a dog looking for some garbage in the trash container at the back of the alley.

"Maybe in the morning we'll be able to find some foot-prints. Though I seriously doubt it. They'll most likely be washed away—if there were any to begin with," he added doubtfully.

Wanting to protest that something—something hu-man—had indeed been there, but having no real proof, Lauren kept her protest to herself. She knew what she'd sensed out there, and it hadn't been a dog.

"Let's go." She led the way. Her flashlight was in her hand and once more pointed toward the floor.

"You go on to bed. I'll stay here awhile and make sure no one tries to get in."

"Don't be silly. You're soaked. You can't stay in those wet things. Come upstairs and I'll find you a towel, and something warm to put on."

He wanted to protest, but followed silently instead. She was right; it was stupid to spend the night in wet clothes just because he was angry with her. His eyes followed the gentle sway of her hips as she climbed the stairs before him.

She looked so small and delicate trudging up the stairs in the long chenille bathrobe. He could feel his anger seeping away. He was cold and unhappy, and the only warm thing he wanted next to his skin he couldn't have. He gave a sud-den violent shiver and sneezed.

Lauren murmured, "Bless you," without stopping, and they reached the top of the stairs.

Dropping his eyes from the curve of her hips, he fought his wayward thoughts. It had been better when he was angry with her; then it hadn't been so hard to forget the feel of her all soft and warm and loving in his arms.

When she had thrown herself against his chest on his arrival he'd felt almost powerless to resist taking her, then and there, in the doorway, despite the wind and the rain. Did she have any idea of how she had turned his life, even his way of thinking, upside down in just a few short weeks?

Lauren entered the sitting room, made certain the blinds were pulled all the way down, then switched on a small lamp and an electric heater. Telling him to wait there, she left the room and passed into her bedroom. There she took a towel from a bottom drawer, picked up the blanket from the foot of her bed and turned once more toward the sitting room.

At the doorway she paused to stare at his back. He stood as she had left him, in the center of the room, his legs slightly spread, his arms lowered before him, the palms of his hands against his thighs.

He was a magnificent sight. Rain had soaked through his clothing, stretching the thin cotton shirt across his broad shoulders like a second skin. The heavy material of his jeans curved like gentle hands around the muscles of his buttocks and thighs. And when, as though sensing her eyes on him, he turned abruptly to face her, her eyes fell to the front of his jeans and she looked swiftly away.

Perhaps now was the time to tell him she was sorry for their misunderstanding earlier that evening. Perhaps conversation would lighten the atmosphere that had turned thick and heavy when he'd caught her eyes on him just now.

"I—I'm sorry you missed your dinner. I didn't invite you as an excuse to pump you for information—"

"Then why did you?" he cut across her words, his gaze intent on her somber face. "Why did you invite me to your room?"

"I didn't! I mean—that is—I felt sorry for you—"

His jaw hardened at the words, and the hands at his sides clenched. "Save your pity for someone who needs it." He pivoted on his heel and stalked toward the door, the angry set of his shoulders indicative of the depth of hurt he was feeling at her words.

Throwing the blanket and towel onto the loveseat, Lauren sought the words to halt his precipitate departure. Why was it that everything she said, every move she made in his direction, was wrong?

"Wait!" she cried, and then on a softer note, "I didn't mean that the way it sounded." Her eyes on her hands clasped nervously before her, she whispered, "I invited you up here—because I was lonely."

Jesse stilled with his hand on the doorknob, waiting.

Licking her lips nervously, she added in an unsteady voice, "I just wanted to see you, spend some time with you alone, without someone else always around. I..." She gave a helpless shrug, lifting her eyes and meeting his glance as he turned slowly to face her.

"That's the truth? You wanted to be with me?" he asked on a husky note, a glow starting deep in his sapphire eyes.

Lauren nodded, unable to continue. She wanted him with an intensity that defied logic, defied her proper upbringing, defied everything but the need to have him hold her, touch her, make her his once more. Dear God, how she loved him!

But their first joining had been at her insistence, born out of terror, out of fear of the unknown. And every time they'd come close after that, it was with that guilty knowledge buried deep in her heart. When she had learned that he'd been sent to stay with her, learned that he had been doing a job the night he'd made love to her, she'd been filled with self-doubts and shame.

And the question, always the question—would he have made love to her, would he *ever* have made love to her, if she hadn't instigated that night's actions? It was a question she needed to have answered before she could be free of her self-condemnation.

Taking the steps that would bring him to within touching distance, Jesse cupped her soft cheek with an unsteady hand. Holding her eyes, he whispered, "That's why I accepted the invitation. I wanted to watch the light spark in your big brown eyes, hear the music of your voice as you spoke my name, feel the warmth of your smile melt the ice around my heart."

Lauren closed her eyes, unable to control the tears that started at his words. He loved her, too. Her heart swelled at the thought; surely his words meant that he loved her, too.

"Lauren—look at me. Lauren..."

The word became a kiss; the kiss became her world.

His mouth moved over hers, devouring its softness, and Lauren raised herself onto her toes to meet his kiss. She trembled in his arms, her response instant and total. Lifting her hands to his shoulders, she clung to him, returning kiss for kiss.

Jesse's mouth massaged hers with provocative insistence; his insides were churning as his hunger for her built. She was everything he'd ever dreamed of as a teenager and as a man, soft, warm and willing in his arms. The tide of desire swamped him, wiping everything else from his mind. Breathing in short gasps, he tried to slow things down a bit. But his need for her was so great...

"God, how I've missed you," he murmured as his mouth moved down past her jaw to the sensitive skin of her neck. "Night after night, you've driven me crazy in my dreams."

A small sound of wonder came from her throat, and she kissed his chin, his cheek, buried her lips against the taut skin of his neck and felt the rough scratch of his beard. She was burning up inside, liquid fire raging through her veins. And no one but Jesse could put out the flames.

With a driving, sensuous move, his tongue entered her mouth, and a wild surge of pleasure erupted through them both. While his tongue ravaged the sweetness of her mouth, she tasted him with a new hunger. Their passions soared to the exploding point as they moved against each other, seeking new heights to explore.

All at once, breathing in short, hard, gasps, Jesse took hold of Lauren's shoulders and forced her back.

"Wait—" he panted. "This is too much, too fast."

Trying to get her own breathing under control, Lauren dropped her head back, exposing the pale, delicate underside of her chin. Jesse's eyes alighted on the tender flesh and couldn't resist. His mouth descended, feather-light, and, his lips like velvet, his tongue explored this new and sensitive area.

Strong and vivid passion coursed through her as she pressed against him, feeling the impatient desire centered below his belly. She caressed him gently with loving fingertips, and a shudder ran through him, only to be echoed in her.

Lifting her hand, his eyes locked onto hers, Jesse centered a hot kiss on her palm before letting it go. With unsteady fingers he parted the loosely closed lapels of the jade robe she wore cinched at the waist.

Lauren shivered and watched, feeling the heat of a blush follow in the wake of his gaze. Down over the lace of the sheer sea-green nightdress, past the hollow of her throat, filled with shadows, and onto the peach-tinted cream of her breasts, his hungry eyes roved.

All at once he bent his head, and Lauren felt the warm whisper of his breath an instant before the touch of his hot, moist tongue. She closed her eyes, and her limbs quaked as she felt the movement of cool air pass over the path his tongue had taken following the line of his slow, soft, damp kisses.

Gripping his wide leather belt, Lauren steadied herself, giving in to the pleasurable sensations pervading her body. He knew how to make every nerve, muscle and fiber sing. Her whole body was a symphony of delight by the time his lips had ended their journey and traveled back to her mouth.

Lauren returned his kisses, drinking of his lips, knowing, without a doubt, she would never get her fill of him.

Jesse's hands slid the robe from Lauren's sloping shoulders, and it dropped slowly, to lie in a solid pool around her ankles. Parting the lacy gown, he freed one small breast and cupped it in his hand.

Lauren's knees began to give way as he began a loving assault, stroking gently around the sensitive bud with the tip of his tongue before drawing it carefully into his mouth. Moaning in pleasure, dizzy with the need for release, Lauren transferred her hands from his belt to his head. Drawing his lips up to hers, she kissed him in total surrender.

Their lips still joined, Jesse lifted her precious weight into his arms and carried her through to the bedroom, laying her gently on the bed. Pausing for a moment, he took in the provocatively lovely picture she made in the glow of a small night lamp on a side table.

Short brown curls flowed about her small shapely head as she turned dark glowing eyes up to his. Her dusky nipples peeked through the transparent lace of the sea-green nightdress that flowed down over her high breasts, trim waist and curved hips before molding the dusky valley between her thighs.

As he straightened and prepared to join her on the bed, Lauren came up onto her knees and stayed his hands as they settled on the belt buckle at his waist. Jesse lowered his hands to his sides, and Lauren's fingers took their place.

Pulling at the heavy buckle, she unfastened it, her eyes on the top snap of his jeans. Suddenly she hesitated, and her eyes slowly traveled upward across the damp expanse of his heaving chest. His shirt hung open, revealing a springy, golden mat of hair. The sight made her want to run her fingers through it, to test its softness.

In a manner reminiscent of the way he'd removed her robe, she slid his shirt back from his husky shoulders, down his brawny arms and left it to drop to the floor at his feet.

Meeting his glance, she smiled slowly, then bent her lips to the task of teasing each small brown nipple in turn, wrenching from him a response not unlike the one he had wrought from her.

Jesse caught his breath sharply, and the muscles of neck and jaw worked as he dropped his head back with a groan. He couldn't keep from sliding his fingers through her short, brown curls and grasping her head to bring it closer.

When he could stand it no longer, he raised her head and, lowering his own, pressed urgent lips to hers.

"You've learned a lot in the last few weeks," he murmured huskily.

"I had a good teacher," she whispered against his throat.

But when he tried to come down onto the bed beside her, she stopped him again. "Not yet," she murmured, "Not just yet."

Her nimble fingers were at the waistband of his jeans. Slowly and methodically she unfastened the metal buttons down the front of the damp, heavy material. Peeling the denim back, an inch at a time, she kissed his hipbone, then the taut muscles of his belly.

Jesse sucked in his breath with a gasp and pushed her back onto the bed. "That's enough, Laurie. Now it's my turn."

Lauren felt a surge of warmth at the way he'd shortened her name, turning it into an endearment.

After sliding the jeans down over his hips, kicking them off, taking his socks and boots along with them, he covered her waiting body with his.

"I'm going to take you to a place no one has ever been," he promised. "And I'm going there along with you."

The words were breathed against her temple as he fitted his body to hers. "It will be our special place," he groaned. "A place no one else can ever enter."

Lauren opened her body to him without question, just as she'd opened her heart. He'd shown her that place once already, and there was nowhere else on earth she'd rather be—and no one else with whom she'd rather share it.

Pressing herself against him, her hips lifting to accommodate him, she felt her impatience slowly give over to the strong, flowing rhythm of love. Glorying in the feel of his naked flesh, she thrust her breasts, the nipples standing out with aching desire, against the coarse hair of his chest.

Her hands slid over the smooth muscles of his back and buttocks, and she felt them flex and tighten with each thrust of his passion. With each deepening thrust she trembled. Finally, unable to hold on to the last threads of separateness, Lauren wrapped her legs around his driving hips and abandoned herself to the spiraling climax.

Jesse caught her lips with his and drove his tongue deep inside her mouth as, with a fevered groan, he jerked suddenly inside her. The earth fell away from them both as he took her to the place he'd promised, a place without fear or deception, a place belonging only to them—a place of total rapture.

When it was over, words were beyond them. Nothing in the English language could come close to expressing what they had just shared, so speech was forsaken.

Spreading the blanket over their sweat-dampened bodies, Jesse settled Lauren close. And then, with his chin against the top of her head, he let sleep take him.

Tomorrow was soon enough to worry about their troubles, to try to sort through all the half-truths and lies. Tomorrow they would get things straightened out between them once and for all and figure out what to do about the man who threatened Lauren's life.

Jesse had a whole lot of unanswered questions to ask someone, for his *own* peace of mind.

Lauren was checking in books when the phone rang at nine-thirty the next morning. She hadn't let her mind dwell too much on the events of the night before. Jesse hadn't yet returned to the library after going to his room at Pete's, and she was almost afraid to see him, for fear things would somehow have reverted to the way they had been before they'd made love last night.

"Hello?"

"Lauren? Rand here. I just wanted to let you know Jesse won't be in this morning. He's off on some important business for me. It may lead to our identifying the man who's been terrorizing you."

Her spirits plunged; there was no way of hiding the letdown, at least not from herself.

"I see," she answered slowly.

He could hear the disappointment in her voice. "He didn't want to go. I wish I hadn't had to send him. I had intended to go myself—but Carrie isn't well this morning—"

"Carrie!" Lauren repeated anxiously.

"Now, don't get upset. It's just some low back pain. It's too early for the baby—"

"Maybe I should get someone to work in my place and come over—"

"I'm taking her in to see Dr. Stillwell in a few minutes," Rand interrupted. "I'll let you know what's happening, okay?"

"All right, but if she needs me, you'd better give me a call."

They hung up, and thoughts of Jesse were pushed aside as Lauren began to worry about her best friend. It was too soon for the baby. There were still two weeks to go to her due date. And the fact that Carrie had miscarried twice before bothered Lauren. She wanted to rush right over to the doctor's office and stay by her friend's side until they knew everything was all right.

Instead she continued to work, though with one eye on the clock for the next couple of hours. Every time the phone rang she hoped it was Rand with word about Carrie—or Jesse.

Lauren replaced the phone receiver slowly. It was almost four, and Rand had just rung to let her know Carrie was being kept in the hospital. Rand had said that the doctor didn't see anything wrong, and the baby should be fine if she ended up delivering now.

When she'd asked rather tentatively about Jesse, Rand had replied that he hadn't heard anything yet. He told her he would be sending Kalan to take Jesse's place in the li-

brary with her that night. Lauren heard his plans with a
frown. No one could take Jesse's place.

Jesse rode his motorcycle south along the canyon road
that bordered the Rio Grande. At times the river was nothing more than a stream no wider than the trunk of a tree.
And then, farther along, it would suddenly widen and rush
like a mad thing over the sandy riverbed, filled with rocks
and debris washed down to the lower levels by the rains of
the day before.

He wanted to get the sheriff's business over as quickly as
possible and get back to Lauren. He'd gotten very little sleep
the night before. Holding Lauren close, listening to her
gentle breathing, his mind had been busy with dark thoughts
that refused to leave him.

Certain facts kept coming to mind, little things that, taken
separately, didn't add up to much. But put them together
and they could identify the man known as *El Personaje no
Presente*, the man who had been terrorizing Lauren.

He was on his way now to get a description of the man
believed to be *El Personaje no Presente* from a former co-
hort of the notorious smuggler. If the man talked, as Jesse
hoped he would, the mystery would soon be over and his
own growing fears laid to rest.

His mind kept refusing to believe that the unpalatable
facts he'd been mentally assimilating over the last few days
were true. They had to be false.

He'd made time to see Paul outside the grade school that
morning, before leaving town. The boy hadn't been very
forthcoming about answering Jesse's questions, but from
what little he did say, and his attitude, Jesse's fears had only
been increased.

He was hoping against hope that the man he was going to interview would have a description that would prove to him his theories were unfounded.

It had taken Jesse longer than he'd expected to get the information out of the man. He had been detained in the small border town all day without results. The man was terrified half out of his wits. He feared *El Personaje no Presente*'s swift and deadly retribution far more than he feared time spent in prison.

It wasn't until some of the man's relatives had arrived late that evening and pleaded with him to talk that he'd finally opened up and given Jesse the information he'd been waiting for.

It was dark by the time Jesse headed his motorcycle back along the gravel road toward Chance. Over an hour's ride stood between him and Lauren, and his fears for her safety were mounting as time passed. He'd called with word about his discovery but had been unable to reach the sheriff.

Rand was with his wife at the hospital. It seemed as though Carrie might be going into labor a couple of weeks early. The man who had answered the phone was not someone Jesse knew well. Kalan, he figured, must be with Lauren. He'd given the deputy the description and told him it was urgent that the sheriff receive it as soon as possible. The man had assured him that he'd see he got it pronto.

That reassurance didn't make Jesse feel any better. He had an uneasy feeling that *El Personaje no Presente* was ready to make his final strike against Lauren.

His speed increased to a dangerous degree as he rounded curves and raced up and down the hills that would slowly flatten out into the valley where the town of Chance lay nestled. He had tried calling the library to warn Lauren of the danger, but there had been no answer, and he figured she must be with Rand at the hospital. He prayed that was where she was, and that she would stay there until he could reach her.

One more time—one final time—he must stand between the woman he loved and the man known as *El Personaje no Presente*—Hank Benton, his best friend.

Chapter 13

Where was Jesse? Why didn't he come?

Lauren paced the floor, moved over to the window and, drawing the curtain aside, lifted the edge of the blind and peered down onto the dark street below.

At least the weather was holding. There hadn't been any rain since late the night before. She worried about the motorcycle speeding along the dangerous curves in the dark.

A sound from somewhere below caused her to pause and listen intently. Kalan Holtzer was down there, hidden. The sound was no doubt of his making. Despite this knowledge, uneasiness crawled through her.

It wasn't that she didn't think Kalan would do everything in his power to protect her, or that she didn't feel safe with him. But she had never felt safer in her life than when Jesse was near. And Jesse must be miles from here.

The phone rang abruptly, causing her to start, then whirl to face it. The only light came from a small lamp on a table beside the loveseat, and the shadows in the room were deep and long. For a moment she couldn't bring herself to answer the phone.

She was afraid that it was *him*—the man who had haunted her these past few weeks, turning her days into waking nightmares. Then again, perhaps it was Rand, with word about Carrie, who had gone into labor. Or Jesse!

"H-hello?"

"Lauren? Rand here. Is Kalan with you? Everything all right?"

"Yes, he's downstairs. Everything's fine. Tell me about Carrie."

"Nothing to tell yet. She's still in labor. Dr. Stillwell said if she doesn't make some progress in the next few hours, he may have to do surgery."

Lauren could hear the concern in his deep voice and sympathized with him. They both wanted this baby so much. They'd waited for over six years for it, and she prayed everything would be all right.

"Have you heard anything from Jesse?" she asked tentatively.

"Not a word. I can't imagine what's taking him so long. The deputy doing office duty said Jesse had called in to leave a description of the suspect and say his business was finished, and as far as he knew, Jesse was headed back to town. That's all he could tell me. God, why do these things have to happen all at once?"

Lauren could imagine him running an impatient hand through his black curls, leaving them standing on end.

"I know there must have been something in that information he went after. I just hope he hasn't had any trouble with that damn motorcycle of his. He's always working on the blasted thing."

"Now don't go paranoid on me, sheriff." Lauren tried a little levity to ease his mind. "Carrie needs you with all your faculties intact right now. Jesse will be all right. You'll see." She sounded a whole lot more confident than she really felt.

"You're right," Rand agreed readily. "He'd make one hell of a good cop. He's cool and calm under pressure. And you already know he's good at keeping a secret," he added without thinking. Then he tried to rectify his blunder by changing the subject. "You know, he worked as an MP in the Marines. And they're one tough group of men."

He figured Jesse wouldn't mind her knowing a few things about him. It was bound to come out after this case was settled, anyway. And he thought it was about time the town knew the real facts about the man. He deserved their gratitude and respect; he'd earned it.

Lauren felt her insides cringe at his words. She didn't like the idea of Jesse working as a cop, or a deputy. She couldn't go through the days and nights of worry she'd seen Carrie endure. But that kind of thinking was jumping the gun. Despite their lovemaking, Jesse hadn't actually told her that he loved her.

"I didn't know that about him," she admitted softly. "Jesse doesn't talk much about himself."

Lauren heard a muffled conversation take place briefly in the background, and Rand came back on the line with the news that Carrie was being taken into surgery. Lauren ordered him to keep his chin up, told him to give Carrie her love and hung up.

Taking a seat in the recliner, she studied the design in the carpet at her feet. Many times in her mind she had gone over that day she had found the note, trying to understand how she had become involved in the deaths of three men. What scrap of information teased her subconscious but refused to surface? What was it that stayed just beyond her memory?

The note had been dropped by one of the fourth-grade boys. Paul? That was a distinct possibility. But had the note been only a prank? No, it had to be for real; three men had been killed by following the directions on the note, and now her own life was in jeopardy.

The message, what had it said? She could no longer remember the exact words. They weren't something she'd wanted to recall—until now. They had, after all, been the death warrant for three men—two of whom she had known very well.

What about the third man? What did she know about him? Could Hernandez Aguilar be the key to solving the puzzle? Aguilar had worked as custodian at the grade school Paul Benton attended. There was nothing sinister about that. He'd been a single man who kept to himself. Everyone in town had been shocked to learn of his death—and his possible association with the smugglers.

Somehow everything kept coming back to Paul Benton. This mystery was like a Chinese puzzle; there was no apparent beginning, and no end to it. It had more twists and turns than a pretzel.

Lauren pushed herself to her feet and moved toward the window once more. Lifting the blind, she studied what little she could see of the street below. It looked dark and silent, deserted. The sight depressed her. Where was Jesse? She needed him.

She turned and walked back across the room. Her skirt brushed against an end table, knocking a small bright object to the floor. Lauren bent to retrieve it.

Holding the red silk rose to her cheek, she recalled the day Paul Benton had given it to her. It had been the day after

Jesse had first made love to her. The day after the man who'd been terrorizing her had tried to put an end to her life.

Lauren pressed a hand to her throat and tried to block the frightening pictures from her mind. She wouldn't think about that now; she would only think about good, pleasant things. Like the glow of Paul Benton's shy smile when he'd given her the flower.

Poor boy, how awful it must be to be ten years old with a crush on an older woman. He'd been so embarrassed that day when he'd dropped his book, and then locked the chain of his necklace around the corner of the desk.

Necklace? Frowning, she remembered that there had been something familiar about its design at the time. She'd been positive that, though the design was unusual, she had seen it before—and not long ago. But when? Where?

Lauren fingered the silk petals of the rose, and though her glance rested on it, her eyes were filled with visions of the medallion. Its strands of beaten, twisted silver with turquoise inlay were vivid in her mind.

All at once she narrowed her eyes and gave a soft murmur. Of course. She remembered exactly where she'd seen it.

In the storeroom. Jesse had found a medallion exactly like it wedged between two boxes. Or *was* it exactly like it? She couldn't remember. She thought it was, but...

She decided that she would have to see it again to be certain they were identical. And if they were, what significance was there in that? She didn't know, unless perhaps it might be important to learn where Paul had come by his.

In any case, she wanted to take another look at the medallion Jesse had found. With luck it would still be in the storeroom where he'd left it that day. Perhaps when she saw it again it would jog her memory.

Lauren patted the electronic signal box resting comfortingly in her pocket. She knew that all she had to do was to push the button and Kalan would receive her distress signal at the same time as whoever was in the sheriff's office. Kalan was closer; he'd reach her in time if anything happened.

Jesse had gotten used to her roaming the library at night when she couldn't sleep, finding a book from the shelves downstairs, taking it upstairs to read. If Kalan heard her and came to investigate she would explain what she was doing. Otherwise, it might be best to leave him to his job.

She took the flashlight from the table by the door and let herself silently out of the room. The stairs creaked beneath her slight weight, and she paused, wondering if Kalan would think she was an intruder and come after her.

Maybe it would be a good idea, after all, to call to him and let him know it was her.

"Kalan?" Her voice floated out on a soft whisper, coming back to her in a hollow ring.

There was no response, so she took another few steps and tried again. "Kalan!" The whisper was louder this time. "It's me, Lauren. Are you there?"

Again the only answer she received was silence. Perhaps, she reasoned, he was in one of the rooms at the back and couldn't hear her, though she would have thought he'd be on the alert for unexpected sounds. Then again, he might have gone outside to check the building's perimeter.

That thought made her stop. What if he *had* gone outside? What if someone had knocked him out, killed him and was now inside? Maybe the sound she had heard earlier was *him*, in the building.

A cold shiver started at the back of her neck and quivered down her spine. The flashlight shook in her icy fingers. Fear made it hard to breathe.

She wanted to scream Kalan's name in panic, but now she was afraid to. If someone had already entered the building, he could be stalking her even now.

Darting a nervous glance over her shoulder, trying to penetrate the deeper shadows outside the line of the flashlight's glare, she took a step back up the stairs.

Stop it! Get a hold of yourself! a voice shouted inside her head. Kalan wouldn't go outside without first telling her so she could lock the door. Her imagination was running away with itself.

Taking a deep breath, getting her fears under control even though her hands shook and her knees felt weak, she moved once more down the stairs toward the storeroom at the back of the building.

Afraid of what she might find, Lauren let herself into the room. She would do what she'd come to do, look at the medallion, then go back upstairs where she belonged. The downstairs would be Kalan's for the remainder of the night.

The flashlight cut a narrow swath through the inky blackness of the room. The air smelled musty, like old books and old wood. She wished she dared to turn on the light. The place gave her the creeps. She had never been able to completely forget what had taken place there a few weeks ago. The specter of the man who had attacked her would always be peering at her from over a shelf, peeking at her around a corner.

Moving swiftly across the floor, refusing to glance into the shadowy depths, Lauren felt around on the shelf where she'd seen Jesse lay the medallion. Her fingers came away empty. Running the beam of light along the top, she searched thoroughly, but in vain. It was gone.

Then, from out of the impenetrable darkness, came a slight sound. Lauren froze. Every fiber of her being screamed for her to get out, to make a dash for the door while she still could. But in the back of her mind she knew it was already too late.

He had found her.

Turning slowly, keeping the flashlight's beam directed toward the floor, she mustered up enough courage to ask in a steady voice, "Who's there?"

Holding her breath and straining her ears, she heard the slight whispery sounds of movement. It was *him*. He'd come back for her. God, where was Kalan!

Where was Jesse?

How stupid she'd been to come out of her room alone. She should have stayed there. She should have barricaded her door and waited for Jesse to come back. And now it was too late. Her room might just as well have been located on the other side of the world for all the good it would do her now.

"I told you I'd be coming for you—and I always keep my promises."

He made no effort to disguise his voice as he had in the past, and suddenly she understood the significance of the nightmare where her father had tried to strangle her.

Jesse made no effort to remain quiet as he rode down the winding lane to the Benton ranch. He had questions that needed answering, and he prayed that Paul—and Hank— would have the right responses.

Chester Benton leaned out of the upstairs window and yelled at the two dogs to stop their barking. Then, catching sight of Jesse on his motorcycle, he turned his attention to the younger man.

"What in tarnation are you doin' out here at this time of the night, Jesse Tyler? Don't you know us workin' folk have to get our rest?"

"I'm sorry, Mr. Benton, but it's important. I need to speak to your sons."

"Paul? And Hank? Why?"

"If you'll wake them, and come downstairs yourself, I'll explain."

"This better not be one of your practical jokes, boy—"

"No sir, no joke, it's serious business."

"All right, all right. Just let me get my pants on. I'll be there in a couple of minutes."

Jesse parked his bike, then stopped to speak in reassuringly familiar tones to Blue, the blue-heeler, and Killer, the German shepherd, before climbing the porch steps.

The front door opened, and Paul stood aside to allow Jesse inside. The hall light was on, and Jesse looked up to see the elder Benton, followed closely by his Spanish wife, emerge from one of the bedrooms, fastening the belt on his trousers.

"Where's Hank?" Jesse asked urgently.

Chester looked from his younger son to Jesse and then turned toward the end of the hall.

Jesse dropped to his knees before the boy and took him by the shoulders. "Paul, where is your brother?"

Paul refused to meet his eyes, his only answer a shrug of his small narrow shoulders.

"Come on, Paul. I have to talk to him. Where is he?" After a moment of silence Jesse asked sadly, "He isn't upstairs, is he?"

"I do not know where he is."

"Paul, is Hank gone a lot at night, especially the last few months?"

"He is gone for days at a time on business for our father—"

"Not business, not ranch business," Jesse corrected him unhappily. "Tell me, the night I brought him home drunk—"

"What the—" Chester Benton expostulated, hearing Jesse's words. "Hank ain't in his room. What's this about his bein' drunk?"

"Paul," Jesse said, ignoring the older man, "you helped me put him to bed that night. Was he really drunk?" His hands tightened on the boy's shoulders. "Was he?"

"I do not know." Jesse shook him a little. "I went to his room later," he admitted reluctantly, "after you left—just to make certain that he was all right—" Tears filled the huge black eyes staring into Jesse's.

"He was gone," Paul whispered brokenly.

"When did he come back?"

"Later..."

Jesse could tell by Paul's attitude that that wasn't all he knew. "What else, Paul?" He gave him another shake. "What else? Lauren Downing almost died in that fire."

The boy's tears spilled over onto his tanned cheeks. "I like Miss Downing. I do not want anything bad to happen to her." Biting his lower lip, he looked away and then back. "I love my brother, Jesse."

"I know, Paul, I know. I love him, too."

"He came home at three in the morning. There was something on his clothes, the smell of kerosene—and smoke." Jesse had to listen hard to hear the barely uttered words.

"I heard about the fire at school and I knew—" He looked up at Jesse. "I knew . . ." he repeated dolefully.

"What's this all about?" the elder Benton asked as he descended the stairs slowly. "If that boy of mine has been in more trouble, I wash my hands of him. I've spent over twenty years tryin' to teach that boy right. I've never spared the rod in this house. No siree, he's felt the just lash of truth and righteousness many a time on his backside."

Jesse stood slowly and turned toward the harsh-faced man. "You ever hear of tempering justice with a little mercy? And what about love? You ever show your kids any love?"

"You tryin' to tell me how to raise my kids, Jesse Tyler?" Chester drew himself up stiffly. "That father of yours should have used a rod of justice on your backside a whole lot more than he did."

Jesse whirled toward the door. There was no talking to the man. He listened to no one. Besides, what mattered now was getting to Lauren—before Hank did.

Straddling his bike, he started the engine and prepared to leave. From the doorway, Paul called to him.

"Jesse—don't hurt him. Please."

The cool wind whipped Jesse's hair across his face, stinging his eyes. He'd left his helmet back at the ranch, or lost it along the way somewhere. The moon was bright, and a bowl of stars filled the black sky. But he had no time to enjoy the beauty. Hank was undoubtedly on his way to the library—if he wasn't there already—to put an end to Lauren, and to the threat he imagined she represented to his cover as *El Personaje no Presente*. It was still hard for him to comprehend that fact. Hank, his buddy, a smuggler, a killer? When had he changed? When had he become so totally different from the shy, tongue-tied boy he'd been?

After leaving his bike in front of the sheriff's office, Jesse ran the rest of the distance to the library on foot. Arriving out of breath, he made his way carefully around to the back of the building. It was dark and silent. Everything looked as it should, but something told him the picture was false.

Skirting the picnic table, he moved toward the back entrance. A soft groan coming from the bushes to one side of the door drew his attention.

Moving cautiously closer, Jesse saw a pair of boots sticking out from behind the leafy branches, which he quickly pulled aside. Kalan Holtzer was just beginning to stir.

Raising his head, he looked up into Jesse's face and muttered, "He's here—inside the building. Lauren . . ."

"I never would have guessed it was you. You've terrorized me for weeks, and I had no idea what you thought I knew."

"And now you do?"

"I'm not sure. Unless it's the fact that the note I found was lost by Paul."

Hank Benton stepped into the circle of light that Lauren's flashlight made as she lifted it slowly toward his face.

"That's right, little librarian. That's exactly right. I'd been passing notes to Hernandez for months in the library books. I checked out the books, put the notes to Hernandez in them with the dates and places where new shipments of illegals were coming in, and Paul returned them to the library for me, after Hernandez got the notes out of Paul's locker without him knowing anything about it. But that last note, the one back in April, Hernandez missed it. And that's how you ended up with it."

"And that explains your sudden interest—and subsequent lack of interest—in reading. I have to admit you had me fooled. I thought you really read all those mysteries you took out."

Hank laughed, and it was an ugly sound. It made Lauren realize she wasn't exchanging a pleasant conversation with Paul's older brother, or Jesse's best friend, but with a murderer.

"You're *El Personaje no Presente*, the smuggler, aren't you? You killed Sheriff Slade and Raul—and Hernandez, your partner. Why?"

She was stalling for time. If she kept him talking, she hoped it would give Kalan time to either discover she wasn't in her room or hear their voices.

"I killed them," he admitted without hesitation. "It wasn't planned. I was only after Hernandez—"

"Your partner?" Lauren gasped. "But why?"

"He was getting too big for his britches. He wanted more than his share—besides, he knew my real identity. That was a mistake—one I don't plan to make in the future. The next time I take a partner, he won't know whose face is hidden behind the mask."

"If all you wanted was to get rid of your partner, then why did you kill the other two? And the man who worked at the convenience store, why him?"

"It was a perfect plan," he began, ignoring the last question. "One that dropped like a peach in my lap. Slade was looking for a smuggler, and I gave him one. Aguilar killed Estevez, then shot the sheriff before the sheriff got him. At least, that's how the town saw it.

"But I don't want you to think I enjoyed killing the sheriff—I liked the man. Now, your boyfriend, I didn't mind wasting him. He was always trying to learn my identity, always talking against me to his people." He sounded almost indignant at the idea of it. "I got a lucrative business going here," he informed her. "I had to protect my interests. You know, I don't force these people to come across the border against their will—they look for me, for the coyotes, the men and women working for me who lead them across the border. They pay to be led across."

"And sold into slavery," she couldn't help accusing angrily. "And into prostitution."

"Look, I'm not going to discuss right and wrong with you. You asked why I did what I did, and I'm telling you. I had to protect my business. Estevez had a big mouth. If he'd stuck to teaching like he was trained, he'd still be alive today. It's his own fault he's dead."

"That's not true!" Lauren protested angrily. "He was a good man, only concerned for the welfare of his people."

Hank took a step closer and removed the flashlight from her unresisting fingers. "Look, I told you—he had a big mouth. I ain't fond of Mexicans overmuch, anyway."

"Your brother is half-Mexican," she reminded him shortly.

"Yeah, well, I don't consider him one of *them*. He's blood. And I'll thank you to keep your nose out of my personal business. You think you can tie every male up in knots, no matter how old he is."

"I don't know what you're talking about," she protested, wondering if she dared make a grab for the alarm in her pocket.

"No? You had that Mex, Estevez, eating out of your hand. And you've got Paul thinking you're better than summer vacation. And Jesse—"

She'd been wondering when he'd mention his best friend, but she was ready for him.

"Yes, let's talk about Jesse, your lifelong friend, the man you've tried to kill twice."

"That's a lie," he snarled, and loomed menacingly closer. "I never tried to kill Jesse. I could have—but I wouldn't. Not over *you*! Not for any reason. You're a slut! You think you can wrap any man around your finger and he'll do your bidding."

Lauren shrank away from his anger. He was growing more disturbed by the moment, and she was afraid of what he might do if he was pushed too far.

"Why did you come after me that first time? I didn't know anything. It had been months since the mur—deaths. I wasn't suspicious of you. I had no idea at all who was responsible for those deaths."

Hank's eyes became dark and glassy. "I should have done it right away, but my old man kept me out of town making business trips for him." His grin was more like a grimace. "Or so he thought. I was busy taking care of my own interests most of the time. Every time I left town I expected to return to find the sheriff waiting for me 'cause you'd talked. I had just gotten back into town that evening, and the first thing I did was get drunk. Drink is evil—I have to remember that—I have wicked ways sometimes. It's the devil coming out of me." His words were becoming disjointed. "I got to quit drinking—you and that Mex—his filthy hands all over you—I'll burn in hell for my evil ways.

"It made me sick to my stomach. I drank—and thought—and saw pictures in my head. You with your big eyes all soft and dreamy —the clothes falling away from your pearly white skin—"

One of his hands came into view with the fingers clenched. The hand moved slowly toward her face, the fingers opening slowly. Lauren took a step back, and the hand fell to his side.

Shaking his head, he looked away and licked his lips—lips that looked suddenly fuller, wider. Lauren wanted to run, but her feet wouldn't move. She couldn't tear her eyes from his face. The skin around his forehead and mouth was suddenly scored with deep lines. He looked as though years had been added to his age in a matter of seconds.

The change frightened Lauren. She felt as though she was seeing another presence superimposed over the man standing only a frighteningly few feet away.

The hard glitter in his gray eyes froze the marrow in her bones. He looked totally insane. Spittle dripped from the corner of his mouth as his lips curled back in a sneer.

"Why did you come back to town if you were afraid of discovery? You had money—why didn't you just keep going?" She had to keep him talking, to give Kalan time to find them.

"Leave?" he asked in amazement, looking almost normal for a moment. "I couldn't do that. Who'd look after Paul? Who'd keep my old man from beating him, like he did me? Not his mother," he jeered. "She's more afraid of the old man than anyone else. I couldn't leave, not yet, not without Paul." His expression underwent another change; a feverish light entered his gray eyes.

"You caused all this. You've been bad. Done bad things. You need to be punished. I don't believe in sparing the rod— no child of mine will be spoiled by the things of this earth—"

Lauren looked at him in amazement. He sounded as though he was repeating a litany he'd memorized over the years. She was astounded at what she was seeing and hearing. She had read of people with multiple personalities; was she meeting one now?

Looking into his eyes, she saw something wild and inhuman with no resemblance to the rational young man of a few minutes before. Not even the horror of the murders, nor his calm relating of his part in them, had been as bad as this.

"I won't tell anyone anything—I promise. You could go away—far, far away. You have money—use it."

"I plan to go, and when I do, I'm taking Paul with me."

Now he seemed rational, the glow of insanity dimmer in his eyes. "No one will touch him as long as I live."

"Then take the money and run—"

"Slut! Whore!" He turned suddenly abusive. "It's all your fault! You had to find that note and give it to your Mexican lover. You should have minded your own business—all of you." A whining note entered his voice. "No one had to die except Aguilar. He was the only one—"

Hank dropped his gaze to his hands. His eyes widened until there was too much white showing. In the flashlight's illumination Lauren saw Hank raise his hands, palms outward. "Look! Blood! Look!" He showed his palms to her. "Look at what you've caused! Stained, marked like Cain—there's blood on my hands!"

If she hadn't been afraid for her life, Lauren might have sympathized with him. Something, perhaps the killings, had pushed him over the edge. Whatever it was, she knew he had lost his ability to reason, to think as a rational human being.

She knew she had only two choices if she wanted to live. She had to either get away from him or make enough noise to draw Kalan's attention.

When Hank had begun his disjointed tirade, she had slipped a hand behind her to the shelf. Surely there was something there that she could use as a weapon. He was coming after her; she was positive of that. And even if she pushed the alarm in her pocket, she was afraid it would be too late by the time someone responded to it. Too late for her.

Suddenly her fingers touched a cold smooth surface. Feeling along its narrow length, she discovered that it was a screwdriver. Jesse must have left it there. Thanking him silently, her fingers closed around it. Please, God, don't make me have to hurt him, she prayed silently. He's been hurt enough.

Hank had finished talking. He was ready for action. Taking Lauren's life didn't seem wrong to him at all; it was justifiable retribution.

To his twisted way of thinking she was the whole cause of his present situation. She had found the note, and made him kill—set the mark of Cain upon him. And for that she *must* pay. Down deep inside, he could admit that he would enjoy making her pay—just as he'd enjoyed making the others pay.

The atmosphere in the room became tense all at once. Lauren saw his muscles contract for the attack. Now. She had to do it *now*.

Hank sprang toward her, and as he lunged, Lauren's arm jerked upward, the screwdriver clutched tightly in her fist. The point of the tool came close to Hank's face, but at the last minute he threw his arm up for protection. The blow was deflected, and the blade only sliced the air near his head. In the struggle she somehow dropped the flashlight, which broke and rolled under one of the shelves. The room was in total blackness now.

Glad for the cover of darkness, Lauren raced toward the door. But Hank, guessing her intention, was there before her. His fingers slid over the side of her neck and fastened onto a handful of her hair.

Lauren's head was jerked back as, with a cry of protest and pain, she fell back against his body. His other arm encircled her throat, and she felt the touch of cold steel against the underside of her chin.

Slowly he dragged her away from the door. She wanted to cry out, to protest, to beg for mercy, but the knife was cutting into her skin. She was afraid to swallow, let alone speak.

This was it. She knew he wouldn't hesitate to kill her now. He'd told her all his secrets, admitted to the murders. Dear God, she began in silent prayer. Forgive me....

The door behind them burst open, and the room was suddenly filled with light from the hall. Hank whirled, dragging Lauren tighter against him, stumbling a step or two back.

The tip of the knife dug into the soft tissue just below Lauren's chin. A trickle of deep red blood oozed from beneath the steel and ran down her neck.

The room was silent except for the sound of labored breathing. The angle of Lauren's head made it impossible for her to see who had entered the room. And then Hank's menacing tones broke forth.

"Get the hell out of here or she's dead."

"Hank..." Lauren recognized Jesse's deep tones with a leap of her heart. "Hank, let her go."

"Jesse? You left—you left me—you went off and didn't care what happened to me. Why should I do what you say?" The whine was back in his voice.

Jesse was stunned by the words. He didn't know what to say. He'd driven hell-for-leather to reach Lauren in time to save her from Hank. But this was a Hank he didn't recognize, and he wasn't certain how to handle him.

"I didn't want to go, buddy—you know that. We were supposed to go into the Marines together. I would've stayed here if you'd asked me to, but you told me to go—said one of us had to do it, and it might as well be me. I'm sorry. I should have stayed. I should have known you couldn't stay out of trouble without me around."

There was a smile in Jesse's words, but not on his lips. It was a standing joke between them that one couldn't walk down the street without getting into trouble, and that it always took the other one to get him out of it.

By now two figures were standing in the hallway behind Jesse. His back was to them, but he knew they were there. Sensing movement, he turned his head slightly and saw that one of the deputies had drawn a bead on Hank.

"Hold your fire," he mouthed in an aside. All he needed now was someone trying to be a hero; that would be sure to get Lauren killed.

Both men relaxed, but their weapons remained trained on Hank as Jesse inched closer to him, covering the move with reminiscences from their childhood. He wasn't positive the other man was listening to the words, but he hoped his tone was getting through to him. He wanted Hank to know he didn't mean him any harm, but at the same time he had to get Lauren as far from Hank as he could.

After a few moments Lauren felt the pressure of the knife relax a fraction. She swallowed and took a mouthful of sweet air. The cadence of Jesse's voice as he talked over old times and how much he had missed his best friend while he was gone in the military had even begun to soothe her own frayed nerves.

Jesse took another step into the room. His chest tightened as Hank glanced down and then up. Would he see the move as a threat to him? Jesse hesitated and held his breath, but Hank stayed where he was.

"Let her go, Hank. Come on, I got my bike outside. We can go for a spin and talk over old times."

"I don't know. You angry at me?" Hank suddenly sounded like a child.

Jesse heard the change in his friend's voice with a great sadness. Hank's mind had snapped. Something, perhaps all the abuse he'd taken from his father over the years, first to protect his mother and then to protect Paul, had taken its final toll.

"I'm not angry."

And he wasn't. How could you be angry with a child? Whatever he had been in the past—*El Personaje no Presente* or just a lonely, confused young man needing love—right now Hank was a child.

"Aw, I wasn't really going to hurt her." Hank loosened his hold on Lauren, giving her a little shove in Jesse's direction.

Jesse's eager arms gathered the shivering woman to him. Closing his eyes in relief, he crushed her close. He could smell her familiar perfume.

"Are you all right?" he asked in an undertone, his lips pressed against the hair above her ear.

"Now I am," she answered, feeling his hands moving over her body to reassure himself of the truth of her words.

"Thank God," he breathed into her neck. "Thank God."

"And you," Lauren added, her arms around his waist, her nose buried in the opening of his leather jacket, pressed against his reassuringly solid chest.

"You gonna' just stand there? Or are we goin' for a ride like you said?" Hank had moved closer to the couple.

Jesse motioned for one of the deputies to get Lauren out of reach. When she had been safely led out of the room, Jesse closed the distance between himself and the other man.

"Hank, give me the knife."

Hank looked from Jesse to his own right hand. A look of surprise spread over his face and his eyes opened wide in astonishment, then narrowed in distaste.

"Here." He shoved the long, wicked-looking blade toward Jesse. "I don't like knives. Remember that time I—"

His voice rose and fell as he recounted some childhood adventure the two of them had shared. Lauren stood back against the wall as they neared the doorway. It was hard to believe this was the same man who had caused her to live in terror, coming close to taking her life.

Hank trotted docilely along at Jesse's side. When one of the deputies stepped up to snap handcuffs on his wrists, Jesse motioned him away. There was no need for that— Hank wasn't even aware of what had taken place a few minutes before. There was no violence left in him; he'd managed to wipe all that from his mind. With one long last look over his shoulder at Lauren, Jesse passed out of her sight.

Kalan met the two men as they left the building. His glance moved over Hank and leveled on Jesse's unreadable expression. He was curious about what had taken place inside, but he knew he'd learn the facts later.

Rubbing a hand along the back of his head, he stepped through the library door. He found Lauren upstairs in her room, every light turned on.

"It's all over." She was looking out the window to the street below. Police cars with flashing red-and-blue lights lined the street.

"Looks like it," Kalan agreed.

"I still can't believe it was him—Hank. He's spent so much time here the last few weeks helping Jesse, sharing lunch and coffee—" Turning abruptly from the window, she looked up at Kalan and asked, "Why?"

He shrugged. What could he say? No one ever completely knew or understood the workings of another's mind. Even the criminal psychologists couldn't always pinpoint causes and effects. And when the mind was as twisted, as warped, as Hank's appeared to be . . .

"I'm sorry I wasn't here when you needed me. I heard something outside and went to the door to investigate. He was waiting for me. I think he must have mistaken me for Jesse in the dark—otherwise I probably wouldn't be standing here."

"He hurt you?" Lauren asked anxiously.

"Just a bump on the head. I'm fine," he assured her quickly.

"What will happen to him now?"

"Hard to say. From what I saw, I seriously doubt he'll stand trial."

Lauren dropped down onto the loveseat. "It's so sad. If I hadn't found that note, maybe none of this would have happened."

Kalan sat down beside her and patted her hand, which was resting on one knee. "Some things are preordained. Hank Benton would still have been *the nameless one*, and through his own choice."

The telephone on the table rang, and Lauren jumped, then reached for it. Jesse!

"Lauren? Rand here. It's a girl!"

"A girl! Oh, Rand, congratulations. How's Carrie?"

"She's fine, great, excited—and beautiful."

Kalan held his hand out for the phone, and Lauren reluctantly handed it over. It was a shame to have to spoil Rand's joy with news of what had been happening here while he was becoming a father.

She didn't listen to the conversation. She went to her bedroom and walked around, touching things at random. Her mind wasn't on what she was doing; she was thinking about Jesse.

When the phone had rung she'd been certain it was him. Where was he? She understood his feelings of compassion for his friend. She felt compassion for him, herself. But *she* needed him, too.

It was no good telling herself she was being selfish, that all his concern had to be for Hank right now. She wanted someone to share her own emotions and relief with. She wanted Jesse.

"Excuse me." Kalan was standing in the doorway. "The sheriff told me to ask if you would like me to stay the night—or the rest of it, at any rate."

"No, thanks. I'll be fine now."

"You're sure?"

Lauren nodded firmly.

"I guess I'll be seeing you in the morning—or rather, later this morning—then."

He felt reluctant to leave her, but she obviously didn't want his company. "Good night. Want to come and lock up after me?"

When he'd gone Lauren bolted the door, fastened the chain and leaned there a moment. She supposed she didn't really need all those locks now. But would she ever feel completely safe again? After all, in a town the size of Chance, where she'd known her neighbors all her life, she hadn't expected one of them to be a deranged killer.

Upstairs, she threw herself across her bed, with her arms on the pillow under her head, and stared at the ceiling. What was wrong with her? She felt so empty. She should be jumping with joy because she was safe now.

Yet all she could see was Hank's face as he'd left the building—and Jesse's. That last look he had given her before leaving, the look in his blue eyes that had warmed her heart, had told that he cared for her—that it wasn't finished between them yet.

Where was Jesse? Why didn't he come?

Chapter 14

It was late when he came to her, but she was waiting for him. He stood below her window, calling to her softly until she raised the sash and leaned out.

"Rapunzel, Rapunzel, let down your hair—or come downstairs and unlock the back door." She could see the flash of white teeth as he grinned, even in the dark.

"I'll be there in a jiffy," she answered, unable to hide her excitement.

She closed the window and left the room at a dead run. Jesse was there. The terror had ended, and Jesse had come back for her.

She was in such a flurry that she could barely unfasten the locks; her hands had suddenly grown two extra thumbs. But finally it was done. The door flew back, and she threw herself against him and felt his arms close tight around her.

"It's over, it's all over." Lauren plastered Jesse's face,

neck and chin with kisses. "Thank God he was caught before anyone else was hurt."

"Yes," Jesse answered gravely. "It's finished."

There was a deeper meaning to his words, and Lauren drew back to get a look at his face in the hall light. In her giddy relief she had lost sight of the fact that he had lost his best friend—to madness.

"I'm sorry, Jesse. I know how you must feel—"

"It's okay," he reassured her. "Hank is where they'll be able to help him now. Maybe someday he'll get better. I hope so, at any rate."

Hank would always remain a treasured part of his youth. The Hank he had watched being taken away in an ambulance to the state mental hospital was not the boy he had loved all his life like a brother.

"So do I," Lauren replied. Poor Hank, abused by his father all those years. What would be his father's punishment? She hoped he wouldn't get away scot-free.

"Can we go upstairs?" Jesse asked, putting the past behind him. "I have something to ask you."

Lauren led the way, her small hand clasped tightly in his larger one. Once inside the sitting room, Jesse pulled her into his arms and kissed her thoroughly. When she had gotten her breath back, she smiled, stars shining from her dark eyes, and asked, "What was that for?"

"Just to reassure myself that it's really over and you're still safe and sound. Last night, when I realized who the killer was, and when I couldn't find Hank, I was so afraid I wouldn't reach you in time."

His hands were everywhere, in her hair, smoothing her cheek, rubbing her shoulders, holding her face up for his kisses.

"God, if I'd lost you—"

Lauren smiled between his kisses, safe and secure in the knowledge that though he hadn't said the words, he loved her as she loved him.

"Jesse, what will happen to Paul?" she questioned, when he allowed her to speak. "Will he have to stay with his parents?"

They had somehow ended up on the loveseat, her head on his shoulder, his arms wrapped around her. She felt invigorated by the depth of his feelings for her, snug in the knowledge of her love for him.

"I talked with Paul's mother for a few moments when I went to tell Chester about Hank's arrest. I guess this really brought everything home to her, she's finally going to do something about the situation. She and Paul are going to Mexico to live with some of her relatives. Chester is staying here."

"Oh, I'm glad. Paul is such a bright little boy, and so affectionate. I'd hate to see him suffer the way Hank did."

"Um-m-m," Jesse agreed, his mind on other matters.

Sensing his lack of attention, Lauren twisted her head and looked up into his face. Her eyes were caught by the sight of the thin blond hairs growing across his upper lip. So, that accounted for the scratchy feel of his kisses.

"What's that?" she asked carefully, keeping the laughter from her eyes.

"What?" Jesse pretended ignorance, suddenly embarrassed.

"That." She raised a hand and wiggled a finger at his mouth.

"Oh, that. A mustache."

"Mustache? Why?"

"I just wanted to see how I'd look with one, that's all."

Turning to face him, pressing against his chest and meeting his eyes with a serious look, she said, "You don't need to grow a mustache to impress me, or to add any years to your appearance. I love you just the way you are."

There, it was out in the open; she'd been the first one to say it. What would his response be?

"You love me? You're sure? It doesn't bother you that I am who I am?" he asked intently.

"And just who are you, Jesse Tyler? You're the man who saved my life, three times. The man who gave up a friend to do it. The man who taught me what it was to be a woman in the fullest sense of the word."

Hauling her up between his legs, he smothered her face with kisses. She was the best thing that had ever happened to him. He'd never be worthy of her.

"I love you," he whispered with his mouth pressed against her breast. "Will you marry me—soon?"

"How soon?" Lauren asked without hesitation.

"As soon as we can get a license."

"What about the mustache?"

Jesse touched his upper lip self-consciously. "Don't you like it?"

"Well . . ." She drew the word out, narrowing her eyes. "You do look a little older with it—about twelve going on thirty-five would be my guess."

"Thanks, that's just what I wanted to hear—I'll shave it tomorrow."

"Jesse." Her expression became pensive. "What about this work you're doing for the sheriff? Will you continue with it after we're married?" The question had to be asked, but she dreaded the answer.

"No. I already told Rand I was finished after this last job," he said quietly. And then he added in a teasing voice,

"I think the life of a gentleman rancher should suit me perfectly." He elevated one blond brow. "What do you think? Will the prudish town librarian like being married to a man who smells of horse manure and cattle?"

"Oh, you." She grabbed his shirtfront and shook him.

"Wait a minute." He held up his hand. "There is one thing that I refuse to give up for you."

"What?" she asked in trepidation, a picture of the lovely dark-skinned Rosalita insinuating itself into her mind.

"My bike. I refuse to give up my motorcycle."

"That's it? That's all?" she asked in relief.

"Yup, that's it."

"Okay," she agreed after a silent moment of pretended contemplation. "Under one condition."

"What's that?"

"You have to teach me to ride. I want to share everything with you." Her eyes grew soft and liquid, and her hand traveled down his broad chest to his thigh.

She was doing it to him again, he thought. She was setting him on fire. All it seemed to take was a look, a touch.

Rolling her over beneath him in a sudden move, he smoothed the dark curls from her cheeks, then bent and took her bottom lip between both of his, stroking it with his tongue. One hand glided beneath the neck of her blouse to supple flesh. The other hand slid lower, under her skirt, then up past her thigh to the waistband of her panties.

Lauren's eyes grew wide, and the blood sang in her veins as she felt him gently stroke her delicate flesh.

"Don't you know that you're in for the ride of your life?" he whispered huskily in her ear.

Hard fingers slid below the soft satin and silky lace. His hips moved, and Lauren felt the evidence of his passion pressing hotly against her thigh.

"But the machine you straddle," he continued, his breath fanning her lips, "won't be made of steel, and the ride you're in for will last a lifetime. Is that a deal?"

"Deal," Lauren agreed, sealing the promise with a kiss.

*   *   *   *   *

Silhouette Intimate Moments®

COMING
NEXT MONTH

#337 RUNAWAY—Emilie Richards
With the help of journalist Jess Cantrell, Kristin Jensen posed as a prostitute to find her missing sister. Despite the constant danger, she found herself attracted to Jess. Was it purely physical . . . or could Kristin's hazardous search be leading to a safe haven of love?

#338 NOT WITHOUT HONOR—
Marilyn Pappano
Held hostage as a political pawn in a steamy South American rebel camp, Brenna Mathis, daughter of a military advisor, discovered that Andrés Montano, leader of the rebel forces and her former lover, had masterminded her abduction! Could the man she'd once loved still be the captor of her heart?

#339 IGUANA BAY—Theresa Weir
Elise Ramsey had been kidnapped—twice in one week! The first man wanted to use her as an alibi at his murder trial. The second, ruggedly handsome bounty hunter Dylan Davis, wanted to prevent her from testifying. To make matters even worse, Elise realized she was falling in love with this madman!

#340 FOREVER MY LOVE—
Heather Graham Pozzessere
Brent McQueen and his ex-wife Kathy were thrown together unexpectedly when smugglers mistakenly believed he had information they needed. Chased by killers and racing to uncover the truth before it was too late, they found passion flaring anew as they discovered that a love like theirs was, indeed, meant to last forever.

AVAILABLE THIS MONTH:

#333 CORRUPTED
Beverly Sommers

#334 SOMEONE TO TURN TO
Marilyn Cunningham

#335 LOVING LIES
Ann Williams

#336 DREAM CHASERS
Mary Anne Wilson

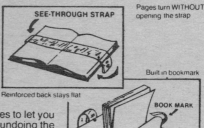

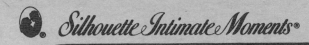

Silhouette Intimate Moments®

Beginning next month,
Intimate Moments will bring you
two gripping stories by Emilie Richards

Coming in June
Runaway
by EMILIE RICHARDS
Intimate Moments #337

Coming in July
The Way Back Home
by EMILIE RICHARDS
Intimate Moments #341

Krista and Rosie Jensen were two sisters who had it all—
until a painful secret tore them apart.

They were two special women who met two very special men
who made life a little easier—and love a whole lot better—
until the day when Krista and Rosie could be sisters once
again.

You'll laugh, you'll cry and you'll never, ever forget. Don't
miss the first book, RUNAWAY, available next month at your
favorite retail outlet.

Silhouette Books®

A BIG SISTER
can take her places

She likes that. Her Mom does too.

HARLEQUIN SUPPORTS BIG SISTERS
For more information, contact your local Big Brothers/Big Sisters agency.

BIG BROTHERS
BIG SISTERS
OF AMERICA

BIG BROTHERS/BIG SISTERS AND HARLEQUIN

Harlequin is proud to announce its official sponsorship of Big Brothers/Big Sisters of America. Look for this poster in your local Big Brothers/Big Sisters agency or call them to get one in your favorite bookstore. Love is all about sharing.

BB/BS-1A